'*Less* is philosophical, poignant, funny, and wise, filled with unexpected turns ... Although Greer is gifted and subtle in comic moments, he's just as adept at ruminating on the deeper stuff. His protagonist grapples with aging, loneliness, creativity, grief, self-pity, and more'

San Francisco Chronicle

'Greer, the author of wonderful, heartfelt novels, including *The Confessions of Max Tivoli*, *The Impossible Lives of Greta Wells*, and *The Story of a Marriage*, shows he has another powerful weapon in his arsenal: comedy. And who doesn't need a laugh right about now?"

Miami Herald

'Seasoned novelist Greer clearly knows whereof he speaks and has lived to joke about it ... This is a very funny and occasionally wise book'

Kirkus Reviews

'The most deftly funny romantic comedy I've read in years. If you have a sentimental bone in your body (I have 206), the ending will make you sob little tears of joy'

Nell Zink, author of *Mislaid*

One of the best books of the year:

New York Times
Washington Post
San Francisco Chronicle

'A reall

stead of
down ..

Ann Patchett

'Greer is an exceptionally lovely writer, capable of mingling humor with sharp poignancy ... Brilliantly funny ... Greer's narration, so elegantly laced with wit, cradles the story of a man who loses everything: his lover, his suitcase, his beard, his dignity'

Ron Charles, *Washington Post*

'I adore this book. It's funny, piquant, bittersweet, and so achingly observant about the vanity of writers that it made me squirm in recognition. I'll probably read it again very soon'

Armistead Maupin, author of *Tales of the City*

'Marvelously, unexpectedly, endearingly funny. A love story focused on the erroneous belief that the second half of life will pale in comparison to the first. Guess what? It won't!'

Gary Shteyngart, author of *Super Sad True Love Story*

'Treat yourself to this book. I missed subway stops. I doubled over in laughter. I experienced more pure reading pleasure than I have in ages. It is hilarious, and wise, and abundantly fun'

Adam Haslett, author of *Imagine Me Gone*

'*Less* is the funniest, smartest, and most humane novel I've read since *The Imperfectionists* ... Greer writes sentences of arresting lyricism and beauty. His metaphors come at you like fireflies ... Like Arthur, Andrew Sean Greer's *Less* is excellent company. It's no less than bedazzling, bewitching, and be-wonderful'

Christopher Buckley, *New York Times Book Review*

'A generous book, musical in its prose and expansive in its structure and range, about growing older and the essential nature of love'

Judges of the Pulitzer Prize for Fiction 2018

'Greer elevates Less's picaresque journey into a wise and witty novel. This is no *Eat, Pray, Love* story of touristic uplift, but rather a grand travelogue of foibles, humiliations, and self-deprecation, ending in joy and a dollop of self-knowledge'

National Book Review

'A fast and rocketing read with everything I want from a story – moments of high humor, moments of genuine wisdom, sharp insights, and gorgeous images. A wonderful, wonderful book!'

Karen Joy Fowler, author of *We Are All Completely Beside Ourselves*

LESS

ANDREW SEAN GREER

ABACUS

First published in the United States in 2017 by Lee Boudreaux Books,
an imprint of Little, Brown and Company
First published in Great Britain in 2018 by Abacus

1 3 5 7 9 10 8 6 4 2

A CIP catalogue record for this book
is available from the British Library.

ISBN 978-0-349-14359-0

Book design by Sean Ford
Illustrations by Lilli Carré

Printed and bound in Great Britain by
Clays Ltd, St Ives plc

Papers used by Abacus are from well-managed forests
and other responsible sources.

Abacus
An imprint of
Little, Brown Book Group
Carmelite House
50 Victoria Embankment
London EC4Y 0DZ

An Hachette UK Company
www.hachette.co.uk

www.littlebrown.co.uk

For Daniel Handler

LESS

LESS AT FIRST

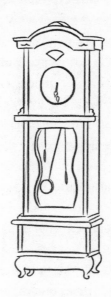

FROM where I sit, the story of Arthur Less is not so bad.

Look at him: seated primly on the hotel lobby's plush round sofa, blue suit and white shirt, legs knee-crossed so that one polished loafer hangs free of its heel. The pose of a young man. His slim shadow is, in fact, still that of his younger self, but at nearly fifty he is like those bronze statues in public parks that, despite one lucky knee rubbed raw by schoolchildren, discolor beautifully until they match the trees. So has Arthur Less, once pink and gold with youth, faded like the sofa he sits on, tapping one finger on his knee and staring at the grandfather clock. The long patrician nose perennially burned by the sun (even in cloudy New York October). The washed-out blond hair too long on the top, too short on the sides—portrait of his grandfather. Those same watery blue eyes. Listen: you might hear anxiety ticking, ticking, ticking away as he stares at that clock, which unfortunately is not ticking itself. It stopped fifteen years ago. Arthur Less is not aware of this; he still believes, at his ripe age, that escorts for literary events arrive on time and bellboys reliably wind the lobby clocks. He wears no watch; his faith is fast. It is mere coincidence that the clock stopped at half past six, almost exactly the hour when he is to be taken to tonight's event. The poor man does not know it, but the time is already quarter to seven.

As he waits, around and around the room circles a young woman in a brown wool dress, a species of tweed hummingbird, pollinating first this group of tourists and then that one. She dips her face into a cluster of chairs, asking a particular question, and then, dissatisfied with the answer, darts away to find another. Less does not notice her as she makes her rounds. He is too focused on the broken clock. The young woman goes up to the lobby clerk, then to the elevator, startling a group of ladies overdressed for the theater. Up and down Less's loose shoe goes. If he paid attention, perhaps he would have heard the woman's eager question, which explains why, though she asks everyone else in the lobby, she never asks it of him:

"Excuse me, but are you Miss Arthur?"

The problem—which will not be solved in this lobby—is that the escort believes Arthur Less to be a woman.

In her defense, she has read only one novel of his, in an electronic form that lacked a photo, and found the female narrator so compelling, so persuasive, that she was certain only a woman could have written it; she assumed the name to be one of those American gender curiosities (she is Japanese). This is, for Arthur Less, a rare rave review. Little good this does him at the moment, sitting on the round sofa, from whose conical center emerges an oiled palm. For it is now ten minutes to seven.

Arthur Less has been here for three days; he is in New York to interview famous science fiction author H. H. H. Mandern onstage to celebrate the launch of H. H. H. Mandern's new novel; in it, he revives his wildly popular Holmesian robot, Peabody. In the world of books, this is front-page news, and a great deal of money is jangling behind the scenes. Money in the voice that called Less out of the blue and asked if he was familiar with the work of H. H. H. Mandern, and if he might be available for an interview. Money in the messages from the publicist instructing Less what questions were absolutely off the table for H. H. H. Mandern (his wife, his daughter, his poorly reviewed poetry collection). Money in the choice of venue, the advertisements plastered all over the Village. Money in the inflatable Peabody battling the wind outside the theater. Money even in the hotel Arthur has been placed in, where he was shown a pile of "complimentary" apples he can feel free to take anytime, day or night, you're welcome. In a world where most people read one book a year, there is a lot of money hoping that *this* is the book and that this night will be the glorious kickoff. And they are depending on Arthur Less.

And still, dutifully, he watches the stopped clock. He does not see the escort standing woefully beside him. He does not see her adjust her scarf, then exit the lobby through the washing machine of its revolving doors. Look at the thinning hair at the crown of his head, the rapid blink of his eyes. Look at his boyish faith.

Once, in his twenties, a poet he had been talking with extinguished her cigarette in a potted plant and said, "You're like a person without skin." A *poet* had said this. One who made her living flaying herself alive in public had said that *he,* tall and young and hopeful Arthur Less, was *without skin.* But it was true. "You need to get an edge," his old rival Carlos constantly told him in the old days, but Less had not known what that meant. To be mean? No, it meant to be protected, armored against the world, but can one "get" an edge any more than one can "get" a sense of humor? Or do you fake it, the way a humorless businessman memorizes jokes and is considered "a riot," leaving parties before he runs out of material?

Whatever it is—Less never learned it. By his forties, all he has managed to grow is a gentle sense of himself, akin to the transparent carapace of a soft-shelled crab. A mediocre review or careless slight can no longer harm him, but heartbreak, real true heartbreak, can pierce his thin hide and bring out the same shade of blood as ever. How can so many things become a bore by middle age—philosophy, radicalism, and other fast foods—but *heartbreak* keeps its sting? Perhaps because he finds fresh sources for it. Even foolish old fears have never been vanquished, only avoided: telephone calls (frenetically dialing like a man decoding a bomb), taxicabs (fumbling the tip and leaping out as from a hostage situation), and talking to attractive men or celebrities at parties (still mentally rehearsing his opening lines, only to realize they are saying their good-byes). He still has these fears, but the passage of time solved them for him. Texting and email saved him from phones forever. Credit card machines appeared in taxis. A missed opportunity could contact you online. But heartbreak—how can you avoid it except to renounce love entirely? In the end, that is the only solution Arthur Less could find.

Perhaps it explains why he gave nine years to a certain young man.

I have neglected to mention that he has, on his lap, a Russian cosmonaut's helmet.

But now a bit of luck: from the world outside the lobby, a chime rings out, one, two, three, four, five, six, seven, causing Arthur Less to pop out of his seat. Look at him: staring at his betrayer, the clock, then running to the front desk and asking—at last—the essential temporal question.

"I don't understand how you could think I was a woman."

"You are such a talented writer, Mr. Less. You tricked me! And what are you carrying?"

"This? The bookstore asked me to—"

"I loved *Dark Matter*. There is a part that reminded me of Kawabata."

"He's one of my favorites! *The Old Capital*. Kyoto."

"I am from Kyoto, Mr. Less."

"Really? I'll be there in a few months—"

"Mr. Less. We are having a problem..."

This conversation takes place as the woman in the brown wool dress leads him down a theater hallway. It is decorated with a lone prop tree, the kind the hero hides behind in comedies; the rest is all brick painted glossy black. Less and his escort have run from the hotel to the event space, and he can already feel the sweat turning his crisp white shirt into a transparency.

Why him? Why did they ask Arthur Less? A minor author whose greatest fame was a youthful association with the Russian River School of writers and artists, an author too old to be fresh and too young to be rediscovered, one who never sits next to anyone on a plane who has heard of his books. Well, Less knows why. It is no mystery. A calculation was made: what literary writer would agree to prepare for an interview and yet not be paid? It had to be someone terribly desperate. How many other writers of his acquaintance said "no chance"? How far down the list did they go before someone said: "What about Arthur Less?"

He is indeed a desperate man.

From behind the wall, he can hear the crowd chanting something. Surely the name H. H. H. Mandern. In the past month, Less has privately gorged on H. H. H. Mandern's works, those space operettas, which at first appalled him, with their tin-ear language and laughable stock characters, and then drew him in with their talent for invention, surely greater than his own. Less's new novel, a serious investigation of the human soul, seems like a minor planet compared with the constellations invented by this man. And yet, what is there to ask him? What does one ever ask an author except: "How?" And the answer, as Less well knows, is obvious: "Beats me!"

The escort is chattering about the theater capacity, the pre-orders, the book tour, the money, the money, the money. She mentions that H. H. H. Mandern seems to have come down with food poisoning.

"You'll see," the escort says, and a black door opens onto a bright clean room where deli meats fan across a folding table. Beside it stands a white-haired lady in shawls, and below her: H. H. H. Mandern, vomiting into a bucket.

The lady turns to Arthur and scans the space helmet: "Who the hell are you?"

New York: the first stop on a trip around the world. An accident, really, of Less trying to find his way out of a sticky situation. He is quite proud he has managed to do so. It was a wedding invitation.

Arthur Less has, for the past decade and a half, remained a bachelor. This came after a long period of living with the older poet Robert Brownburn, a tunnel of love he entered at twenty-one and exited, blinking in the sunlight, in his thirties. Where was he? Somewhere in there he lost the first phase of youth, like the first phase of a rocket; it had fallen, depleted, behind him. And here was the second. And last. He swore he would not give it to anyone; he would enjoy it. He would enjoy it alone. But: how to live alone and yet not be alone? It was solved for him by the most surprising person: his one-time rival Carlos.

If asked about Carlos, Less always calls him "one of my oldest friends." The date of their first encounter can be pinpointed precisely: Memorial Day, 1987. Less can even remember what each of them wore: he, a green Speedo, Carlos, the same in bright banana. Each with a white-wine spritzer in hand, like a pistol, eyeing the other from across the deck. A song was playing, Whitney Houston wanting to dance with somebody. Shadow of a sequoia falling between them. With somebody who loved her. Oh, to have a time machine and a video camera! To capture thin pink-gold Arthur Less and brawny nut-brown Carlos Pelu in their youth, when your narrator was only a child! But who needs a camera? Surely, for each of them, that scene replays itself whenever the other's name is mentioned. Memorial Day, spritzer, sequoia, somebody. And each smiles and says the other is "one of my oldest friends." When of course they hated each other on sight.

Let us take that time machine after all, but to a destination almost twenty years later. Let us land ourselves in mid-2000s San Francisco, a house in the hills, on Saturn Street. One of those creatures on stilts, a glass wall revealing a never-used grand piano and a crowd of mostly men celebrating one of a dozen fortieth-birthday parties that year. Among them: a thicker Carlos, whose longtime lover left him real estate when he died, and who turned those few lots into a property empire, including far-flung holdings in Vietnam, Thailand, even some ridiculous resort Less heard about in India. Carlos: same dignified profile, but no trace anymore of that muscled young man in a banana Speedo. It was an easy walk for Arthur Less, from his little shack on the Vulcan Steps, where he now lived alone. A party; why not? He chose a Lessian costume—jeans and a cowboy shirt, only slightly wrong—and made his way south along the hillside, toward the house.

Meanwhile, imagine Carlos, enthroned in a peacock chair and holding court. Beside him, twenty-five years old, in black jeans, T-shirt, and round tortoiseshell glasses, with dark curly hair: his son.

My son, I recall Carlos telling everyone when the boy first appeared, then barely in his teens. But he was not his son—he was an orphaned nephew, shipped off to his next of kin in San Francisco. How do I describe him? Big eyed, with brown sun-streaked hair and a truculent demeanor in those days, he refused to eat vegetables or to call Carlos anything but Carlos. His name was Federico (Mexican mother), but everybody called him Freddy.

At the party, Freddy stared out the window, where the fog erased downtown. These days he ate vegetables but still called his legal father Carlos. In his suit he was painfully thin, with a concave chest, and, while lacking youth's verve, Freddy had all of youth's passions; one could sit back with a bag of popcorn and watch the romances and comedies of his mind projected onto his face, and the lenses of his tortoiseshell glasses swirled with his thoughts like the iridescent membranes of soap bubbles.

Freddy turned at the sound of his name; it was a woman in a white silk suit and amber beads, with a cool Diana Ross demeanor: "Freddy, honey, I heard you were back in school." What was he studying to be? she asked gently. Proud smile: "A high school English teacher."

This caused her face to flower. "God, that's nice to hear! I never see young people going into teaching."

"To be honest, I think it's mostly that I don't like people my age."

She picked the olive from her martini. "That'll be hard on your love life."

"I suppose. But I don't really have a love life," Freddy said, taking a long gulp from his champagne, finishing it.

"We just have to find you the right man. You know my son, Tom—"

From beside them: "He's actually a poet!" Carlos, appearing with a listing glass of white wine.

The woman (courtesy requires introductions: Caroline Dennis, in software; Freddy would come to know her very well) yipped.

Freddy eyed her carefully and gave a shy smile. "I'm a terrible poet. Carlos is just remembering that's what I wanted to be when I was a kid."

"Which was last year," Carlos said, smiling.

Freddy stood silently; his dark curls quivered with whatever shook his mind.

Mrs. Dennis gave a sequined laugh. She said she loved poetry. She had always been into Bukowski "and that bag."

"You like Bukowski?" Freddy asked.

"Oh no," said Carlos.

"I'm sorry, Caroline. But I think he's even worse than I am."

Mrs. Dennis's chest flushed, Carlos drew her attention to a painting done by an old pal of the Russian River School, and Freddy, unable to swallow even the vegetables of small talk, stalked to the bar for another champagne.

Arthur Less at the front door, one of those low walls with a white door, concealing the house that drops down the hill behind it, and what will people say? *Oh, you look well. I heard about you and Robert. Who is keeping the house?*

How could he know that nine years lay beyond that door?

"Hello, Arthur! What is that you're wearing?"

"Carlos."

Twenty years later and still, that day, in that room: old rivals at battle.

Beside him: a young man with curly hair and glasses, standing at attention.

"Arthur, you remember my son, Freddy..."

It was so easy. Freddy found Carlos's house intolerable and so often, after a long Friday teaching and hitting a happy hour with a few of his college friends, would show up at Less's, tipsy and eager to crawl into bed for the weekend. The next day would be Less nursing a hungover Freddy with coffee and old movies until Less kicked him out on Monday morning. This happened once a month or so when they first began but grew into a habit, until Less found himself disappointed when one Friday evening, the doorbell never rang. How strange to wake up in his warm white sheets, the sunlight through the trumpet vine, and sense something missing. He told Freddy, the next time he saw him, that he should not drink so much. Or recite such terrible poetry. And here was a key to his house. Freddy said nothing but pocketed the key and used it whenever he liked (and never returned it).

An outsider would say: *That's all fine, but the trick is not to fall in love.* They would have both laughed at that. Freddy Pelu and Arthur Less? Freddy was as uninterested in romance as a young person should be; he had his books, and his teaching, and his friends, and his life as a single man. Old, easy Arthur asked nothing. Freddy also suspected that it drove his father nuts that he was sleeping with Carlos's old nemesis, and Freddy was still young enough to take pleasure in torturing his foster parent. It never occurred to him that Carlos might be relieved to have the boy off his hands. As for Less, Freddy was not even his type. Arthur Less had always fallen for older men; they were the real danger. Some kid who couldn't even name the Beatles? A diversion; a pastime; a hobby.

Less of course had other, more serious lovers in the years he saw Freddy. There was the history professor at UC–Davis who would drive two hours to take Less to the theater. Bald, red bearded, sparkling eyes and wit; it was a pleasure, for a while, to be a grown-up with another grown-up, to share a phase of life—early forties—and laugh about their fear of fifty. At the theater, Less looked over and saw Howard's profile lit by the stage and thought: *Here is a good companion, here is a good choice.* Could he have loved Howard? Very possibly. But the sex was awkward, too specific ("Pinch that, okay, now touch there; no, higher; no, *higher;* no, HIGHER!") and felt like an audition for a chorus line. Howard was nice, however, and he could cook; he brought ingredients over and made sauerkraut soup so spicy, it made Less a little high. He held Less's hand a lot and smiled at him. So Less waited it out for six months, to see if the sex would change, but it didn't, and he never said anything about it, so I suppose he knew it wasn't love, after all.

There were more; many, many more. There was the Chinese banker who played the violin and made fun noises in bed but who kissed like he'd only seen it in movies. There was the Colombian bartender whose charm was undeniable but whose English was impossible ("I want to wait on your hand and on your foot"); Less's Spanish was even worse.

There was the Long Island architect who slept in flannel pajamas and a cap, as in a silent movie. There was the florist who insisted on sex outdoors, leading to a doctor's visit during which Less had to ask for both an STD test and a remedy for poison oak. There were the nerds who assumed Less followed every news item about the tech industry but who felt no obligation to follow literature. There were the politicians sizing him up as for a suit fitting. There were the actors trying him on the red carpet. There were the photographers getting him in the right lighting. They might have done, many of them. So many people will do. But once you've actually been in love, you can't live with "will do"; it's worse than living with yourself.

No surprise that again and again, Less returned to dreamy, simple, lusty, bookish, harmless, youthful Freddy.

They went on in this way for nine years. And then, one autumn day, it ended. Freddy had changed, of course, from a twenty-five-year-old to a man in his midthirties: a high school teacher, in blue short-sleeved button-ups and black ties, whom Less jokingly called Mr. Pelu (often raising his hand as if to be called on in class). Mr. Pelu had kept his curls, but his glasses were now red plastic. He could no longer fit his old slim clothes; he had filled out from that skinny youngster into a grown man, with shoulders and a chest and a softness just beginning on his belly. He no longer stumbled drunk up Less's stairs and recited bad poetry every weekend. But one weekend he did. It was a friend's wedding, and he did show up, tipsy and red faced, leaning into Less as he staggered, laughing, into his mudroom. A night when he clung to Less, radiating heat. And a morning when, sighing, Freddy announced that he was seeing someone who wanted him to be monogamous. He had promised to be, about a month earlier. And he thought it was about time he stayed true to his promise.

Freddy lay on his stomach, resting his head on Less's arm. The scratch of his stubble. On the side table, his red glasses magnified a set of cuff links. Less asked, "Does he know about me?"

Freddy lifted his head. "Know what about you?"

"This." He gestured to their naked bodies.

Freddy met his gaze directly. "I can't come around here anymore."

"I understand."

"It would be fun. It has been fun. But you know I can't."

"I understand."

Freddy seemed about to say something more, then stopped himself. He was silent, but his gaze was that of someone memorizing a photograph. What did he see there? He turned from Less and reached for his glasses. "You should kiss me like it's good-bye."

"Mr. Pelu," Less said. "It's not really good-bye."

Freddy put on his red glasses, and in each aquarium a little blue fish swam.

"You want me to stay here with you forever?"

A bit of sun came through the trumpet vine; it checkered one bare leg.

Less looked at his lover, and perhaps a series of images flashed through his mind—a tuxedo jacket, a Paris hotel room, a rooftop party—or perhaps what appeared was just the snow blindness of panic and loss. A dot-dot-dot message relayed from his brain that he chose to ignore. Less leaned down and gave Freddy a long kiss. Then he pulled away and said, "I can tell you used my cologne."

The glasses, which had amplified the young man's determination, now magnified his already wide pupils. They darted back and forth across Less's face as in the act of reading. He seemed to be gathering up all his strength to smile, which, at last, he did.

"Was that your best good-bye kiss?" he said.

Then, a few months later, the wedding invitation in the mail: *Request your presence at the marriage of Federico Pelu and Thomas Dennis.* How awkward. He could under no circumstances accept, when everyone knew he was Freddy's old paramour; there would be chuckles and raised eyebrows, and, while normally Less wouldn't have cared, it was just too much to imagine the smile on Carlos's face. The smile of pity. Less had already run into Carlos at a Christmas benefit (a firetrap of pine branches), and he had pulled Less aside and thanked him for being so gracious in letting Freddy go: "Arthur, you know my son was never right for you."

Yet Less could not simply decline the invitation. To sit at home while all the old gang gathered up in Sonoma to drink Carlos's money—well, they would cackle about him all the same. Sad young Arthur Less had become sad old Arthur Less. Stories would be brought out of mothballs for ridicule; new ones would be tested, as well. The thought was unbearable; he could under no circumstances decline. Tricky, tricky, this life.

Along with the wedding invitation came a letter politely

reminding him of an offer to teach at an obscure university in Berlin, along with the meager remittance and the meager time remaining for an answer. Less sat at his desk, staring at the offer; the rearing stallion on the letterhead seemed to be erect. From the open window came the song of roofers hammering and the smell of molten tar. Then he opened a drawer and pulled out a pile of other letters, other invitations, unanswered; more were hidden deep within his computer; still more lay buried beneath a pile of phone messages. Less sat there, with the window rattling from the workers' din, and considered them. A teaching post, a conference, a writing retreat, a travel article, and so on. And, like those Sicilian nuns who, once a year, appear behind a lifted curtain, singing, so that their families can gaze upon them, in his little study, in his little house, for Arthur Less a curtain lifted upon a singular idea.

My apologies, he wrote on the RSVP, *but I will be out of the country. My love to Freddy and Tom.*

He would accept them all.

What a ramshackle itinerary he has nailed together!

First: this interview with H. H. H. Mandern. This gets him plane fare to New York City, with two days before the event to enjoy the city, aflame with autumn. And there is at least one free dinner (the writer's delight): with his agent, who surely has word from his publisher. Less's latest novel has been living with his publisher for over a month, as any modern couple lives together before a marriage, but surely his publisher will pop the question any day now. There will be champagne; there will be money.

Second: a conference in Mexico City. It is the kind of event that for years, Less has refused: a symposium on Robert's work. He and Robert split up a decade and a half ago, but once Robert became ill and unable to travel, the directors of literary festivals began to contact Less. Not as a novelist in his own right; rather, as a kind of witness. A Civil War widow, as Less thinks of it. These festivals want one last glimpse of the famous Russian River School of writers and artists, a 1970s bohemian world long receded over the horizon, and they will accept a reflected one. But Less has always refused. Not because it would diminish his own reputation—this is impossible, since Less feels almost subterranean in stature—but because it seems parasitic to make money off what was really Robert's world. And this time, even the money isn't enough. It's not enough by half. But it neatly kills the five days between New York and the prize ceremony in Turin.

Third: Turin. Less is dubious. He is supposedly up for a *prestigioso* award for a book recently translated into Italian. Which book? It took some searching to discover it is *Dark Matter*. A pang of love and regret; the name of an old amour on your cruise ship's passenger list. *Yes, we are happy to provide airfare from Mexico City to Turin; your driver will await*—as glamorous a sentence as Less has ever read. He wonders who funds such European excesses, considers they are perhaps laundering ill-gotten gains, and finds, printed at the bottom of the invitation, the name of an Italian soap conglomerate. Laundering indeed. But it gets him to Europe.

Fourth: the Wintersitzung at the Liberated University of Berlin—a five-week course "on a subject of Mr. Less's choosing." The letter is in German; the university is under the impression Arthur Less is fluent in German, and Arthur Less's publisher, who recommended him, is also under this impression. So is Arthur Less. *With God's happiness,* he writes back, *I accept the pedestal of power,* and sends it off with a flush of pleasure.

Fifth: a sojourn across Morocco, his single indulgence on the itinerary. He would be tacking onto another birthday celebration, for someone he has never met named Zohra, who has planned an expedition from Marrakech into the Sahara Desert and from thence northward to Fez. His friend Lewis insisted; they were looking to fill one spot on the trip—how perfect! The wine would be copious, the conversation scintillating, and the amenities deluxe. How could he say no? The answer, as always: money, money, money. Lewis relayed the cost, all inclusive, and, though the amount was staggering (Less checked twice to be sure it was not in Moroccan dirhams), he was, as always, already too much in love. Bedouin music was already playing in his ears; camels were already grunting in the darkness; he was already standing up from embroidered pillows and walking out into the desert night, champagne in hand, to let the floury Sahara warm his toes as, above him, the Milky Way glowed with his birthday candles.

For it was somewhere in the Sahara that Arthur Less would turn fifty.

He swore he would not be alone. Memories of his fortieth, wandering the broad avenues of Las Vegas, still came to him in worser moments. He would not be alone.

Sixth: to India. Who gave him this peculiar idea? Carlos,

of all unlikely people. It was at the very Christmas party where his old rival first discouraged Less in one field ("My son was never right for you") and then encouraged him in another ("You know, there's a retreat center very close to a resort I'm fixing up, friends of mine, beautiful place, on a hill above the Arabian Sea; it would be a wonderful place for you to write"). India: perhaps he could rest at last; he could polish the final draft of his novel, the one whose acceptance his agent will surely be celebrating in New York with that champagne. When was monsoon season again?

And, finally: to Japan. He was, improbable as it seems, at a writer's poker game in San Francisco when it fell into his lap. Needless to say, these were heterosexual writers. Even in his green eyeshade, Less was not a convincing player; the first game, he lost every hand. But he was a good sport. It was during the third game—when Less began to think he could not bear another minute of the cigarette smoke and grunting and warm Jamaican beer—when one man looked up and said his wife was pissed at all his travel, he had to stay home and pass on an article, and could anyone could go to Kyoto in his stead? "I can!" Less shrieked. The poker faces all looked up, and Less was reminded of volunteering for the school play in junior high: the same expressions on the faces of the football players. He cleared his throat and lowered his voice: "I can." A piece for an in-flight magazine about traditional kaiseki cuisine. He hoped he would not be too early for the cherry blossoms.

From there, he will head back to San Francisco and return, once again, to his house on the Vulcan Steps. Paid for, almost all of it, by festivals, prize committees, universities, residency programs, and media conglomerates. The rest, he has found, he can cover with free airline points that, neglected over the decades, have multiplied into a digital fortune, as in a sorcerer's magic chest. After prepaying for the Morocco extravagance, he has just enough in his savings to cover necessities, providing he practices the Puritanical thrift drilled into him by his mother. No clothing purchases. No nights on the town. And, God help him, no medical emergencies. But what could possibly go wrong?

Arthur Less, encircling the globe! It feels cosmonautical in nature. The morning he left San Francisco, two days before the event with H. H. H. Mandern, Arthur Less marveled that he would not be returning, as he had his entire life, from the east but from the mysterious west. And during this odyssey, he was certain he would not think about Freddy Pelu at all.

New York is a city of eight million people, approximately seven million of whom will be furious when they hear you were in town and didn't meet them for an expensive dinner, five million furious you didn't visit their new baby, three million furious you didn't see their new show, one million furious you didn't call for sex, but only five actually available to meet you. It is completely reasonable to call none of them. You could instead sneak off to a terrible, treacly Broadway show that you will never admit you paid two hundred dollars to see. This is what Less does on his first night, eating a hot dog dinner to make up for the extravagance. You cannot call it a guilty pleasure when the lights go down and the curtain goes up, when the adolescent heart begins to beat along with the orchestra, not when you feel no guilt. And he feels none; he feels only the shiver of delight when there is no-body around to judge you. It is a bad musical, but, like a bad lay, a bad musical can still do its job perfectly well. By the end, Arthur Less is in tears, sobbing in his seat, and he thinks he has been sobbing quietly until the lights come up and the woman seated beside him turns and says, "Honey, I don't know what happened in your life, but I am so so sorry," and gives him a lilac-scented embrace. *Nothing happened to me,* he wants to say to her. *Nothing happened to me. I'm just a homosexual at a Broadway show.*

Next morning: the coffeemaker in his hotel room is a hungry little mollusk, snapping open its jaws to devour pods and subsequently secreting coffee into a mug. The instructions on care and feeding are clear, and yet somehow Less manages to produce, on the first go, nothing but steam and, on the second, a melted version of the pod itself. A sigh from Less.

It is an autumn New York morning, and therefore glorious; it is his first day of his long journey, the day before the interview, and his clothes are still clean and neat, socks still paired, blue suit unwrinkled, toothpaste still American and not some strange foreign flavor. Bright-lemon New York light flashing off the skyscrapers, onto the quilted aluminum sides of food carts, and from there onto Arthur Less himself. Even the mean delighted look from the lady who would not hold the elevator, the humor-free girl at the coffee shop, the tourists standing stock-still on busy Fifth Avenue, the revved-up accosting hawkers ("Mister, you like comedy? Everybody likes comedy!"), the toothache sensation of jackhammers in concrete—none of it can dull the day. Here is a shop that sells only zippers. Here are twenty of them. The Zipper District. What a glorious city.

"What are you going to wear?" the bookstore employee asks when Less stops by to say hello. He has walked twenty wonderful blocks to get here.

"What am I going to *wear?* Oh, just my blue suit."

The employee (in pencil skirt, sweater, and glasses: a burlesque librarian) laughs and laughs. Her mirth settles into a smile. "No, but *seriously,*" she says, "what are you going to *wear?*"

"It's a great suit. What do you mean?"

"Well, it's H. H. H. Mandern! And it's almost Halloween! I found a NASA jumpsuit. Janice is coming as the Queen of Mars."

"I was under the impression he wanted to be taken seriously—"

"But it's H. H. H. Mandern! Halloween! We have to dress up!"

She does not know how carefully he packed his luggage. It is a clown car of contradictory possessions: cashmere sweaters yet light linen trousers, thermal underwear yet suntan lotion, a tie yet a Speedo, his workout set of rubber bands, and so on. What shoes do you pack for the university and the beach? What sunglasses for northern European gloom and South Asian sun? He would be passing through Halloween, Día de los Muertos, Festa di San Martino, Nikolaustag, Christmas, New Year's, Eid al-Mawlid, Vasant Panchami, and Hina Matsuri. The hats alone could fill a shopwindow. And then there is the suit.

•   •   •

There is no Arthur Less without the suit. Bought on a whim, in that brief era of caprice three years ago when he threw caution (and money) to the wind and flew to Ho Chi Minh City to visit a friend on a work trip, searching for air-conditioning in that humid, moped-plagued city, found himself in a tailor shop, ordering a suit. Drunk on car exhaust and sugarcane, he made a series of rash decisions, gave his home address, and by the next morning had forgotten all about it. Two weeks later, a package arrived in San Francisco. Perplexed, he opened it and pulled out a medium blue suit, lined in fuchsia, and sewn with his initials: *APL*. A rose-water smell from the box summoned, instantly, a dictatorial woman with a tight bun, hectoring him with questions. The cut, the buttons, the pockets, the collar. But most of all: the blue. Chosen in haste from a wall of fabrics: not an ordinary blue. Peacock? Lapis? Nothing gets close. Medium but vivid, moderately lustrous, definitely bold. Somewhere between ultramarine and cyanide salts, between Vishnu and Amon, Israel and Greece, the logos of Pepsi and Ford. In a word: bright. He loved whatever self had chosen it and after that wore it constantly. Even Freddy approved: "You look like someone famous!" And he does. Finally, at his advanced age, he has struck the right note. He looks good, and he looks like himself. Without it, somehow he does not. Without the suit, there is no Arthur Less.

But apparently the suit is not enough. Now, with a schedule crammed with lunches and dinners, he will have to find...what? A *Star Trek* uniform? He wanders down from the bookstore to his old neighborhood, where he lived after college, and it gives him a chance to reminisce about the old West Village. All gone now: the soul food restaurant that used to hold Less's extra key underneath the coconut cake, the string of fetish stores whose window displays of rubberized equipment gave young Less terrors, the lesbian bars Less used to frequent on the theory he would have a better chance with the men there, the seedy bar where a friend once bought what he thought was cocaine and emerged from the bathroom announcing he had just snorted Smarties, the piano bars stalked, one summer, by what the *New York Post* inaccurately called "the Karaoke Killer." Gone, replaced by prettier things. Beautiful shops of things made of gold, and lovely little chandelier restaurants that served only hamburgers, and shoes on display as if at a museum. Sometimes it seems only Arthur Less remembers how downright filthy this place used to be.

From behind him: "Arthur! Arthur Less?"

He turns around.

"Arthur Less! I can't believe it! Here I was, *just talking about you!*"

He has embraced the man before he can fully take in whom he is embracing, instead finding himself immersed in flannel, and over his shoulder a sad big-eyed young man with dreadlocks looks on. The man releases him and starts to talk about what an amazing coincidence this is, and all the while Less is thinking: *Who the hell is this?* A jolly round bald man with a neat gray beard, in plaid flannel and an orange scarf, standing grinning outside a grocery-store-used-to-be-a-bank on Eighth Avenue. In a panic, Less's mind races to put this man before a series of backgrounds—blue sky and beach, tall tree and river, lobster and wineglass, disco ball and drugs, bedsheets and sunrise—but nothing is coming to mind.

"I can't believe it!" the man says, not releasing his grip on Less's shoulder. "Arlo was just telling me about his breakup, and I was saying, you know, give it time. It seems impossible now, but give it time. Sometimes it takes years and years. And then I saw you, Arthur! And I pointed down the street, I said, *Look!* There's the man who broke my heart; I thought I'd never recover, I'd never want to see his face again, or hear his name, and look! There he is, out of nowhere, and I have no rancor. How long has it been, six years, Arthur? No rancor at all."

Less stands and studies him: the lines on his face like origami that has been unfolded and smoothed down with your hand, the little freckles on the forehead, the white fuzz from his ears to his crown, the coppery eyes flashing with anything but rancor. Who the hell is this old man?

"You see, Arlo?" the man says to the young man. "Nothing. No feelings at all! You just get over all of them. Arlo, will you take a picture?"

And Less finds himself embracing this man again, this chubby stranger, and smiling for a picture that young Arlo moves to take until the man begins instructing him: "Take it again; no, take it from over there, hold the camera higher; no, *higher;* no, HIGHER!"

"Howard," Less says to his old lover, smiling. "You look wonderful."

"And so do you, Arthur! Of course, we didn't know how young we were, did we? Look at both of us now, old men!"

Less steps back, startled.

"Well, good to see you!" Howard says, shaking his head and repeating, "Isn't that lovely? Arthur Less, right here on Eighth Avenue. Good to see you, Arthur! You take care, we've got to run!"

A kiss on the cheek is misaimed and lands on the history professor's mouth; he smells of rye bread. Brief flash to six years ago, seeing his silhouette in the theater and thinking: *Here is a good companion.* A man he almost stayed with, almost loved, and now he does not even recognize him on the street. Either Less is an asshole, or the heart is a capricious thing. It is not impossible both are true. A wave to poor Arlo, to whom none of this is a comfort. The two are about to cross the street when Howard stops, turns back, and, with a bright expression, says: "Oh! You were a friend of Carlos Pelu, weren't you? Isn't it a small world! Maybe I'll see you at the wedding?"

Arthur Less did not publish until he was in his thirties. By then, he had lived with the famous poet Robert Brownburn for years in a small house—a shack, they always called it— halfway up a steep residential stairway in San Francisco. The Vulcan Steps, they're called, curving from Levant Street at the top, down between Monterey pines, ferns, ivy, and bottle-brush trees, to a brick landing with a view east to downtown. Bougainvillea bloomed on their porch like a discarded prom dress. The "shack" was only four rooms, one of them expressly Robert's, but they painted the walls white and hung up paintings Robert had gotten from friends (one of them of an almost-identifiable Less, nude, on a rock), and planted a seedling trumpet vine below the bedroom window. It took five years for Less to take Robert's advice and write. Just labored short stories at first. And then, almost at the end of their lives together, a novel. *Kalipso:* a retelling of the Calypso myth from *The Odyssey,* with a World War II soldier washed ashore in the South Pacific and brought back to life by a local man who falls in love with him and must help him find a way back to his world, and to his wife back home. "Arthur, this book," Robert said, taking off his glasses for effect. "It's an honor to be in love with you."

It was a moderate success; none other than Richard Champion deigned to review it in the pages of the *New York Times.* Robert read it first and then passed it to Less, smiling, his glasses on his forehead for his poet's second pair of eyes; he said it was a good review. But every author can taste the poison another has slipped into the punch, and Champion ended by calling the author himself "a magniloquent spoony." Less stared at those words like a child taking a test. *Magniloquent* sounded like praise (but was not). But a spoony? What the hell was a spoony?

"It's like a code," Less said. "Is he sending messages to the enemy?"

He was. "Arthur," Robert said, holding his hand, "he's just calling you a faggot."

Yet, like those impossible beetles that survive years in the dunes, living only on desert rains, his novel somehow, over the years, kept selling. It sold in England, and France, and Italy. Less wrote a second novel, *The Counterglow,* which got less attention, and a third, *Dark Matter,* which the head of Cormorant Publishing pushed hard, giving it an enormous publicity budget, sending him to over a dozen cities. At the launch, in Chicago, he stood offstage and listened to his introduction ("Please welcome the magniloquent author of the critically acclaimed *Kalipso*...") and heard the whimpering applause of perhaps fifteen, twenty people in the auditorium—that dreadful harbinger, like the dark rain spots one notices on a sidewalk before the storm—and he was brought back to his high school reunion. The organizers had convinced him to do a reading billed, on the mailed invitation, as "An Evening with Arthur Less." No one in high school had ever wanted an evening with Arthur Less, but he took them at their word. He showed up at low squat Delmarva High School (even squatter than in memory), thinking of how far he had come. And I will let you guess how many alumni came to "An Evening with Arthur Less."

By the publication of *Dark Matter,* he and Robert had parted, and since then, Less has had to live on desert rains alone. He did get the "shack" when Robert decamped to Sonoma (mortgage paid off after Robert's Pulitzer); the rest he has patched together, that crazy quilt of a writer's life: warm enough, though it never quite covers the toes.

But this next book! This is the one! It is called *Swift* (to whom the race does not go): a peripatetic novel. A man on a walking tour of San Francisco, and of his past, returning home after a series of blows and disappointments ("All you do is write gay *Ulysses*," said Freddy); a wistful, poignant novel of a man's hard life. Of broke, gay middle age. And today, at dinner, surely over champagne, Less will get the good news.

In his hotel room, he puts on the blue suit (freshly dry-cleaned) and smiles before the mirror.

•   •   •

Nobody came to "An Evening with Arthur Less."

Freddy once joked that Less's agent was his "great romance." Yes, Peter Hunt knows Less intimately. He handles the struggles and fits and joys that no one else witnesses. And yet, about Peter Hunt, Less knows almost nothing at all. He cannot even recall where he is from. Minnesota? Is he married? How many clients does he have? Less has no idea, and yet, like a schoolgirl, he lives on Peter's phone calls and messages. Or, more precisely, like a mistress waiting for word from her man.

And here he is, coming into the restaurant: Peter Hunt. A basketball star in his college days, and his height still commands a room when he enters it, though now instead of a crew cut, he has white hair as long as a cartoon conductor's. As he crosses the restaurant, Peter telepathically shakes hands with friends on all sides of the room, then locks his gaze with poor smitten Less. Peter is wearing a beige corduroy suit, and it purrs as he sits. Behind him, a Broadway actress makes an entrance in black lace while on either side of her, two lobsters thermidor are revealed in clouds of steam. Like any diplomat at a tense negotiation, Peter never discusses business until the eleventh hour, so for the whole meal it is literary talk about authors Less feels obliged to pretend he has read. Only as they are having their coffee does Peter say: "I hear you'll be traveling." Less says yes, he's on a trip around the world. "Good," Peter says, signaling for the bill. "It will take your mind off things. I hope you're not too attached to Cormorant." Less stutters, then falls silent. Peter: "Because they passed on *Swift*. I think you should fiddle with it while you're traveling. Let new sights bring new ideas."

"What did they offer? They want changes?"

"No changes. No offer."

"Peter, am I being dumped?"

"Arthur, it is not to be. Let's think beyond Cormorant."

It is as if a trapdoor has opened beneath his dining chair. "Is it too . . . spoony?"

"Too wistful. Too poignant. These walk-around-town books, these day-in-the-life stories, I know writers love them. But I think it's hard to feel bad for this Swift fellow of yours. I mean, he has the best life of anyone I know."

"Too *gay?*"

"Use this trip, Arthur. You're so good at capturing a place. Tell me when you're back in town," Peter says, giving him a hug, and Less realizes that he is leaving; it is over; the bill was delivered and paid for all while Less was grappling in the dark, bottomless, slick-walled pit of this bad news. "And good luck tomorrow with Mandern. I hope his agent's not there. She's a monster."

His white hair whips around like a horse's tail, and he strides across the room. Less watches the actress accept Peter's kiss on her hand. Then he is gone, Less's great romance, off to charm another smitten writer.

Back in his room, he is surprised to find, in the Lilliputian bathroom, a Brobdingnagian tub. So, even though it is ten o'clock, he runs a bath. As it fills, he looks out at the city: the Empire State Building, twenty blocks down, is echoed, below, by an Empire Diner with a card stock sign: PASTRAMI.

From the other window, near Central Park, he sees the sign for the Hotel New Yorker. They are not kidding, no sir. No more than the New England inns called the Minuteman and the Tricorner are kidding, with their colonial cupolas topped with wrought iron weather vanes, their cannonball pyramids out front, or the Maine lobster pounds called the Nor'easter, hung with traps and glass buoys, are kidding, or the moss-festooned restaurants in Savannah, or the Western Grizzly Dry Goods, or the Florida Gator This and Gator That, or even the Californian Surfboard Sandwiches and Cable Car Cafés and Fog City Inn, are kidding. Nobody is kidding. They are dead serious. People think of Americans as easy-going, but in fact they are all dead serious, especially about their local culture; they name their bars "saloons" and their shops "Ye Olde"; they wear the colors of the local high school team; they are Famous for Their Pies. Even in New York City.

Perhaps Less, alone, is kidding. Here, looking at his clothes—black jeans for New York, khaki for Mexico, blue suit for Italy, down for Germany, linen for India—costume after costume. Each one is a joke, and the joke is on him: Less the gentleman, Less the author, Less the tourist, Less the hipster, Less the colonialist. Where is the real Less? Less the young man terrified of love? The dead-serious Less of twenty-five years ago? Well, he has not packed him at all. After all these years, Less doesn't even know where he's stored.

He turns off the water and gets into the tub. Hot hot hot hot hot! He steps out, red to his waist, and lets the cold run a little longer. Mist haunts the surface and the reflection of the white tiles, with their single stripe of black. He slips back in, the water only slightly too hot now. His body ripples beneath the reflection.

Arthur Less is the first homosexual ever to grow old. That is, at least, how he feels at times like these. Here, in this tub, he should be twenty-five or thirty, a beautiful young man naked in a bathtub. Enjoying the pleasures of life. How dreadful if someone came upon naked Less today: pink to his middle, gray to his scalp, like those old double erasers for pencil and ink. He has never seen another gay man age past fifty, none except Robert. He met them all at forty or so but never saw them make it much beyond; they died of AIDS, that generation. Less's generation often feels like the first to explore the land beyond fifty. How are they meant to do it? Do you stay a boy forever, and dye your hair and diet to stay lean and wear tight shirts and jeans and go out dancing until you drop dead at eighty? Or do you do the opposite—do you forswear all that, and let your hair go gray, and wear elegant sweaters that cover your belly, and smile on past pleasures that will never come again? Do you marry and adopt a child? In a couple, do you each take a lover, like matching nightstands by the bed, so that sex will not vanish entirely? Or do you let sex vanish entirely, as heterosexuals do? Do you experience the relief of letting go of all that vanity, anxiety, desire, and pain? Do you become a Buddhist? One thing you certainly do not do. You do not take on a lover for nine years, thinking it is easy and casual, and, once he leaves you, disappear and end up alone in a hotel bathtub, wondering what now.

From nowhere, Robert's voice:

I'm going to grow too old for you. When you're thirty-five I'll be sixty. When you're fifty I'll be seventy-five. And then what will we do?

It was in the early days; he was so young, maybe twenty-two. Having one of their serious conversations after sex. *I'm going to grow too old for you.* Of course Less said this was ridiculous, the age difference meant nothing to him. Robert was hotter than those stupid boys, surely he knew that. Men in their forties were so sexy: the calm assurance of what a man liked and didn't, where he set limits and where he set none, experience and a sense of adventure. It made the sex so much better. Robert lit another cigarette and smiled. *And then what will we do?*

And then comes Freddy, twenty years later, standing in Less's bedroom: "I don't think of you as old."

"But I am," Less says from where he lies in the bed. "I will be." Our hero resting sideways on his elbows. The dappled sunlight showing how the trumpet vine has grown, over the years, to lattice the window. Less is forty-four. Freddy, twenty-nine, wearing his red glasses, Less's tuxedo jacket, and nothing else. In the center of his furred chest, barely an indent where the hollow used to be.

Freddy looks at himself in the mirror. "I think I look better in your tuxedo than you do."

"I want to make sure," Less says, lowering his voice, "that I'm not preventing you from meeting anyone."

Freddy catches Arthur Less's gaze in the mirror. The young man's face tightens slightly, as if he had a toothache. At last, he says, "You don't have to worry about it."

"You're at an age—"

"I know." Freddy has the look of someone paying very

close attention to every word. "I understand where we are. You don't have to worry about it."

Less settles back in the bed, and they look at each other silently for a moment. The wind sets the vine tapping against the window, scrambling the shadows. "I just wanted to talk—" he begins.

Freddy turns around. "We don't need to have a long talk, Arthur. You don't have to worry about it. I just think you should give me this tuxedo."

"Absolutely not. And stop using my cologne."

"I will when I'm rich." Freddy gets onto the bed. "Let's watch *The Paper Wall* again."

"Mr. Pelu, I just want to make sure," Less goes on, unable to let go until he is certain he has made his point, "that you don't get attached to me." He wonders when their conversations had begun to sound like a novel in translation.

Freddy sits up again, very serious. A strong jaw, the kind an artist would sketch, a jaw that reveals the man he has become. His jaw, and the eagle of dark hair on his chest—they belong to a man. A few details—the small nose and chipmunk smile and blue eyes in which his thoughts can so easily be read— are all that remains of that twenty-five-year-old watching the fog. Then he smiles.

"It's incredible how vain you are," Freddy says.

"Just tell me you think my wrinkles are sexy."

Crawling closer: "Arthur, there isn't a part of you that isn't sexy."

The water has grown cold, and the tiled windowless room feels like an igloo now. He sees himself reflected in the tiles, a wavering ghost on the shiny white surface. He cannot stay in here. He cannot go to bed. He has to do something not sad.

When you're fifty I'll be seventy-five. And then what will we do?

Nothing to do but laugh about it. True for everything.

I remember Arthur Less in his youth. I was twelve or so and very bored at an adult party. The apartment itself was all in white, as was everyone invited, and I was given some kind of colorless soda and told not to sit on anything. The silver-white wallpaper had a jasmine-vine repetition that fascinated me for long enough to notice that every three feet, a little bee was kept from landing on a flower by the frozen nature of art. Then I felt a hand on my shoulder—"Do you want to draw something?" I turned, and there was a young blond man smiling down at me. Tall, thin, long hair on top, the idealized face of a Roman statue, and slightly pop eyed as he grinned at me: the kind of animated expression that delights children. I must have assumed he was a teenager. He brought me to the kitchen, where he had pencils and paper, and said we could draw the view. I asked if I could draw him. He laughed at that, but he said all right and sat on a stool listening to the music playing from the other room. I knew the band. It never occurred to me that he was hiding from the party.

No one could rival Arthur Less for his ability to exit a room while remaining inside it. He sat, and his mind immediately left me behind. His lean frame in pegged jeans and a big speckled white cable-knit sweater, his long flushed neck stretched as he listened—"So *lonely,* so *lonely*"—too big a head for his frame, in a way, too long and rectangular, lips too red, cheeks too rosy, and a thick glossy head of blond hair buzzed short on the sides and falling in a wave over his forehead. Staring off at the fog, hands in his lap, and mouthing along to the lyrics—"So *lonely*, so *lonely*"—I blush to think of the tangle of lines I made of him. I was too much in awe of his *self-sufficiency*, of his *freedom*. To disappear within himself for ten or fifteen minutes while I drew him, when I could barely sit still to hold the pencil. And after a while, his eyes brightened, and he looked at me and said, "What do you got?" and I showed him. He smiled and nodded and gave me some tips, and asked if I wanted more soda.

"How old are you?" I asked him.

His mouth screwed into a smile. He brushed the hair out of his eyes. "I'm twenty-seven."

For some reason, I found this to be a terrible betrayal. "You're not a kid!" I told him. "You're a man!"

How inconceivable to watch the man's face blush with injury. Who knows why what I said wounded him; I suppose he liked to think of himself as a boy still. I had taken him for confident when he was in truth full of worry and terror. Not that I saw all that then, when he blushed and his eyes went down. I knew nothing of anxiety or other pointless human suffering. I only knew I had said the wrong thing.

An old man appeared in the doorway. He seemed old to me: white oxford shirt, black spectacles, something like a pharmacist. "Arthur, let's get out of here." Arthur smiled at me and thanked me for a nice afternoon. The old man glanced at me and nodded briefly. I felt the need to fix whatever I had done wrong. Then, together, they left. Of course

I did not know that it was the Pulitzer Prize–winning poet Robert Brownburn. With his young lover, Arthur Less.

"Another Manhattan, please."

It is later the same night; Arthur Less had better not be hungover for the interview tomorrow with Mandern. And he had better find something space operatic to wear.

He is talking: "I'm traveling around the world."

This conversation takes place in a Midtown bar close to the hotel. Less used to frequent it as a very young man. Nothing has changed about the joint: not the doorman, dubious of anyone wanting to enter; not the framed portrait of an older Charlie Chaplin; not the lounge whose curved bar serves the young swiftly and the old tardily; not the black grand piano whose player (as in a Wild West saloon) dutifully plays whatever he is ordered to (Cole Porter, mostly); not the striped wallpaper, nor the shell-shaped sconces, nor the clientele. It is known as a place for older men to meet younger ones; two antiquities are interviewing a slick-haired man on a couch. Less is amused to think that now he is on the other end of the equation. He is talking to a balding but handsome young man from Ohio, who for some reason is listening intently. Less has not yet noticed, displayed above the bar, a Russian cosmonaut's helmet.

"Where to next?" the fellow asks brightly. He has a redhead's missing lashes and freckled nose.

"Mexico. Then I'm up for a prize in Italy," Less says. He is drinking Manhattan number two, and it has done its job. "I'm not going to win it. But I had to leave home."

The redhead rests his head on his hand. "Where's home, handsome?"

"San Francisco." Less is having a memory from nearly thirty years before: walking out of an Erasure concert with his friend, stoned, learning that the Democrats had retaken the Senate, and walking into this bar and declaring: "We want to sleep with a Republican! Who's a Republican?" And every man in the place raising his hand.

"San Francisco's not too bad," the young man says with a smile. "Just a little smug. Why leave?"

Less leans against the bar and looks directly at his new friend. Cole Porter is still alive in that piano, and Less's cherry is still alive in his Manhattan; he plucks it from the drink. Charlie Chaplin stares down (why Charlie Chaplin?). "What do you call a guy who you're sleeping with—let's say you do that for nine years, you make breakfast and have birthday parties and arguments and wear what he tells you to wear, for nine years, and you're nice to his friends, and he's always at your place, but you know all the time it can't go anywhere, he's going to find someone, it won't be you, that's agreed on from the start, he's going to find someone and marry him—what do you call that guy?"

The piano moves into "Night and Day" with a furious tom-tom beat.

His barmate lifts an eyebrow. "I don't know, what do you call him?"

"Freddy." Less takes the cherry stem in his mouth and, within a few seconds, removes it tied into a knot. He places the knot on the bar napkin before him. "He found someone, and he's marrying him."

The young man nods and asks, "What are you drinking, handsome?"

"Manhattans, but I'm buying. Excuse me, bartender," he says, pointing to the space helmet above them, "what's that over the bar?"

"Sorry, mister, not tonight," the redheaded man says, putting his hand on Less's. "It's on me. And the cosmonaut helmet is mine."

Less: "It's yours?"

"I work here."

Our hero smiles, looking down at his hand, then up at the redhead. "You'll think I'm nuts," he says. "I have a crazy favor to ask. I'm interviewing H. H. H. Mandern tomorrow, and I need—"

"I also live nearby. Tell me your name again?"

"Arthur Less?" the white-haired woman asks in the green room of the theater, while H. H. H. Mandern vomits into a bucket. "Who the hell is Arthur Less?"

Less stands in the doorway, space helmet under his arm, a smile imprinted on his face. How many times has he been asked this question? Certainly enough for it not to sting; he has been asked it when he was very young, back in the Carlos days, when he could overhear someone explaining how Arthur Less was that kid from Delaware in the green Speedo, the thin one by the pool, or later, when it was explained he was the lover of Robert Brownburn, the shy one by the bar, or even later, when it was noted he was his ex-lover and maybe shouldn't be invited over anymore, or when he was introduced as the author of a first novel, and then a second novel, and then as that fellow someone knew from somewhere long ago. And at last: as the man Freddy Pelu had been sleeping with for nine whole years, until Freddy married Tom Dennis. He has been all those things, to all those people who did not know who he was.

"I said, who the hell are you?"

No one out there in the theater will know who he is; when he will help H. H. H. Mandern, sick with food poisoning but unwilling to let down his fans, onto the stage, he will be introduced merely as "a huge fan." When he leads that hour-and-a-half-long interview, filling it with extended descriptions when he sees the writer is failing, answering some questions from the audience when Mandern turns his weary eyes to Less, when he saves this event, saves this poor man's career, still nobody will know who he is. They are there for H. H. H. Mandern. They are there for his robot Peabody. They have come dressed as robots or space goddesses or aliens because a writer has changed their lives. That other writer, sitting beside him, face partly visible in the open visor of a space helmet, is inconsequential; he will not be remembered; no one will know, or even wonder, who he is. And later tonight, when he boards a plane for Mexico City, and the young Japanese tourist beside him, hearing he is a writer, grows excited and asks who he is, Less, still in free fall from the broken bridge of his last hopes, will answer as he has so many times before.

A magniloquent spoony.

No rancor. No feelings at all.

Arthur, you know my son was never right for you.

"Nobody," says our hero to the city of New York.

LESS MEXICAN

FREDDY *Pelu is a man who doesn't need to be told, before take-off, to secure his own oxygen mask before assisting others.*

It was just a game they were playing, waiting for friends to join them at the bar. One of those San Francisco bars that is neither gay nor straight, just odd, and Freddy still wore his blue shirt and tie from teaching, and they were having some new kind of beer that tasted like aspirin and smelled like magnolias and cost more than a hamburger. Less was in a cable-knit sweater. They were trying to describe each other in a single sentence. Less had gone first and said the sentence written above.

Freddy frowned. "Arthur," he said. Then he looked down at the table.

Less took some candied pecans from the bowl before him. He asked what the problem could be. He thought he'd come up with a good one.

Freddy shook his head so that his curls bounced, and he sighed. "I don't think that's true. Maybe when you met me. But that was a long time ago. You know what I was going to say?"

Less said he did not know.

The young man stared at his lover and, before taking a sip of his beer, said: "'Arthur Less is the bravest person I know.'"

Arthur thinks of this on every flight. It always ruins everything. It has ruined this flight from New York to Mexico City, which is well on the way to ruining itself.

Arthur Less has heard it is traditional, in Latin American countries, to applaud an airplane's safe arrival. In his mind, he associates it with the miracles of Our Lady of Guadalupe, and indeed, while the plane suffers a prolonged bout of turbulence, Less finds himself searching for an appropriate prayer. He was, however, raised Unitarian; he has only Joan Baez to turn to, and "Diamonds and Rust" gives no solace. On and on the plane convulses in the moonlight, like a man turning into a werewolf. And yet, Arthur Less appreciates life's corny metaphors; a transformation, yes. Arthur Less, leaving America at last; perhaps, beyond its borders, he will change, like the aged crone who is rescued by a knight and who, once she is carried across the river, becomes a princess. Not Arthur Less the nobody, but Arthur Less the Distinguished Featured Speaker at this conference. Or was it a princess into a crone? The young Japanese tourist seated beside Less, impossibly hip in a yellow neon sweatsuit and moon-landing sneakers, is sweating and breathing through his mouth; at one point, he turns to Less and asks if this is normal, and Less says, "No, no, this is not normal." More throes, and the young man grabs his hand. Together they weather the storm. They are perhaps the only passengers literally without a prayer. And when the plane lands at last—the windows revealing the vast nighttime circuit board of Mexico City—Less finds himself, alone, applauding their survival.

What had Freddy meant, "the bravest person I know"? For Less, it is a mystery. Name a day, name an hour, in which Arthur Less was not afraid. Of ordering a cocktail, taking a taxi, teaching a class, writing a book. Afraid of these and almost everything else in the world. Strange, though; because he is afraid of everything, nothing is harder than anything else. Taking a trip around the world is no more terrifying than buying a stick of gum. The daily dose of courage.

What a relief, then, to emerge from customs and hear his name called out: "Señor Less!" There stands a bearded man, perhaps thirty, in the black jeans, T-shirt, and leather jacket of a rock musician.

"I am Arturo," says Arturo, holding out a hairy hand. This is the "local writer" who will be his escort for the next three days. "It is an honor to meet a man who knew the Russian River School."

"I am also Arturo," says Less, shaking it garrulously.

"Yes. You were fast through the customs."

"I bribed a man to take my bags." He gestures to a small man in a Zapata mustache and blue uniform standing arms akimbo.

"Yes, but that is not a bribe," says Arturo, shaking his head. "That is a *propina*. A tip. That is the luggage man."

"Oh," says Less, and the mustached man gives a smile.

"Is it your first time in Mexico?"

"Yes," Less says quickly. "Yes, it is."

"Welcome to Mexico." Arturo hands him a conference packet and looks up at him wearily; violet streaks curve beneath his eyes, and lines are grooved into his still-young brow. Less notices now that what he had taken for gleaming bits of pomade in his hair are streaks of gray. Arturo says, "There follows, I am sad to say, a very long ride on a very slow road . . . to your final place of rest."

He sighs, for he has spoken the truth for all men.

Less understands: he has been assigned a poet.

Of the Russian River School, Arthur Less missed all the fun. Those famous men and women took mallets to the statues of their gods, those bongo-drumming poets and action-painting artists, and scrambled from the sixties onto the mountaintop of the seventies, that era of quick love and quaaludes (is there any more perfect spelling than with that lazy superfluous vowel?), basking in their recognition and arguing in cabins on the Russian River, north of San Francisco, drinking and smoking and fucking into their forties. And becoming, some of them, models for statues themselves. But Less came late to the party; what he met were not young Turks but proud bloated middle-aged artists who rolled in the river like sea lions. They seemed over-the-hill to him; he could not understand they were in the prime of their minds: Leonard Ross, and Otto Handler, even Franklin Woodhouse, who did that nude of Less. Less also owns a framed excision poem, made for his birthday by Stella Barry out of a tattered copy of *Alice in Wonderland*. He heard bits of Handler's *Patty Hearst* on an old piano in a rainstorm. He saw a draft of Ross's *Love's Labors Won* and watched him scratch out an entire scene. And they were always kind to Less, especially considering (or was it because of?) the scandal: Less had stolen Robert Brownburn from his wife.

But perhaps it is fitting, at last, for someone to praise them and to bury them, now that almost all of them are dead (Robert is still kicking but is barely breathing, in a facility in Sonoma—all those cigarettes, darling; they chat once a month on a video call). Why not Arthur Less? He smiles in the taxi as he weighs the packet: lapdog yellow, with its leash of red string. Little Arthur Less, sitting in the kitchen with the wives and watering down the gin while the fellows roared beside the fire. *And I alone have lived to tell the tale.* Tomorrow on the university stage: the famous American writer Arthur Less.

It takes an hour and a half in traffic to get to the hotel; the rivers of red taillights conjure lava flows that destroyed ancient villages. Eventually, the smell of greenery bursts into the cab; they have entered Parque México, once so open that Charles Lindbergh supposedly landed his plane here. Now: chic young Mexican couples strolling, and on one lawn, ten dogs of various breeds being trained to lie perfectly still on a long red blanket. Arturo strokes his beard and says, "Yes, the stadium in the middle of the park is named for Lindbergh, who was of course a famous father and a famous fascist. We are here."

To Less's delight, the name of the hotel is the Monkey House, and it is filled with art and music: in the front hallway is an enormous portrait of Frida Kahlo holding a heart in each hand. Below her, a player piano works through a roll of Scott Joplin. Arturo speaks in rapid Spanish to a portly older man, his hair slick as silver, who then turns to Less and says, "Welcome to our little home! I hear you are a famous poet!"

"No," Less said. "But I knew a famous poet. That seems to be enough, these days."

"Yes, he knew Robert Brownburn," Arturo gravely explains, hands clasped.

"Brownburn!" the hotel owner shouts. "To me he is better than Ross! When did you meet him?"

"Oh, a long time ago. I was twenty-one."

"Your first time in Mexico?"

"Yes, yes, it is."

"Welcome to Mexico!"

What other desperate characters have they invited to this shindig? He dreads the appearance of any acquaintances; he can bear only a private humiliation.

Arturo turns to Less with the pained expression of one who has just broken something beloved of yours. "Señor Less, I am so sorry," he begins. "I think you speak no Spanish, am I correct?"

"You are correct," Less says. He is so weary, and the festival packet is so heavy. "It's a long story. I chose German. A terrible mistake in my youth, but I blame my parents."

"Yes. Youth. And so tomorrow the festival is completely in Spanish. Yes, I can take you in the morning to the festival center. But you are not to speak until the third day."

"I'm not on until the third day?" His face takes on the expression of a bronze-medal winner in a three-man race.

"Perhaps"—here Arturo takes a deep breath—"I take you downtown to see our city instead? With a compatriot?"

Less sighs and smiles. "Arturo, that is a wonderful suggestion."

At ten the next morning, Arthur Less stands outside his hotel. The sun shines brightly, and overhead in the jacarandas three fantailed black birds make peculiar, merry noises. It takes a moment before Less understands they have learned to imitate the player piano. Less is in search of a café; the hotel's coffee is surprisingly weak and American flavored, and a poor night's sleep (Less painfully fondling the memory of a good-bye kiss) has led to an exhausted state.

"Are you Arthur Less?"

North American accent, coming from a lion of a man in his sixties, with a shaggy gray mane and a golden stare. He introduces himself as the festival organizer. "I'm the Head," he says, holding out a surprisingly dainty paw for a handshake. He names the midwestern university at which he is a professor. "Harold Van Dervander. I helped the director shape this year's conference and put together the panels."

"That's wonderful, Professor Vander...van..."

"Van Dervander. Dutch German. We had a very esteemed list. We had Fairborn and Gessup and McManahan. We had O'Byrne and Tyson and Plum."

Less swallows this piece of information. "But Harold Plum is dead."

"There were changes to the list," the Head admits. "But

the original list was a thing of beauty. We had Hemingway. We had Faulkner and Woolf."

"So you didn't get Plum," Less contributes. "Or Woolf, I assume."

"We didn't get anyone," says the Head, lifting his massive chin. "But I had them print out the original list; you should have found it in your packet."

"Wonderful," Less says, blinking in perplexity.

"Your packet also includes a donation envelope to the Haines Scholarship. I know you have just arrived, but after a weekend in this country he loved, you may be so moved."

"I don't—" says Arthur.

"And there," the Head says, pointing to the west, "are the peaks of Ajusco, which you will remember from his poem 'Drowning Woman.'" Less sees nothing in the smoggy air. He has never heard of this poem, or of Haines. The Head begins to quote from memory: 'Say you fell down the coal-chute one Sunday afternoon . . .' Remember?"

"I can't—" says Arthur.

"And have you seen the *farmacias?*"

"I haven't—"

"Oh, you must go, there's one just around the corner. Farmicias Similares. Generic drugs. It's the whole reason I throw this festival in Mexico. Did you bring your prescriptions? You can get them so much cheaper here." The Head points, and Less can now make out a pharmacy sign; he watches a small round woman in a white lab coat dragging the shop gate open. "Klonopin, Lexapro, Ativan," he coos. "But really I come down here for the Viagra."

"I won't—"

The Head gives a cat grin. "At our age, you've got to stock up! I'll try a pack this afternoon and tell you if it's legit." He puts his fist down at his crotch level, then springs his erectile thumb upward.

The mynah birds above mock them in ragtime.

"Señor Less, Señor Banderbander." It is Arturo; he seems not to have changed clothes or demeanor from the night before. "Are you ready to go?"

Less, still bewildered, turns to the Head. "You're coming with us? Don't you have to see the panels?"

"I really have put together some wonderful panels! But I never go," he explains, spreading his hands on his chest. "I don't speak Spanish."

Is it his first time in Mexico? No.

Arthur Less visited Mexico nearly thirty years ago, in a beat-up white BMW fitted with an eight-track tape player and only two tapes, two suitcases of hurriedly packed clothes, a bag of marijuana and mescaline taped under the spare tire, and a driver who sped down the length of California as if he were running from the law. That driver: the poet Robert Brownburn. He awakened young Arthur Less with a call early that morning, telling him to pack for three days, then showed up an hour later, motioning him quickly into the car. What caper was this? Nothing more than a fancy of Robert's. Less would grow used to these, but at the time he had known Robert for only a month; their encounters for drinks had turned into rented hotel rooms, and now, suddenly, this. Being whisked away to Mexico: it was the thrill of his young life. Robert shouting above the noise of the motor as they sped between the almond groves of Central California, then long stretches of quiet while they switched the tapes around again, and the rest stops where Robert would take young Arthur Less off behind the oak trees and kiss him until there were tears in his eyes. It all startled Less. Looking back, he understood that surely Robert was on something; probably some amphetamine one of his artist friends had given him up in Russian River. Robert was excited and happy and funny. He never offered whatever he was on to Less; he only handed him a joint. But he kept driving, with hardly a stop, for twelve hours, until they reached the Mexican border at San Ysidro, then another two hours through Tijuana and down toward Rosarito, where, at last, they drove along an ocean set on fire by a sunset that cooled to a line of neon pink, and finally arrived in Ensenada, at a seaside hotel where Robert was slapped on the back in welcome and given two shots of tequila. They smoked and made love all weekend, barely escaping the hot room except for food and a mescaline walk on the beach. From below, a mariachi band endlessly played a song that only constant repetition had allowed Less to memorize, and he sang along to the *llorar*s as Robert smoked and laughed:

> *Yo se bien que estoy afuera*
> *Pero el día que yo me muera*
> *Se que tendras que llorar*
> *(Llorar y llorar, llorar y llorar)*

> *I know I'm out of your life*
> *But the day that I die*

I know you are going to cry
(Cry and cry, cry and cry)

On Sunday morning, they bid good-bye to the hotel staff and headed in another speed streak back toward home; this time, they made it in eleven hours. Weary and dazed, young Arthur Less was dropped off at his apartment building, where he stumbled in for a few hours' sleep before work. He was deliriously happy, and in love. It did not occur to him until later that during the entire trip, he never asked the crucial question—*Where is your wife?*—and so decided never to mention the weekend around Robert's friends, fearing he would give something away. Less grew so used to covering up their scandalous getaway that even years later, when it can't possibly matter anymore, when asked if he has ever been to Mexico, Arthur Less always answers: no.

The tour of Mexico City begins with a subway ride. Why did Less expect tunnels filled with Aztec mosaics? Instead, he descends, with wonder, into a replica of his Delaware grammar school: the colorful railings and tiled floors, primary yellows and blues and oranges, the 1960s cheerfulness that history revealed to be a sham but that still lives on here, as it does in the teacher's-pet memory of Arthur Less. What retired principal has been brought down to design a subway on Less's dreams? Arturo motions for him to take a ticket, and Less duplicates his motions of feeding it to a robot as red-bereted police officers look on in groups large enough to make *futbol* teams.

"Señor Less, here is our train." Along comes an orange

Lego monorail, running along on rubber wheels before it comes to a stop and he steps inside and takes hold of a cold metal pole. He asks where they are going, and when Arturo answers "the Flower," Less feels he is indeed living now inside a dream—until he notices above his head a map, each stop represented by a pictograph. They are indeed headed to "the Flower." From there, they switch lines to head to "the Tomb." Flower to tomb; it is always thus. When they arrive, Less feels gentle pressure on his back from the woman behind him and is ejected smoothly onto the platform. The station: a rival grammar school, this time in bright blues. He follows Arturo and the Head closely through the tiled passages, the crowds, and finds himself on an escalator gliding upward into a square of peacock sky . . . and then he is in an enormous city square. All around, buildings of cut stone, tilting slightly in the ancient mud, and a massive cathedral. Why did he always assume Mexico City would be like Phoenix on a smoggy day? Why did no one tell him it would be Madrid?

They are met by a woman in a long black dress patterned with hibiscus blossoms, their guide, who leads them to one of Mexico City's markets, a stadium of blue corrugated steel, where they are met by four young Spanish men, clearly friends of Arturo's. Their guide stands before a table of candied fruits and asks if anyone has allergies or things they will not or cannot eat. Silence. Less wonders if he should mention make-believe foods like bugs and slimy Lovecraftian sea horrors, but she is already leading them between the stalls. Bitter chocolates wrapped in paper, piled in ziggurats beside a basket of Aztec whisks, shaped like wooden maces, and jars of multicolored salts such as those Buddhist monks might use to paint mandalas, along with plastic bins of rust- and cocoa-colored seeds, which their guide explains are not seeds but crickets; crayfish and worms both live and toasted, alongside the butcher's area of rabbits and baby goats still wearing their fluffy black-and-white "socks" to prove they are not cats, a long glass butcher's case that for Arthur Less increases in horrors as he moves along it, such that it seems like a contest of will, one he is sure to fail, but luckily they turn down the fish aisle, where somehow his heart grows colder among the gray speckled bodies of octopuses coiled in ampersands, the unnamable orange fish with great staring eyes and sharp teeth, the beaked parrotfish whose flesh, Less is told, is blue and tastes of lobster (he smells a lie); and how very close this all is to childhood haunted houses, with their jars of eyeballs, dishes of brains and jellied fingers, and that gruesome delight he felt as a boy.

"Arthur," the Head says as their guide leads them on between the icy shoals. "What was it like to live with genius? I understand you met Brownburn in your distant youth."

No one is allowed to say "distant youth" but you, isn't that a rule? But Less merely says, "Yes, I did."

"He was a remarkable man, playful, merry, tugging critics this way and that. And his movement was sublime. Full of joy. He and Ross were always one-upping each other, playing a game of it. Ross and Barry and Jacks. They were pranksters. And there's nothing more serious than a prankster."

"You knew them?"

"I *know* them. I teach every one of them in my course on middle-American poetry, by which I don't mean the middle America of small minds and malt shops, or midcentury America, but rather the middle, the muddle, the *void,* of America."

"That sounds—"

"Do you think of yourself as a genius, Arthur?"

"What? Me?"

Apparently the Head takes that as a no. "You and me, we've met geniuses. And we know we're not like them, don't we? What is it like to go on, knowing you are not a genius, knowing you are a mediocrity? I think it's the worst kind of hell."

"Well," Less said. "I think there's something between genius and mediocrity—"

"That's what Virgil never showed Dante. He showed him Plato and Aristotle in a pagan paradise. But what about the lesser minds? Are we consigned to the flames?"

"No, I guess," Less offers, "just to conferences like this one."

"You were how old when you met Brownburn?"

Less looks down into a barrel of salt cod. "I was twenty-one years old."

"I was forty when I happened upon Brownburn. Very late for us to meet. But my first marriage had ended, and suddenly there was humor and invention. He was a great man."

"He's still alive."

"Oh yes, we invited him to the festival."

"But he's bedridden in Sonoma," Less says, his voice finally taking on the fish market's chill.

"It was an earlier list. Arthur, I should tell you, we have a wonderful surprise for you—"

Their guide stops and addresses the group:

"These chilis are the center of Mexican cuisine, which has been labeled by UNESCO as a World Heritage intangible." She stands beside a row of baskets, all filled with dried chilis in various forms. "Mexico is the main Latin American country that uses hot peppers. You," she says to Less, "are probably more used to chilis than a Chilean." One of Arturo's friends who has joined them for the day is Chilean and nods in agreement. When asked which is the spiciest, the guide consults the vendor and says the tiny pink ones in a jar from Veracruz. Also the most expensive. "Would you like to taste some relishes?" A chorus of *Sí!* What follows is a contest of escalating difficulty, like a spelling bee. One by one, they taste the relishes, increasing in heat, to see who fails first. Less feels his face flush with each bite, but by the third round he has already outlasted the Head. When given a taste of a five-chili relish, he announces to the group:

"This tastes just like my grandmother's chow-chow."

They all look at him in shock.

The Chilean: "What did you say?"

"Chow-chow. Ask Professor Van Dervander. It is a relish in the American South." But the Head says nothing. "It tastes like my grandmother's chow-chow."

Slowly, the Chilean begins to guffaw, hand over his mouth. The others seem to be holding something in.

Less shrugs, looking from face to face. "Of course, her chow-chow wasn't so spicy."

At that, the dam breaks; all the young men burst into howls of laughter, hooting and weeping beside the chili bins. The vendor looks on with raised eyebrows. And even when it begins to subside, the men keep stoking their laughter, asking Less how often he tastes his grandmother's chow-chow. And does it taste different at Christmas? And so on. It does not take long for Less to understand, sharing a pitying glance with the Head, feeling the burn of the relish beginning anew in the back of his mouth, that there must be a false cognate in Spanish, yet another false friend...

What was it like to live with genius? Well, then there was the time he lost his ring in the mushroom bin at Happy Produce.

Less wore a ring, one Robert gave him on their fifth anniversary, and, while it was long before the days of gay marriage, they both knew it meant a kind of marriage: it was a thin gold Cartier Robert had found in a Paris flea market. And so young Arthur Less wore it always. While Robert wrote, locked in his room with the view of Eureka Valley, Less often went grocery shopping. This day he was in the mushrooms. He had pulled out a plastic bag and had just begun choosing mushrooms when he felt something spring from his finger. He knew instantly what it was.

In those days, Arthur Less was far from faithful. It was the way of things among the men they knew, and it was something he and Robert never spoke of. If on his errands he met a handsome man with a free apartment, Less might be willing to dally for half an hour before he came home. And once he took a real lover. Someone who wanted to talk, who came just short of asking for promises. At first it was a wonderful, casual connection not very far from his home, something easy to grab on an afternoon or when Robert was on a trip. There was a white bed beside a window. There was a parakeet that warbled. There was wonderful sex, and no talk afterward of *I forgot to tell you Janet called,* or *Did you put the parking permit on the car?* or *Remember, I'm going to LA tomorrow.* Just sex and a smile: *Isn't it wonderful to get what you want and pay no price?* Someone very unlike Robert, someone cheerful and bright, with affection, and, maybe, not terribly smart. It took a long time for it to be sad. There were fights and phone calls and long walks with little said. And it ended; Less ended it. He knew he had hurt someone terribly, unforgivably. That happened not long before he lost his ring in the mushroom bin.

"Oh shit," he said.

"Are you okay?" a bearded man asked, farther down the row of vegetables. Tall, glasses, holding a baby bok choy.

"Oh shit, I just lost my wedding ring."

"Oh shit," the man said, looking over at the bin. Maybe sixty cremini mushrooms—but, of course, it could have gone anywhere! It could be in the buttons! In the shiitakes! It could have flown into the chili peppers! How could you paw through chili peppers? The bearded man came over. "Okay, buddy. Let's just do this," he said, as if they were setting a broken arm. "One by one."

Slowly, methodically, they put each mushroom into Less's bag.

"I lost mine once," the man offered as he held the bag. "My wife was furious. I lost it twice, actually."

"She's going to be pissed," Arthur said. Why had he made Robert into a woman? Why was he so willing to go along? "I can't lose it. She got it in a Paris flea market."

Another man chimed in: "Use beeswax. To keep it tight

until you get it fitted." The kind of guy who wore his bicycle helmet while shopping.

The bearded man asked, "Where do you get it fitted?"

"Jeweler," the bike guy said. "Anywhere."

"Oh, thanks," Arthur said. "If I find it."

At the grim prospect of loss, the bike guy started to pick through the mushrooms along with them. A male voice from behind him: "Lose your ring?"

"Yep," said the bearded guy.

"When you find it, use chewing gum till you get it fixed."

"I said beeswax."

"Beeswax is good."

Was this how men felt? Straight men? Alone so often, but if they faltered—if they lost a wedding ring!—then the whole band of brothers would descend to fix the problem? Life was not hard; you shouldered it bravely, knowing all the time that if you sent the signal, help would arrive. How wonderful to be part of such a club. Half a dozen men gathered around, engaged in the task. To save his marriage and his pride. So they did have hearts, after all. They were not cold, cruel dominators; they were not high school bullies to be avoided in the halls. They were good; they were kind; they came to the rescue. And today Less was one of them.

They reached the bottom of the bin. Nothing.

"Ooh, sorry, buddy," the bike guy said, and grimaced. The bearded man: "Tell her you lost it swimming." One by one they shook his hand and shook their heads and left.

Less wanted to cry.

What a ridiculous person he was. What a terrible writer, to get caught up in a metaphor like this. As if it would reveal anything to Robert, signify anything about their love. It was just a ring lost in a bin. But he could not help himself; he was too attracted to the bad poetry of it all, of his one good thing, his life with Robert, undone by his carelessness. There was no way to explain it that would not sound like betrayal. Everything would show in his voice. And Robert, the poet, would look up from his chair and see it. That their time had come to an end.

Less leaned against the Vidalia onions and sighed. He took the bag, now empty of mushrooms, to crumple it up and toss it in the trash bin. A glint of gold.

And there it was. In the bag all along. Oh, wonderful life.

He laughed, he showed it to the shop owner. He bought all five pounds of mushrooms the men had handled and went home and made a soup with pork ribs and mustard greens and all the mushrooms and told Robert everything that had happened, from the ring, to the men, to the discovery, the great comedy of it all.

And in the telling, laughing at himself, he watched as Robert looked up from his chair and saw everything.

That's what it was like to live with genius.

The subway ride back to the hotel is made half as charming by being filled with twice as many people, and the heat of the afternoon has made Less self-conscious that he smells of fish and peanuts. They pass the Farmacias Similares on the way to the hotel, and the Head tells them he will catch up with them in a minute. They continue to the Monkey House (missing its mynahs), and, though Less bows a quick good-bye, Arturo will not let him go. He insists that the

American must taste mescal, that it might change his writing, or perhaps his life. There are some other writers waiting. Less keeps saying he has a headache, but nearby construction noise drowns him out and Arturo cannot understand. The Head returns, beaming in the late-afternoon light, a white bag in his hand. So Arthur Less goes along. Mescal turns out to be a drink that tastes as if someone has put their cigarette out in it. You drink it, he is informed, with an orange slice that has been coated in toasted worms. "You are kidding me," Less says, but they are not kidding him. Again: no one is kidding. They have six rounds. Less asks Arturo about his event at the festival, now a mere two days away. Arturo, his dour mood unchanged even after a bath of mescal, says, "Yes. I am sorry to say tomorrow the festival is also entirely in Spanish; shall I take you to Teotihuacán?" Less has no idea what this is, agrees, and asks again about his own event. Will he be onstage alone, or in conversation?

"I hope there will be conversation," Arturo states. "You will be there with your friend."

Less asks if his fellow panelist is a professor or a fellow writer.

"No, no, *friend,*" Arturo insists. "You are speaking with Marian Brownburn."

"Marian? *His wife?* She's here?!"

"*Sí.* She arrives tomorrow night."

Less tries to assemble the wayward congress of his mind. Marian. The last words she ever said to him were *Take care of my Robert.* But she had not known then that he would take him from her. Robert kept Less away from the divorce, found the shack on the Vulcan Steps, and he never met her again. Would she be seventy? Finally given a stage to say what she thinks of Arthur Less? "Listen listen listen, you can't have us together. We haven't seen each other in almost thirty years."

"Señor Banderbander thinks it is a nice surprise for you."

Less does not remember what he replies. All he knows is that he has been fooled into returning to Mexico, to the scene of the crime, to be impaneled before the world beside the woman he has wronged. Marian Brownburn, with a microphone. Surely this is how gay men are judged in Hell. By the time he returns to the hotel, he is drunk and stinks of smoke and worms.

The next morning Less is awakened at six, as planned, introduced to a cup of coffee, and led into a black van with smoked windows; Arturo is there with two new friends, who seem to speak no English. Less looks for the Head, to forestall disaster, but the Head is nowhere in sight. All of this is in the predawn darkness of Mexico City, with the sound of awakening birds and pushcarts. Arturo has also hired another guide (presumably at the festival's expense): a short athletic man with gray hair and wire glasses. His name is Fernando, and he turns out to be a history professor at the university. He tries to engage Arthur in a discussion of the highlights of Mexico City and whether Less is interested in seeing them, perhaps after Teotihuacán (which has not yet been described). There are, for example, the twin houses of Diego Rivera and Frida Kahlo, surrounded by a fence of spineless cactus. Arthur Less nods, saying this morning he feels like a spineless cactus. "Sorry?" the guide asks. Yes, Less says, yes, he would like to see that.

"I am afraid it is closed to mount a new exhibit."

And there is, as well, the house of the architect Luis Bar-ragán, designed for a lifestyle of monkish mystery, where low ceilings lead to vaulted spaces, and Madonnas watch over the guest bed, and his private changing room is overseen by a Christ crucified without a cross. Less says that sounds lonely, but he would like to see that as well.

"Yes, ah, but it too is closed."

"You are a terrible tease, Fernando," Less says, but the man does not seem to know what this means and goes on to describe the National Museum of Anthropology, the city's greatest museum, which can take days or even weeks to see completely but, with his guidance, can be done in a number of hours. By this point, the van has clearly taken them out of Mexico City proper, the parks and mansions replaced by concrete shantytowns, painted all in taffy colors that Less knows belie their misery. A sign points to TEOTIHUACÁN Y PIRÁMIDES. The museum of anthropology, Fernando insists, is not to be missed.

"But it is closed," Less offers.

"On Mondays, I am sorry, yes."

As the van rounds the corner of an agave grove, he is aware of an enormous structure, with the sun pulsing behind it and striping it in shadows of green and indigo: the Temple of the Sun. "It is not the Temple of the Sun," Fernando informs him. "That is what the Aztecs thought it was. It is most probably the Temple of the Rain. But we know almost nothing about the people who built it. The site was long abandoned by the time the Aztecs came through. We believe they burned their own city to the ground." A cold blue silhouette of a long-lost civilization. They spend the morning climbing the two massive pyramids, the Temple of the Sun and the Temple of the Moon, walking the Avenue of the Dead ("It is not the Avenue of the Dead, really," Fernando informs him, "and it is not the Temple of the Moon"), imagining all of it covered in painted stucco, miles and miles, every wall and floor and roof in the ancient city that once held hundreds of thousands of people, about whom literally nothing is known. Not even their names. Less imagines a priest covered in peacock feathers walking down the steps as in an MGM musical, or a drag show, arms spread wide, as music plays from conch shells all around and Marian Brownburn, standing at the top, holds the beating heart of Arthur Less. "They chose this spot, we think, because it was far from the volcano that destroyed villages in ancient times. That volcano there," Fernando said, pointing to a peak barely visible in the morning haze.

"Is it still active, that volcano?"

"No," Fernando says sadly, shaking his head. "It is closed."

What was it like to live with genius?

Like living alone.

Like living alone with a tiger.

Everything had to be sacrificed for the work. Plans had to be canceled, meals had to be delayed; liquor had to be bought, as soon as possible, or else all poured into the sink. Money had to be rationed or spent lavishly, changing daily. The sleep schedule was the poet's to make, and it was as often late nights as it was early mornings. The habit was the demon pet in the house; the habit, the habit, the habit; the morning coffee and books and poetry, the silence until noon. Could he be tempted by a morning stroll? He could, he always could; it was the only addiction where the sufferer longed for anything *but* the desired; but a morning walk meant work undone, and suffering, suffering, suffering. Keep the habit, help the habit; lay out the coffee and poetry; keep the silence; smile when he walked sulkily out of his office to the bathroom. Taking nothing personally. And did you sometimes leave an art book around with a thought that it would be the key to his mind? And did you sometimes put on music that might unlock the doubt and fear? Did you love it, the rain dance every day? Only when it rained.

Where did the genius come from? Where did it go?

Like allowing another lover into the house to live with you, someone you'd never met but whom you knew he loved more than you.

Poetry every day. A novel every few years. Something happened in that room, despite everything; something beautiful happened. It was the only place in the world where time made things better.

Life with doubt. Doubt in the morning, with the oil beading on a cup of coffee. Doubt in the pee break, not catching his eye. Doubt in the sound of the front door opening and closing—a restless walk, no good-bye—and in the return. Doubt in the slow sound of typewriter keys. Doubt at lunchtime, taken in his room. Doubt vanishing in the afternoon like the fog. Doubt driven away. Doubt forgotten. Four in the morning, feeling him stirring awake, knowing he is staring at the darkness, at Doubt. *Life with Doubt: A Memoir.*

What made it happen? What made it not happen?

Thinking of a cure, a week away from the city, a dinner party with other geniuses, a new rug, a new shirt, a new way to hold him in bed, and failing and failing and somehow, at random, succeeding.

Was it worth it?

Luck in days of endless golden words. Luck in checks in the mail. Luck in prize ceremonies and trips to Rome and London. Luck in tuxedos and hands secretly held beside the mayor or the governor or, one time, the president.

Peeking in the room while he was out. Rooting through the trash bin. Looking at the blanket heaped on the napping couch, the books beside it. And, with dread, what sat half-written in the typewriter's gap-toothed mouth. For at the beginning, one never knew what he was writing about. Was it you?

Before a mirror, behind him, tying his tie for a reading while he smiles, for he knows perfectly well how to tie it.

Marian, was it worth it for you?

The festival takes place in University City, in a low-ceilinged concrete building associated with the Global Linguistics and Literature Department, whose famous mosaics have for some reason been removed for restoration, leaving it as barren as an old woman without her teeth. Again, the Head does not make an appearance. Less's day of judgment has arrived; he finds he is shaking with fear. Color-coded carpets lead to various subdepartments, and around any corner Marian Brownburn might appear, tanned and sinewy, as he remembers her on a beach, but when Less is led to a green room (painted a pastel green, supplied with a tower of fruit), he is introduced only to a friendly man in a harlequin tie. "Señor Less!" the man says, bowing twice. "What an honor for you to come to the festival!"

Less looks around for his personal Fury; there is no one in the room but him, this man, and Arturo. "Is Marian Brownburn here?"

The man bows. "I am sorry it was so much in Spanish."

Less hears his name shouted from the doorway and flinches. It is the Head, his curly white hair in disarray, his face a grotesque shade of red. He motions Less over; Less quickly approaches. "Sorry I missed you yesterday," says the Head. "I had other business, but I wouldn't miss this panel for the world."

"Is Marian here?" Less asks quietly.

"You'll be fine, don't worry."

"I'd just like to see her before we—"

"She isn't coming." The Head puts his heavy hand on Less's shoulder. "We got a note last night. She broke her hip; she's nearly eighty, you know. A shame, because we had so many questions for you both."

Less experiences not a helium-filled sense of relief, but a horrible deflating sorrow. "Is she okay?"

"She sends her love to you."

"But is she okay?"

"Sure. We had to make a new plan. I'm going to be up there with you! I'll talk for maybe twenty minutes about my work. Then I'll ask you about meeting Brownburn when you were twenty-one. Do I have that right? You were twenty-one?"

• • •

"I'm twenty-five," Less lies to the woman on the beach.

Young Arthur Less sitting on a beach towel, perched with three other men above the high-tide line. It is San Francisco in October 1987, it is seventy-five degrees, and everyone is celebrating like children with a snow day. No one goes to work. Everyone harvests their pot plants. Sunlight flows as sweet and yellow as the cheap champagne sitting, half-finished and now too warm, in the sand beside young Arthur Less. The anomaly causing the hot weather is also responsible for extraordinarily high waves that send men scrambling from the rockier gay section over to the straight section of Baker Beach, and there they all huddle together, united in the dunes. Before them: the ocean wrestles with itself in silver-blue. Arthur Less is a little drunk and a little high. He is naked. He is twenty-one.

The woman beside him, tanned to alder wood, topless, has begun to talk to him. She wears sunglasses; she is smoking; she is somewhere past forty. She says, "Well, I hope you're making good use of youth."

Less, cross-legged on his towel and pink as a boiled shrimp: "I don't know."

She nods. "You should waste it."

"What's that?"

"You should be at the beach, like today. You should get stoned and drunk and have loads of sex." She takes another drag off her cigarette. "I think the saddest thing in the world is a twenty-five-year-old talking about the stock market. Or *taxes.* Or real estate, goddamn it! That's *all* you'll talk about when you're forty. Real estate! Any twenty-five-year-old who says the word *refinance* should be taken out and shot. Talk about love and music and poetry. Things everyone forgets they ever thought were important. Waste every day, that's what I say."

He laughs goofily and looks over at his group of friends. "I guess I'm doing pretty good at that."

"You queer, honey?"

"Oh," he says, smiling. "Yeah."

The man beside him, a broad-chested Italianate fellow in his thirties, asks for young Arthur Less to "do my back." The lady seems amused, and Less turns to apply cream to the man's back, the color of which reveals it is far too late. Dutifully, he does his job anyway and receives a pat on the rump. Less takes a swig of warm champagne. The waves are growing in intensity; people leap in there, laughing, screaming with delight. Arthur Less at twenty-one: thin and boyish, not a muscle on him, his blond hair bleached white, his toes painted red, sitting on a beach on a beautiful day in San Francisco, in the awful year of 1987, and terrified, terrified, terrified. AIDS is unstoppable.

When he turns, the lady is still staring at him and smoking.

"Is that your guy?" she asks.

He looks over at the Italian, then turns back and nods.

"And the handsome man beyond him?"

"My friend Carlos." Naked, muscled, and browned by the sun, like a polished redwood burl: young Carlos lifting his head from the towel as he hears his name.

"You boys are all so beautiful. Lucky man to have snatched you up. I hope he fucks you silly." She laughs. "Mine used to."

"I don't know about that," Less says softly, so that the Italian will not hear.

"Maybe what you need at your age is a broken heart."

He laughs and runs a hand through his bleached hair. "I don't know about that either!"

"Ever had one?"

"No!" he shouts, still laughing, bringing his knees up to his chest.

A man stands up from behind the woman; her pose has hidden him all this time. The lean body of a runner, sunglasses, a Rock Hudson jaw. Also naked. He looks down first at her, then at young Arthur Less, then says aloud to everybody that he is going in.

"You're an idiot!" the lady says, sitting straight up. "It's a hurricane out there."

He says he has swum in hurricanes before. He has a faint British accent, or perhaps he's from New England.

The lady turns to Less and lowers her sunglasses. Her eye shadow is hummingbird blue. "Young man, my name's Marian. Will you do me a favor? Go in the water with my ridiculous husband. He may be a great poet, but he's a terrible swimmer, and I can't bear to watch him die. Will you go with him?"

Young Arthur Less nods yes and stands up with the smile he saves for grown-ups. The man nods in greeting.

Marian Brownburn grabs a large black straw hat, puts it on her head, and waves to them. "Go on, boys. Take care of my Robert!"

The sky takes on a shimmer as blue as her eye shadow, and as the men approach the waves they seem to redouble in violence like a fire that has been fed a bundle of kindling. Together they stand in the sun before those terrible waves, in the fall of that terrible year.

By spring, they will be living together on the Vulcan Steps.

"We had to do a quick change to the program. You can see it has a new title." But Less, conversant only in German, can make nothing of the words on the paper he has just been handed. People are coming and going now, clipping a microphone to his lapel, offering him water. But Arthur Less is still halfway lit by beach sunshine, halfway in the water of the Golden Gate in 1987. *Take care of my Robert.* And now, an old woman falling and breaking her hip.

She sends her love. No rancor, no feelings at all.

The Head leans forward with a whisper and a comradely wink: "By the way. Wanted you to know, those pills work great!"

Less looks over at the man. Is it the pills that make him so flushed and grotesque? What else do they sell here for middle-aged men? Is there a pill for when the image of a trumpet vine comes into your head? Will it erase it? Erase the voice saying, *You should kiss me like it's good-bye*? Erase the tuxedo jacket, or at least the face above it? Erase the whole nine years? Robert would say, *The work will fix you.* The work, the habit, the words, will fix you. Nothing else can be depended on, and Less has known genius, what genius can do. But what if you are not a genius? What will the work do then?

"What's the new title?" Less asks. The Head passes the program to Arturo. Less consoles himself that tomorrow he will board a plane to Italy. The language is getting to him. The lingering taste of mescal is getting to him. The tragicomic business of being alive is getting to him.

Arturo studies the program for a moment, then looks up gravely:

"Una Noche con Arthur Less."

LESS ITALIAN

ALONG with the other drugs Arthur Less bought at Mexico City's airport farmacia, Less has obtained a new variety of sleeping pill. He recalls Freddy's advice from years before: "It's a hypnotic instead of a narcotic. They serve you dinner, you sleep seven hours, they serve you breakfast, you're there." Thus armed, Less boards the Lufthansa aircraft (he will have a fairly rushed layover in Frankfurt), settles into his window seat, chooses the Tuscan chicken (whose ravishing name reveals itself, like an internet lover, to be mere chicken and mashed potatoes), and with his Thumbelina bottle of red wine takes a single white capsule. His remaining anxiety from "Una Noche con Arthur Less" is working against his exhaustion; the sound of the Head's amplified voice loops in his brain, saying again and again, *We were talking backstage about mediocrity;* he hopes the drug will do its duty. It does: he does not remember finishing the Bavarian cream in its little eggcup, nor the removal of his dinner, nor setting his watch to a new time zone, nor a dozing talk with his seatmate: a girl from Jalisco. Instead, Less awakens to a plane of sleeping citizens under blue prison blankets. Dreamily happy, he looks at his watch and panics: only two hours have passed! There are still nine more to go. On the monitors, a recent American cop comedy plays soundlessly. As with any silent movie, it needs no sound for him to imagine its plot. A heist by amateurs. He tries to fall back asleep, his jacket as a pillow; his mind plays a movie of his present life. A heist by amateurs. Less takes a deep breath and fumbles in his bag. He finds another pill and puts it in his mouth. An endless process of dry swallowing he remembers from being a boy with his vitamins. Then it is done, and he places the thin satin mask again over his eyes, ready to reenter the darkness—

"Sir, your breakfast. Coffee or tea?"

"What? Uh, coffee."

Shades are being opened to let in the bright sun above the heavy clouds. Blankets are being put away. Has any time passed? He does not remember sleeping. He looks at his watch—what madman has set it? To what time zone: Singapore? Breakfast; they are about to descend into Frankfurt. And he has just taken a hypnotic. A tray is placed before him: a microwaved croissant with frozen butter and jam. A cup of coffee. Well, he will have to push through. Perhaps the coffee will counteract the sedative. You take an upper for a downer, right? *This,* Less thinks to himself as he tries to butter the bread with its companion chunk of ice, *is how drug addicts think*.

He is going to Turin for a prize ceremony, and in the days leading into the ceremony there will be interviews, something called a "confrontation" with high school students, and many luncheons and dinners. He looks forward to escaping, briefly, into the streets of Turin, a town unknown to him. Contained deep within the invitation was the information that the greater prize has already been awarded to the famous British author Fosters Lancett, son of the famous British author Reginald Lancett. He wonders if the poor man is actually coming. Because of his fear of jet lag, Less requested to arrive a day before all these events, and for some reason they acceded to his request. A car, he has been told, will be waiting for him in Turin. If he manages to make it there.

He floats through the Frankfurt airport in a dream, thinking: *Passport, wallet, phone, passport, wallet, phone.* On a great blue screen he finds his flight to Turin has changed terminals. Why, he wonders, are there no clocks in airports? He passes through miles of leather handbags and perfumes and whiskeys, miles of beautiful Turkish retail maids, and in this dream, he is talking to them about colognes and letting them giggle and spritz him with scents of leather and musk; he is looking through wallets and fingering the ostrich leather as if some message were written in braille; he imagines standing at the counter of a VIP lounge and talking to the receptionist, a lady with sea-urchin hair, about his childhood in Delaware, charming his way into the lounge where businessmen of all nationalities are wearing the same suit, and he sits in a cream leather chair, drinks champagne, eats oysters, and there the dream fades...

He awakens in a bus, headed somewhere. But where? Why is he holding so many bags? Why is there the tickle of champagne in his throat? Less tries to listen, among the straphangers, for Italian; he must find the flight to Turin. Around him seem to be only American businessmen, talking about sports. Less recognizes the words but not the names. He feels un-American. He feels homosexual. Less notes there are at least five men on the bus taller than he, which seems like a life record. His mind, a sloth making its slow way across the forest floor of necessity, is taking in the fact that he is still in Germany. Less is due to be back in Germany in just a week's time, to teach a five-week course at the Liberated University. And it is while he is in Germany that the wedding will take place. Freddy will marry Tom somewhere in Sonoma. The shuttle crosses the tarmac and deposits them at an identical terminal. Nightmarishly: passport control. Yes, he still has his in his front left pocket. "Geschäftlich," he answers the muscular agent (red hair cut so close, it seems painted on), secretly thinking: *What I do is hardly business.* Or pleasure. Security, again. Shoes, belt, off, again. What is the logic here? Passport, customs, security, again? Why do today's young men insist on marrying? Was this why we all threw stones at the police, for weddings? Submitting to his bladder at last, Less enters a white tiled bathroom and sees, in the mirror: an old balding *Onkel* in wrinkled, oversized clothes. It turns out there is no mirror: it is the businessman across the sink. A Marx Brothers joke. Less washes his own face, not the businessman's, finds his gate, and boards the plane. *Pass-*

port, wallet, phone. He sinks into his window seat with a sigh and never gets his second breakfast: he has fallen instantly to sleep.

Less awakens to a feeling of peace and triumph: "Stiamo iniziando la discesa verso Torino. We are beginning our descent into Turin." His seatmate seems to have moved across the aisle. He removes his eye mask and smiles at the Alps below, an optical illusion making them into craters and not mountains, and then he sees the city itself. They land serenely, and a woman in the back applauds—he is reminded of landing in Mexico. He recalls smoking on an airplane once when he was young, checks his armrest, and finds an ashtray in it still. Charming or alarming? A chime rings, passengers stand up. *Passport, wallet, phone.* Less has manned his way through the crisis; he no longer feels mickeyed or dull. His bag is the first to arrive on the luggage roller coaster: a dog eager to greet its master. No passport control. Just an exit, and here, wonderfully, a young man in an old man's mustache, holding a sign lettered *SR. ESS.* Less raises his hand, and the man takes his luggage. Inside the sleek black car, Less finds his driver speaks no English. *Fantastico,* he thinks as he closes his eyes again.

Has he been to Italy before? He has, twice. Once when he was twelve, on a family trip that took the path of a Pachinko game by beginning in Rome, shooting up to London, and falling back and forth among various countries until they landed, at last, in Italy's slot. Of Rome, all he remembers (in his childish exhaustion) are the stone buildings stained as if hauled from the ocean, the heart-stopping traf-

fic, his father lugging old-fashioned suitcases (including his
mother's mysterious makeup kit) across the cobblestones, and
the nighttime click-click-click of the yellow window shade
as it flirted with the Roman wind. His mother, in her final
years, often tried to coax other memories from Less (sitting
bedside): "Don't you remember the landlady with the wig
that kept falling off? The handsome waiter who offered to
drive us to his mother's house for lasagna? The man at the
Vatican who wanted to charge you for an adult ticket because you were so tall?" There with her head wrapped in a
scarf with white seashells. "Yes," he said every time, just as he
always did with his agent, pretending to read books he had
never even heard of. The wig! Lasagna! The Vatican!

The second time he went with Robert. It was in the middle of their time together, when Less was finally worldly
enough to be of help with travel and Robert had not become
so filled with bitterness that he was a hindrance, the time
when any couple has found its balance, and passion has qui-
eted from its early scream, but gratitude is still abundant;
what no one realizes are the golden years. Robert was in a
rare mood for travel and had accepted an invitation to read
at a literary festival in Rome. Rome was itself enough, but
showing Rome to Less was like having the chance to introduce someone to a beloved aunt. Whatever happened would
be memorable. What they did not realize until they arrived
was that the event was to take place in the ancient Forum,
where thousands would gather in the summer wind to listen
to a poet read before a crumbling arch; he would be standing on a dais lit by pink spotlights, with an orchestra playing
Philip Glass between each poem. "I will never read anywhere

like this again," Robert whispered to Less, standing backstage as a brief biographical clip played for the audience on
an enormous screen—Robert as a boy in a cowboy costume;
as a serious Harvard student with his pal Ross; then he and
Ross in a San Francisco café, a woodland setting—picking up
more and more artistic companions until Robert reached the
face recognizable from his *Newsweek* photograph: hair gone
gray and wild, retaining that monkey-business expression of
a capering mind (he would not frown for a photo). The
music swelled, his name was called. Four thousand people
applauded, and Robert, in his gray silk suit, readied himself
to stride onto a pink-lit stage below the ruins of the centuries, and let go of his lover's hand like someone falling from
a cliff...

Less opens his eyes to a countryside of autumn vineyards,
endless rows of the crucified plants, a pink rosebush always
planted at the end. He wonders why. The hills roll to the
horizon, and atop each hill, a little town, silhouetted with its
single church spire, and no visible way of approach except
with rope and a pick. Less senses by the sun's shift that at least
an hour has passed. He is not headed to Turin, then; he is
being taken somewhere else. Switzerland?

Less understands at last what is happening: he is in the
wrong car.

SR. ESS—he anagrams in his mind what he took, in his
lingering hypnosis and pride, for *signor* and a childlike mis-
spelling of *Less.* Sriramathan Ess? Srovinka Esskatarinavitch?
SRESS—Società di la Repubblica Europea per la Sexualité
Studentesca? Almost anything makes sense to Less at this alti-

tude. But it is obvious: having cleared the problems of travel, he let his guard slip, waved at the first sign resembling his name, and was whisked away to an unknown location. He knows life's commedia dell'arte and how he has been cast. He sighs in his seat. Staring out at a shrine to an auto accident, placed at a particularly rough curve in the road. He feels the Madonna's plastic eyes meet his for an instant.

And now the signs for a particular town become more frequent, and a particular hotel: something called Mondolce Golf Resort. Less stiffens in fear. His narrating mind whittles the possibilities down: he had taken the car of a Dr. Ludwig Ess, some vacationing Austrian doctor who is off to a golf resort in Piemonte with his wife. He: brown skulled, with white hair in puffs over his ears, little steel glasses, red shorts and suspenders. Frau Ess: short, blond hair with a streak of pink, rough linen tunics and chili pepper leggings. Walking sticks packed in their luggage for jaunts to the village. She has signed up for courses in Italian cooking, while he dreams of nine holes and nine Morettis. And now they stand in some hotel lobby in Turin, shouting with the proprietor while a bellboy waits, holding the elevator. Why did Less come a day early? There will be no one from the prize foundation to straighten out the misunderstanding; the poor Ess voices will echo emptily up to the lobby chandelier. BENVENUTO, a sign reads as they pull into a drive, A MONDOLCE GOLF RESORT. A glass box on a hill, a pool, golf holes all around. "Ecco," the driver announces as they pull to the front; the last sunlight flashes on the pool. Two beautiful young women emerge from the entryway's hall of mirrors, hands clasped. Less readies himself for full mortification.

But life has pardoned him at the scaffold steps:

"Welcome," says the tall one in the sea-horse-print dress, "to Italy and to your hotel! Mr. Less, we are greet you from the prize committee..."

The other finalists do not arrive until late the following day, so Less has almost twenty-four hours in the golf resort by himself. Like a curious child, he tries the pool, then the sauna, the cold plunge, the steam room, the cold plunge again, until he is as scarlet as a fever victim. Unable to decipher the menu at the restaurant (where he dines alone in a shimmering greenhouse), for three meals he orders something he recalls from a novel: steak tartare of the local *Fassona*. For three meals he orders the same Nebbiolo. He sits in the glass sunlit room like the last human on earth, with a wine cellar to last him a lifetime. There is an amphora of petunia-like flowers on his private deck, worried day and night by little bees. On closer inspection, Less sees that instead of stingers, they have long noses to probe the purple flowers with. Not bees: pygmy hummingbird moths. The discovery delights him to his core. Less's pleasures are tinted only slightly the following afternoon, when a mixed group of teenagers appears at the edge of the pool and stares as he does his laps. He returns to his room, all Swedish whitened wood, with a steel fireplace hanging on the wall. "There is wood in the room," the sea horse lady said. "You know how to light a fire, yes?" Less nods; he used to go camping with his father. He stacks the wood in a little Cub Scout tepee, and stuffs the underspace with *Corriere della Sera,* and lights the thing. Time for his rubber bands.

Less has, for years, traveled with a set of rubber bands that he thinks of as his portable gym. The set is multicolored, with interchangeable handles, and he always imagines, when he coils them into his luggage, how toned and fit he will be when he returns. The ambitious routine begins in earnest the first night, with dozens of special techniques recommended in the manual (lost long ago in Los Angeles but remembered in parts), Less wrapping the bands around the legs of beds, columns, rafters, and performing what the manual called "lumberjacks," "trophies," and "action heroes." He ends his workout lacquered in sweat, feeling he has beat back another day from time's assault. Fifty is further than ever. The second night, he advises himself to let his muscles repair. The third, he remembers the set and begins the routine with half a heart; the thin walls of the room might tremble with a neighbor's television, or the dead bathroom light might depress him, or the thought of an unfinished article. Less promises himself a better workout in two days. In return for this promise: a dollhouse whiskey from the room's dollhouse bar. And then the set is forgotten, abandoned on the hotel's side table: a slain dragon.

Less is no athlete. His single moment of greatness came one spring afternoon when he was twelve. In the suburbs of Delaware, spring meant not young love and damp flowers but an ugly divorce from winter and a second marriage to buxom summer. August's steam-room setting came on automatically in May, cherry and plum blossoms made the slightest wind into a ticker-tape parade, and the air filled with pollen. Schoolteachers heard the boys giggling at the sweat shine of their bosoms; young roller skaters found themselves stuck in softening asphalt. It was the year the cicadas returned; Less had not been alive when they buried themselves in the earth. But now they returned: tens of thousands of them, horrifying but harmless, drunk driving through the air so they bumped into heads and ears, encrusting telephone poles and parked cars with their delicate, amber-hued, almost Egyptian discarded shells. Girls wore them as earrings. Boys (Tom Sawyer descendants) trapped the live ones in paper bags and released them at study hour. All day, the creatures hummed in huge choruses, the sound pulsing around the neighborhood. And school would not end until June. If ever.

Then picture young Less: twelve years old, his first year wearing the gold-rimmed glasses that would return to him, thirty years later, when a shopkeeper recommended a pair in Paris and a thrill of sad recognition and shame would course through his body—the short boy in glasses in right field, his hair as gold-white as old ivory, covered now by a black-yellow baseball cap, wandering in the clover with a dreamy look in his eyes. Nothing has happened in right field all season, which is why he was put there: a kind of athletic Canada. His father (though Less would not know this for over a decade) had had to attend a meeting of the Public Athletics Board to defend his son's right to participate in the league despite his clear lack of talent at baseball and obliviousness on the field. His father actually had to remind his son's coach (who had recommended Less's removal) that it was a *public* athletic league and, like a public library, was open to all. Even the fumbling oafs among us. And his mother, a softball champ in her day, has had to pretend none of this matters to her at all and drives Less to games with a speech about sportsmanship that is more a dismantling of her own beliefs than a relief to the boy. Picture Less with his leather glove weighing down his left hand, sweating in the spring heat, his mind lost in the reverie of his childhood lunacies before they give way to adolescent lunacies—when an object appears in the sky. Acting almost on a species memory, he runs forward, the glove before him. The bright sun spangles his vision. And—thwack! The crowd is screaming. He looks into the glove and sees, gloriously grass-bruised and double-stitched in red, the single catch of his life span.

From the stands: his mother's ecstatic cry.

From his bag in Piemonte: the famous rubber bands uncoiled for the famous childhood hero.

From the cabin's doorway: the sea horse lady bursting in, opening windows to let out the smoke from Less's botched attempt at a fire.

Arthur Less was up for a prize only once before: something called the Wilde and Stein Literary Laurels. He was informed of the mysterious honor through his agent, Peter Hunt. Less, perhaps hearing "Wildenstein," replied he wasn't Jewish. Peter coughed and said: "I believe it is something gay." It was, and yet Less was surprised; he had spent half a lifetime living with a writer whose sexuality was never mentioned, much less his half life as a married man. To be called a gay writer! Robert scorned the idea; it was like elevating the importance of his childhood in Westchester, Connecticut. "I don't write about Westchester," he would say. "I don't think about Westchester. I'm not a Westchester poet"— which would have surprised Westchester, whose council had placed a plaque on the middle school Robert had attended. Gay, black, Jewish; Robert and his friends thought they were beyond all that. So Less was surprised to know this kind of award even existed. His first response to Peter was to ask: "How did they even know I was gay?" He asked this from his front porch, wearing a kimono. But Peter persuaded him to attend. Less and Robert had split by then, and, anxious about how he would appear to this mysterious gay literary world, and desperate for a date, he panicked and asked Freddy Pelu.

Who knew Freddy, then only twenty-six, would be such a boon? They arrived to a college auditorium (banners everywhere: *Hopes Are the Ladders to Dreams!*), on whose stage six wooden chairs were arranged as in a court of law. Less and Freddy took their seats. ("Wilde and Stein," Freddy said. "It sounds like a vaudeville act.") Around them, people were shouting recognition and hugging and having intense conversations. Less recognized none of them. It seemed so strange; here, his contemporaries, his peers, and they were strangers. But not to bookish Freddy, suddenly come alive in literary company—"Look, there's Meredith Castle; she's a language poet, Arthur, you should know her, and that one is Harold Frickes," and so on. Freddy peering through his red glasses at these oddities and naming each with satisfaction. It was like being with a bird-watcher. The lights went down, and six men and women walked onstage, some of them so elderly, they seemed to be automatons, and sat in the chairs. One small bald man in tinted glasses stepped to the microphone. "That's Finley Dwyer," Freddy whispered. Whoever that was.

The man began to welcome them all, and then his face

brightened: "I admit I will be disappointed tonight if we reward the assimilationists, the ones who write the way straight people write, who hold up heterosexuals as war heroes, who make gay characters suffer, who set their characters adrift in a nostalgic past that ignores our present oppression; I say we purge ourselves of these people, who would have us vanish into the bookstore, the assimilationists, who are, at their core, ashamed of who they are, who we are, who *you* are!" The audience applauded wildly. War heroes, suffering characters, adrift in a nostalgic past—Less recognized these elements as a mother might recognize the police description of a serial killer. It was *Kalipso*! Finley Dwyer was talking about *him*. Him, harmless little Arthur Less: the *enemy!* The audience roared on, and Less turned and whispered shakily, "Freddy, I have to get out of here." Freddy looked at him with surprise. "Hopes are the ladders to dreams, Arthur." But then he saw Less was serious. When the award for Book of the Year came up, Less did not hear the announcement; he was lying on his bed, while Freddy was saying not to worry. Their lovemaking had been ruined by the bedroom bookcase, from which dead writers stared at him like dogs at the foot of the bed. Perhaps Less *was* ashamed, as Finley Dwyer had accused. A bird outside the window seemed to be mocking him. He had not, in any case, won.

Less has read (in the packet the beautiful women handed him before vanishing into the glasswork) that, while the five finalists were chosen by an elderly committee, the final jury is made up of twelve high school students. The second night, they appear in the lobby, dressed up in elegant flowered dresses (the girls) or their dad's oversized blazers (the boys). Why did it not occur to Less these were the same teens by the pool? The teens move like a tour group into the greenhouse, formerly Less's private dining room, which now bustles with caterers and unknown people. The beautiful Italian women reappear and introduce him to his fellow finalists. Less feels his confidence drop. The first is Riccardo, a young unshaven Italian man, incredibly tall and thin, in sunglasses, jeans, and a T-shirt that reveals the Japanese carp tattoos on both arms. The other three are all much older: Luisa, glamorously white-haired and dressed in a white cotton tunic, with gold alien bracelets for fending off critics; Alessandro, a cartoon villain, with streaks of white at his temples, a pencil mustache, and black plastic spectacles that narrow his look of disapproval; and a short rose-gold gnome from Finland who asks to be called Harry, though his name on the books is something else entirely. Their works, Less is told, are a Sicilian historical novel, a retelling of Rapunzel in modern-day Russia, an eight-hundred-page novel of a man's last minute on his deathbed in Paris, and an imagined life of St. Margory. Less cannot seem to match each novel with its author; has the young one made the deathbed novel or Rapunzel? Either seems likely. They are all so intellectual. Less knows at once he hasn't a chance.

"I read your book," says Luisa, her left eye batting away a loose scrap of mascara while her right one stares straight into his heart. "It took me to new places. I thought of Joyce in outer space." The Finn seems to be brimming with mirth.

The cartoon villain adds: "He would not live long, I think."

"*Portrait of the Artist as a Spaceman!*" the Finn says at last, and covers his teeth as he ticks away with silent laughter.

"I have not read it, but...," says the tattooed author, moving restlessly, hands in pockets. The others wait for more. But that is all. Behind them, Less recognizes Fosters Lancett walking alone into the room, very short and heavy headed and looking as soaked in misery as a trifle pudding is soaked in rum. And perhaps also soaked in rum.

"I don't think I have a chance of winning" is all Less can say. The prize is a generous amount of euros and a bespoke suit made in Turin proper.

Luisa flings a hand into the air. "Oh, but who knows? It is up to these students! Who knows what they love? Romance? Murder? If it's murder, Alessandro has us beat."

The villain raises first one eyebrow, then the other. "When I was young, all I wanted to read were pretentious little books. Camus and Tournier and Calvino. If it had a plot, I hated it."

"You remain this way," Luisa chides, and he shrugs. Less senses a love affair from long ago. The two switch gears to Italian, and so begins what sounds like a squabble but could really be anything at all.

"Do any of you happen to speak English or have a cigarette?" It is Lancett, glowering under his eyebrows. The young writer immediately pulls a pack from his jeans and produces one, slightly flattened. Lancett eyes it with trepidation, then takes it. "You are the finalists?" he asks.

"Yes," Less says, and Lancett turns his head, alert to an American accent.

His eyelids flutter closed in disgust. "These things are *not cool.*"

"I guess you've been to a lot of them." Less hears himself saying this inane thing.

"Not many. And I've never won. It's a sad little cockfight they arrange because they have no talent themselves."

"You have won. You won the main prize here."

Fosters Lancett stares at Less for moment, then rolls his eyes and stalks off to smoke.

For the next two days, the crowd moves in packs—teenagers, finalists, elderly prize committee—smiling at each other from auditoriums and restaurants, passing peacefully by each other at catering buffets, but never seated together, never interacting, with only Fosters Lancett moving freely among them as the skulking lone wolf. Less now feels a new shame that the teenagers have seen him nearly naked and avoids the pool if they are present; in his mind he sees the horror of his middle-aged body and cannot bear the judgment (when in fact his anxiety has kept him almost as lean as in his college years). He also shuns the spa. And so the old rubber bands are brought out again, and each morning Less gives his Lessian best to the "trophies" and "action heroes" of the long-lost manual (itself a poor translation from Italian), each day doing fewer and fewer, asymptotically approaching, but never reaching, zero.

Days, of course, are crowded. There is the sunny town square luncheon alfresco where Less is cautioned not once, not twice, but *ten times* by various Italians to apply sunscreen to his pinkening face (of *course* he has applied sunscreen, and what the hell did they know about it, with their luscious mahogany skin?). There is the speech by Fosters Lancett on Ezra

Pound, in the middle of which the bitter old man pulls out
an electronic cigarette and begins to puff away; its little green
light, at this time alien to the Piemontesi, makes some journalists present conjecture he is smoking their local *marijuana.*
There are numerous baffling interviews—"I am sorry, I need
the *interprete,* I cannot understand your American accent"—
in which dowdy matrons in lavender linen ask highly intellectual questions about Homer, Joyce, and quantum physics.
Less, completely below the journalistic radar in America, and
unused to substantive questions, keeps to a fiercely merry-
making persona at all times, refusing to wax philosophical
about subjects he chose to write about precisely *because* he
does not understand them. The ladies leave amused but without enough copy for a column. From across the lobby, Less
hears journalists laughing at something Alessandro is saying;
clearly he knows how to handle these things. And there is the
two-hour bus ride up a mountain, when Less turns to Luisa
with a question and she explains that the roses at the ends of
the vineyard rows are to detect disease. She shakes her finger
and says, "The roses will be taken first. Like a bird...what is
the bird?"

"A canary in a coal mine."

"*Sì. Esatto.*"

"Or like a poet in a Latin American country," Less offers.
"The new regime always kills them first." The complex triple
take of her expression: first astonishment, then wicked com-
plicity, and last shame for either the dead poets, themselves,
or both.

And then there is the prize ceremony itself.

·   ·   ·

Less was in the apartment when Robert received the call, back in 1992. "Well, holy fuck," came the cry from the bedroom, and Less rushed in, thinking Robert had injured himself (he carried on a dangerous intrigue with the physical world, and chairs, tables, shoes, all came rushing into his path as to an electromagnet), but found Robert basset faced, the phone in his lap, staring straight ahead at Woodhouse's painting of Less. In a T-shirt, and with tortoiseshell glasses on his forehead, the newspaper spread around him, a cigarette dangerously close to lighting it, Robert turned to face Less. "It was the Pulitzer committee," he said evenly. "It turns out I've been pronouncing it wrong all these years."

"You won?"

"It's not *Pew*-lit-sir. It's *Pull*-it-sir." Robert's eyes took another survey of the room. "Holy fuck, Arthur, I won."

A party was called for, of course, and the old gang all came back together—Leonard Ross, Otto Handler, Franklin Woodhouse, Stella Barry—piled into the shack on the Vulcan Steps, and patted Robert on the back; Less had never seen him so bashful with his pals, so obviously delighted and proud. Ross went right up to him, and Robert bowed his head, leaning into the tall Lincolnesque writer, and Ross rubbed his scalp as if for good luck or, more probably, as if they had done this when they were young. They laughed and talked about it ceaselessly—what they were like when they were young—which baffled Less, because they seemed just the same age as when he met them. A number had given up drink, including Robert by then, so what they drank was coffee, from a beat-up metal urn, and some of them passed around a joint. Less resumed his old role and stood to the side, admiring them. At some point, Stella saw him from across the room and went over with her stork walk; she was all bones and sharp edges, a too-tall, unpretty woman who celebrated her flaws with confidence and grace, so they became, to Less, beautiful. "I hear you've taken up writing too, Arthur," she said in her scratchy voice. She took his glass of wine and sipped from it, then handed it back to him, her eyes full of devilry. "Here's my only advice. Don't win one of these prizes." She herself had won several, of course; she was in the *Wharton Anthology of Poetry,* which meant she was immortal. Like Athena coming down to advise young Telemachus. "You win a prize, and it's all over. You lecture for the rest of your life. But you never write again." She tapped a nail on his chest. "Don't win one." Then she kissed him on his cheek.

That was the last time they ever were together, the Russian River School.

It takes place not in the ancient monastery itself, where one can buy honey from cloistered bees, but in a municipal hall built in the rock beneath the monastery. Being a place of worship, it lacks a dungeon, and so the region of Piemonte has built one. In the auditorium (whose rear access door is open to different weather: a sudden storm brewing), the teenagers are arrayed exactly as Less imagines the hidden monks to be: with devout expressions and vows of silence. The elderly chairpeople sit at a kingly table; they also do not speak. The only speaker is a handsome Italian (the mayor, it turns out) whose appearance on the podium is announced by a crack of thunder; the sound goes out on his microphone;

the lights go out. The audience goes "Aaaah!" Less hears the young writer, seated beside him in the darkness, lean over and speak to him at last: "This is when someone is murdered. But who?" Less whispers "Fosters Lancett" before realizing the famous Brit is seated just behind them.

The lights awake the room again, and no one has been murdered. A movie screen begins to unroll noisily from the ceiling like a mad relative wandering downstairs and has to be sent back into hiding. The ceremony begins again, and as the mayor begins his speech in Italian, those mellifluous, see-sawing, meaningless harpsichord words, Less feels his mind drifting away like a spaceman from an airlock, off into the asteroid belt of his own concerns. For he does not belong here. It seemed absurd when he got the invitation, but he saw it so abstractly, and at such a remote distance in time and space, that he accepted it as part of his getaway plan. But here, in his suit, sweat already beginning to dot the front of his white shirt and bead on his thinning hairline, he knows it is utterly wrong. He did not take the wrong car; the wrong car took him. For he has come to understand this is not a strange funny Italian prize, a joke to tell his friends; it is very real. The elderly judges in their jewelry; the teens in their jury box; the finalists all quivering and angry with expectation; even Fosters Lancett, who has come all this way, and written a long speech, and charged his electronic cigarette and his dwindling battery of small talk—it is very real, very important to them. It cannot be dismissed as a lark. Instead: it is a vast mistake.

Less begins to imagine (as the mayor doodles on in Italian) that he has been mistranslated, or—what is the word?—*super-*

translated, his novel given to an unacknowledged genius of a poet (Giuliana Monti is her name) who worked his mediocre English into breathtaking Italian. His book was ignored in America, barely reviewed, without a single interview request by a journalist (his publicist said, "Autumn is a bad time"), but here in Italy he understands he is taken seriously. In autumn, no less. Just this morning, he was shown the articles in *la Repubblica, Corriere della Sera,* local papers, and Catholic papers, with photographs of him in his blue suit, gazing upward at the camera with the same worried unsophisticated sapphire gaze he showed to Robert on that beach. But it should be a photograph of Giuliana Monti. *She* has written this book. Rewritten, upwritten, outwritten Less himself. For he has known genius. He has been awakened by genius in the middle of the night, by the sound of genius pacing the halls; he has made genius his coffee, and his breakfast, and his ham sandwich and his tea; he has been naked with genius, coaxed genius from panic, brought genius's pants from the tailor and ironed his shirts for a reading. He has felt every inch of genius's skin; he has known genius's smell and felt genius's touch. Fosters Lancett, a knight's move behind him, for whom an hour-long talk on Ezra Pound is a simple matter— he is a genius. Alessandro, in his Oil Can Harry mustache, the elegant Luisa, the perverted Finn, the tattooed Riccardo: possible geniuses. How has it come to this? What god has enough free time to arrange this very special humiliation, to fly a minor novelist across the world so that he can feel, in some seventh sense, the minusculitude of his own worth? Decided by *high school students,* in fact. Is there a bucket of blood hanging high in the auditorium rafters, waiting to be dropped on his bright-blue suit? Will this become a dungeon at last? It is a mistake, or a setup, or both. But there is no escaping it now.

Arthur Less has left the room while remaining in it. Now he is alone in the bedroom of the shack, standing before the mirror and tying his bow tie. It is the day of the Wilde and Stein awards, and he is thinking, briefly, of what he will say when he wins, and, briefly, his face grows golden with delight. Three raps on the front door and the sound of a key in the lock. "Arthur!" Less is adjusting both the tie and his expectations. "Arthur!" Freddy comes around the corner, then produces, from the pocket of his Parisian suit (so new it is still partially sewn shut) a flat little box. It is a present: a polka-dot bow tie. So now the tie must be undone and this new one knotted. Freddy, looking at his mirror image. "What will you say when you win?"

And further: "You think it's love, Arthur? It isn't love." Robert ranting in their hotel room before the lunchtime Pulitzer ceremony in New York. Tall and lean as the day they met; gone gray, of course, his face worn with age ("I'm dog-eared as a book"), but still the figure of elegance and intellectual fury. Standing here in silver hair before the bright window: "Prizes aren't love. Because people who never met you can't love you. The slots for winners are already set, from here until Judgment Day. They know the kind of poet who's going to win, and if you happen to fit the slot, then bully for you! It's like fitting a hand-me-down suit. It's luck, not love. Not that it isn't nice to have luck. Maybe the only way to think about it is being at the center of all beauty. Just by chance, today we get to be in the center of all beauty. It doesn't mean I don't want it—it's a desperate way to get off—but I do. I'm a narcissist; desperate is what we do. Getting off is what we do. You look handsome in your suit. I don't know why you're shacked up with a man in his fifties. Oh, I know, you like a finished product. You don't want to add a pearl. Let's have champagne before we go. I know it's noon. I need you to do my bow tie. I forget how because I know you never will. Prizes aren't love, but this is love. What Frank wrote: *It's a summer day, and I want to be wanted more than anything in the world.*"

More thunder unsettles Less from his thoughts. But it isn't thunder; it is applause, and the young writer is pulling at Less's coat sleeve. For Arthur Less has won.

LESS GERMAN

A phone call, translated from German into English:

"Good afternoon, Pegasus Publications. This is Petra."

"Good morning. Here is Mr. Arthur Less. There is a fence in my book."

"Mr. Less?"

"There is a fence in my book. You are to correct, please."

"Mr. Arthur Less, our writer? The author of *Kalipso*? It is wonderful to speak with you at last. Now, how can I help you?"

(Sound of keys on a keyboard) "Yes, hello. It is nice to speak. I call over a fence. Not *fence*." (More keyboard sounds) "An *error.*"

"An error in the book?"

"Yes! I call over an error in my book."

"I apologize. What is the nature of this error?"

"My birth year is written one nine sex four."

"Again?"

"My birth year is sex five."

"Do you mean you were born in 1965?"

"Exactly. The journalists write that I have fifty years. But I have forty-nine years!"

"Oh! We wrote your birth year wrong on the flap copy, and so journalists have been reporting that you're fifty. When you're only forty-nine. I'm so sorry. That must be so frustrating!"

(Long pause) "Exactly exactly exactly." (Laughter) "I am not an old man!"

"Of course not. I'll make a note for the next printing. And may I say in your photograph you look under forty? All the girls in the office are in love with you."

(Long pause) "I do not understand."

"I said all the girls in the office are in love with you."

(Laughter) "Thank you, thank you, that is very very nice." (Another pause) "I like love."

"Yes, well, call me if you have any other concerns."

"Thank you and good-bye!"

"Have a good day, Mr. Less."

What a delight, for Arthur Less, to be in a country where he at last speaks the language! After the miraculous reversal of his Italian fortunes, in which he stood up in a daze and accepted a heavy golden statuette (which would now have to be figured into his luggage weight allowance)—the journalists shrieking as in an operatic finale—he is to arrive in Germany on the winds of success. Added to this: his fluency in German, and his esteemed position of professor, and how forgotten are the cares of *Gestern!* Chatting with the stewards, babbling freely with passport control, it seems almost possible he has forgotten that Freddy's wedding is a matter of mere weeks away. How heartening it is to watch him speak; how disconcerting, however, to listen.

Less has studied German since he was a boy. His first teacher, when he was nine, was Frau Fernhoff, a retired piano instructor, who had them all (him, sharp-witted Georgia beanpole Anne Garret, and odd-smelling but sweet Giancarlo Taylor) stand up and shout, "Guten Morgen, Frau Fernhoff!" at the beginning of each afternoon lesson. They learned the names of fruits and vegetables (the beautiful *Birne* and *Kirsche,* the faux-ami *Ananas,* the more-resonant-than-"onion" *Zwiebel*), and described their own prepubescent bodies, from their *Augenbrauen* to their *großer Zehen.* High school led to more sophisticated conversation ("Mein Auto wurde gestohlen!") and was led by buxom Fräulein Church, an enthusiastic teacher in wrap dresses and scarves who had grown up in a German district of New York City and who often spoke of her dream of following the Von Trapp trail in Austria. "The key to speaking a new language," she told them, "is to be bold instead of perfect." What Less did not know was that the charming Fräulein had never been to Germany, nor spoken German with Germans outside of Yorkville. She was ostensibly German speaking, just as seventeen-year-old Less was ostensibly gay. Both had the fantasy; neither had carried it out.

Bold instead of perfect, Less's tongue is bruised with errors. Male friends tend to switch to girls in the Lessian plural, becoming *Freundin* instead of *Freund;* and, by using *auf den Strich* instead of *unterm Strich,* he can lead intrigued listeners to believe he is going into prostitution. But, even at four and nine, Less has yet to be disabused of his skills. Perhaps the fault lies with Ludwig, the folk-singing German exchange student who lived with his family, took Less's ostensibility away, and never corrected his German—for who corrects what is spoken in bed? Perhaps it was the grateful, *dankbaren* East Berliners whom Less met on a trip with Robert—escaped poets living in Paris—astonished to hear their mother tongue working in the mouth of this slim young American. Perhaps it was too much *Hogan's Heroes.* But Less arrives in Berlin, taxiing to his temporary apartment in Wilmersdorf, swearing he will not speak a word of English while he is here. Of course, the real challenge is to speak a word of German.

Again, a translation:

"Six greetings, class. I am Arthur Less."

This is the class he will be teaching at the Liberated University. In addition, he is expected to give a reading in five weeks, open to the public. Delighted he was fluent in German, the department offered Less the chance to teach a course of his choosing. "With a visiting professor," wrote the kind Dr. Balk, "we can often have as few as three students, which is a nice intimate room." Less dusted off a writing course he had given at a Jesuit college in California, put the entire syllabus through a computer translation, and considered himself prepared. He called the course Read Like a Vampire, Write Like Frankenstein, based on his own notion that writers read other works in order to take their best parts. This was, especially translated into German, an unusual title. When his teaching assistant, Hans, brings him to the classroom this first morning, he is astounded to find not three, not fifteen, but a hundred and thirty students waiting to take his extraordinary course.

"I am your Mr. Professor."

He is not. Unaware of the enormous difference between the German *Professor* and *Dozent,* the former being a rank achieved only through decades of internment in the academic prison, the latter a mere parolee, Less has given himself a promotion.

"And now, I am sorry, I must kill most of you."

With this startling announcement, he proceeds to weed out any students who are not registered in the Global Linguistics and Literature Department. To his relief, this removes all but thirty. And so he begins the class.

"We start at a sentence in Proust: *For a long time, I used to go to bed early.*"

But Arthur Less has not gone to bed early; in fact, it is a miracle he has even made it to the classroom. The problem: a surprise invitation, a struggle with German technology, and, of course, Freddy Pelu.

Back to his arrival at the Tegel Airport, the day before:

A baffling series of glass chambers, sealing and unsealing automatically like air locks, where he is met by his tall serious teaching assistant and escort: Hans. Though about to sit for his doctorate exam on Derrida and therefore, in Less's mind, his intellectual superior, curly-headed Hans willingly takes all of Less's luggage and brings him, via his beat-up Twingo, to the university apartment he will call home for the next five weeks. It is on a high floor of an eighties building whose open staircases, and open walkways, are exposed to the chill Berlin air; in its goldenrod-and-glass severity, it resembles the airport. Additionally, there is no apartment key but instead a circular fob with a button—like a mating bird, the door chirps in response, then opens. Hans demonstrates this quickly; the door chirps; it seems simple. "You take the stairs to the walkway, you use the fob. You understand?" Less nods, and Hans leaves Less with his luggage, explaining that he will be back at nineteen hours to take him to dinner, and then at thirteen hours the next day to take him to the university. His curly head bobs good-bye, and he disappears down the open staircase. It occurs to Less that the graduate student never met his gaze. And that he should learn military time.

He cannot imagine that the next morning before class, he will find himself hanging from the ledge outside his apartment building, forty feet above the courtyard, inching his way toward the only open window.

Hans arrives precisely at nineteen hours (Less keeps repeating to himself: *seven p.m., seven p.m., seven p.m.*). Unable to find an iron in the apartment, Less has hung up his shirts in the bathroom and run a hot shower to steam out the wrinkles, but the billowing steam somehow sets off the fire alarm, which of course brings a burly, cheerful, English-free man from the lower depths to tease him ("Sie wollen wohl das Haus mit Wasser abfackeln!") and return with a sturdy German iron. Windows are opened. Less is in the process of ironing when he hears the Bach chimes of the doorbell. Hans bobs his head again. He has changed from a hoodie into a denim blazer. In the Twingo (evidence of cigarettes but no actual cigarettes), the young man drives him into another mysterious district, parking beneath a concrete railway where a sad Turkish man sits in a kiosk, selling curried hot dogs. The restaurant is called Austria and is decorated everywhere with beer steins and antlers. As is true everywhere else: they are not kidding.

They are shown to a leather booth where two men and a young woman are waiting. These are Hans's friends, and, while Less suspects the grad student is cagily sponging from the department's expense account, it is a relief to have someone other than a Derridean to talk with: a composer named Ulrich, whose brown eyes and shaggy beard give him the alert appearance of a schnauzer, his girlfriend, Katarina, similarly canine in her Pomeranian puff of hair, and Bastian, a business student whose dark good looks and voluminous kinky hairstyle make Less assume he is African; he is Bavarian. Less judges them to be around thirty. Bastian keeps picking a fight with Ulrich about sports, a conversation difficult for Less to follow not because of the specific vocabulary (*Verteidiger, Stürmer, Schienbeinschützer*) or obscure sports figures but because he simply does not care. Bastian seems to be arguing that danger is essential to sports: The thrill of death! *Der Nervenkitzel des Todes!* Less stares at his schnitzel (a crisp map of Austria). He is not here, in Berlin, in the Schnitzelhaus. He is in Sonoma, in a hospital room: windowless, yellowish, encurtained for privacy like a stripper before her entrance. In the hospital bed: Robert. He has a tube in his arm and a tube in his nose, and his hair is that of a madman.

"It's not the cigarettes," Robert says, his eyes framed by his same old thick glasses. "It's the poetry that's done it. It kills you now. But later," he says, shaking a finger, "immortality!" A husky laugh, and Less holds his hand. This is only a year ago. And Less is in Delaware, at his mother's funeral, a hand softly pressing on his back to keep him from collapsing. He is so grateful for that hand. And Less is in San Francisco, on the beach, in the fall of that terrible year.

"You boys don't know anything about death."

Someone has said this; Less discovers it is he. This one time, his German is perfect. The entire table sits silent, and Ulrich and Hans look away. Bastian merely stares at Less, his mouth hanging open.

"I'm sorry," Less says, putting down his beer. "I'm sorry, I do not know why I said that."

Bastian is silent. The sconces behind him light every kink in his hair.

The bill comes, and Hans pays with a department credit card, and Less cannot be persuaded a tip is unnecessary, and then they are out on the street, where street lamps shine on black lacquered trees. He has never been this cold in his life. Ulrich stands with his hands in his pockets, swaying back and forth to a private symphony, Katarina clutching him, and Hans looks at the rooftops and says he will bring Less back to the apartment. But Bastian says no, it is the American's first night, and he should be taken for a drink. The conversation takes place as if Less were not there. It feels like they are arguing about something else. At last, it is decided Bastian will bring Less to his favorite bar, close by. Hans says, "Mr. Less, you can find your way home?" and Bastian says a taxi will be simple. It is all happening very quickly. The others vanish into the Twingo; Less turns and sees Bastian looking at him with an indecipherable frown. "Come with me," the young man says. But he does not lead him to a bar. He leads him to his own apartment, in Neukölln, where Less—to his surprise—spends the night.

The problem comes the next morning. Less, sleepless from his evening with Bastian, sweating out all the alcohol he's been served over the past twelve hours, still dressed in the black shirt and jeans grease-spotted from dinner, is able to climb the stairs to his building's exterior walkway but unable to work the lock to his apartment. Over and over he presses the button on the fob, over and over he listens for the chirp of the door. But it is mute. It will not mate. Frantically looking around the courtyard, he sees birds gathering on the balcony of an upstairs maisonette. Here, of course, is the bill for last night. Here is the shame built into living. How did he imagine he would escape it? Less pictures himself sleeping in his doorway when Hans arrives to take him to the university. He imagines teaching his first class stinking of vodka and cigarette smoke. And then his eye falls upon an open window.

At ten, we climb the tree higher even than our mothers' fears. At twenty, we scale the dormitory to surprise a lover asleep in bed. At thirty, we jump into the mermaid-green ocean. At forty, we look on and smile. At four and nine?

Over the walkway railing, he rests one scuffed wingtip on the decorative concrete ledge. It is only five feet away, the narrow window. A matter of flinging out his arm to catch the shutter. The smallest of leaps to the adjoining ledge. Pressed against the wall, and already yellow paint is flaking onto his

shirt, and already he can hear his audience of birds coo-
ing appreciatively. A Berlin sunrise glows over the rooftops,
bringing with it a smell of bread and car exhaust. *Arthur Less,
minor American author known mostly for his connection to the Russian River School of artists, especially the poet Robert Brownburn,
took his own life this morning in Berlin,* Pegasus's press release
will read. *He was fifty years old.*

What witness is there to see your Mr. Professor dangling
from the fourth floor of his apartment building? Throwing
out a foot, then a hand, to edge himself toward the kitchen
window? Using all his upper-body strength to pull himself
over the protective railing and to fall, in a cloud of dust, into
the darkness beyond? Just a new mother, walking her baby
around her apartment in the early morning. Seeing a scene
perhaps out of a foreign comedy. She knows he is not a thief;
he is clearly just an American.

Less is not *known* as a teacher, in the same way Melville
was not *known* as a customs inspector. And yet both held
the respective positions. Though he was once an endowed
chair at Robert's university, he has no formal training except
the drunken, cigarette-filled evenings of his youth, when
Robert's friends gathered and yelled, taunted, and played
games with words. As a result, Less feels uncomfortable lec-
turing. Instead, he re-creates those lost days with his students.
Remembering those middle-aged men sitting with a bottle
of whiskey, a Norton book of poetry, and scissors, he cuts
up a paragraph of *Lolita* and has the young doctoral students reassemble the text as they desire. In these collages,
Humbert Humbert becomes an addled old man rather than

a diabolical one, mixing up cocktail ingredients and, instead of confronting the betrayed Charlotte Haze, going back for more ice. He gives them a page of Joyce and a bottle of Wite-Out—and Molly Bloom merely says "Yes." A game to write a persuasive opening sentence for a book they have never read (this is difficult, as these diligent students have read *everything*) leads to a chilling start to Woolf's *The Waves: I was too far out in the ocean to hear the lifeguard shouting, "Shark! Shark!"*

Though the course features, curiously, neither vampires nor Frankenstein monsters, the students adore it. No one has given them scissors and glue sticks since they were in kindergarten. No one has ever asked them to translate a sentence from Carson McCullers (*In the town there were two mutes, and they were always together*) into German (*In der Stadt gab es zwei Stumme, und sie waren immer zusammen*) and pass it around the room, retranslating as they go, until it comes out as playground gibberish: *In the bar there were two potatoes together, and they were trouble.* What a relief for their hardworking lives. Do they learn anything about literature? Doubtful. But they learn to love language again, something that has faded like sex in a long marriage. Because of this, they learn to love their teacher.

It is in Berlin that Less begins to grow a beard. You could blame the approach of a certain wedding date. You could also blame his new German lover, Bastian.

One would not expect them to become lovers. Less certainly did not. After all, they are not well suited. Bastian is young, vain, arrogant, and incurious, even contemptuous, of literature and art; instead, he follows sports avidly, and

Germany's losses leave him in a depression not seen since Weimar days. This, despite the fact that he does not consider himself German; he is Bavarian. This means nothing to Less, who associates this nation more with München's beer fests and lederhosen than with the graffiti heaven of Berlin. But it means a great deal to Bastian. He frequently wears T-shirts proclaiming his heritage, and these, along with light-colored jeans and a puffy cotton jacket, are his typical costume. He is not intellectual about, interested in, or kind with words. But he is, Less is to discover, surprisingly softhearted.

It so happens that Bastian visits Less every few nights. Waiting outside Less's apartment building in his jeans, neon T-shirt, puffy jacket. What on earth does he want with your Mr. Professor? He does not say. He merely pins Less against the wall the moment they are inside, paraphrasing in a whisper from the Checkpoint Charlie sign: *Entering American Sector.* . . . Sometimes they don't even leave the apartment, and Less is forced to make dinner from his meager fridge: bacon, eggs, and walnuts. One night two weeks into the Wintersitzung, they watch Bastian's favorite TV show, something called *Schwiegertochter gesucht,* about country people looking to play matchmaker for their children, until the young man falls asleep with his body wrapped tight around Less's, his nose docked in Less's ear.

Around midnight, the fever begins.

It is a puzzling experience, dealing with a stranger in his illness. Bastian, so confident as a young man, becomes a sickly child, calling for Less to pull his covers down, then up, as his temperature soars and plummets (the apartment comes with a thermometer, but, alas, it's in alien Centigrade), asking for foods Less has never heard of and ancient (possibly fever invented) Bavarian remedies of plasters and hot *Rosenkohl-Saft* (Brussels-sprout juice). And Less, not known for his bedside manner (Robert accused him of abandoning the weak), finds himself heartsick for the poor Bavarian. No *Mami,* no *Papi.* Less tries to banish the memory of another man, sick in another European bed. How long ago was it? He gets on his bicycle and rides the streets of Wilmersdorf in search of anything to help. He returns with what one usually returns with in Europe: powder in a folded packet. This he puts in water; it smells atrocious, and Bastian will not drink it. So Less puts on *Schwiegertochter gesucht* and tells Bastian he has to drink every time the lovebirds remove their glasses to kiss. And when Bastian drinks, he stares into Less's eyes with his own: each as light brown as an acorn. The next day, Bastian has recovered.

"You know what my friends call you?" Bastian asks in the morning light, tangled in Less's ivy-patterned bedsheets. He is his old self, red cheeked, alert with a little smile. His wild hair seems the only part of him still asleep, like a cat on the pillow.

"Mr. Professor," Less says, toweling himself from a shower.

"That's what I call you. No, they call you Peter Pan."

Less laughs in his backward way: *AH ah ah.*

Bastian reaches for the coffee beside him. The windows are open and blowing the cheap white curtains around; the sky is foxed and gray above the linden trees. "'How is Peter Pan?' they ask me."

Less frowns and makes his way to the closet, catching a

glimpse of himself in the mirror: his flushed face, his white body. Like a statue pieced together with the wrong head. "Tell me why I am this called."

"You know, your German is pretty terrible," Bastian tells him.

"Not true. It is not perfect, perhaps," Less tells him, "but it is excited."

The young man laughs freely, sitting up in bed. Brown skin, reddened on his shoulders and his cheeks from his time in the solarium. "See, I don't know what you're talking about. Excited?"

"Excited," Less explains, pulling on his underwear. "Enthusiastic."

"Yes, you talk like a child. You look and act very young." He reaches one hand out to catch Less's arm and pulls him to the bed. "Maybe you never grew up."

Maybe he never did. Less knows so well the pleasures of youth—danger, excitement, losing oneself in a dark club with a pill, a shot, a stranger's mouth—and, with Robert and his friends, the pleasures of age—comfort and ease, beauty and taste, old friends and old stories and wine, whiskey, sunsets over the water. His entire life, he has alternated between the two. There is his own distant youth, that daily humiliation of rinsing out your one good shirt and putting on your one good smile, along with the daily rush of newness: new pleasures, new people, new reflections of yourself. There is Robert's late middle age of selecting his vices as carefully as ties in a Paris shop, napping in the sunlight on an afternoon and getting up from a chair and hearing the creak of death. The city of youth, the country of age. But in between, where

Less is living—that exurban existence? How has he never learned to live it?

"I think you should grow a beard," the young man murmurs later. "I think you would be very handsome."

So he does.

A truth must now be told: Arthur Less is no champion in bed.

Anyone would guess, seeing Bastian staring up at Less's window each night, waiting to be buzzed in, that it is the sex that brings him. But it is not precisely the sex. The narrator must be trusted to report that Arthur Less is—technically—not a skilled lover.

He possesses, first of all, none of the physical attributes; he is average in every way. A straightforwardly American man, smiling and blinking with his pale lashes. A handsome face, but otherwise ordinary. He has also, since his early youth, suffered an anxiety that leaves him sometimes too eager in the sexual act, sometimes not eager enough. Technically: bad in bed. And yet—just as a flightless bird will evolve other tactics for survival, Arthur Less has developed other traits. Like the bird, he is unaware of these.

He kisses—how do I explain it? Like someone in love. Like he has nothing to lose. Like someone who has just learned a foreign language and can use only the present tense and only the second person. Only now, only you. There are some men who have never been kissed like that. There are some men who discover, after Arthur Less, that they never will be again.

Even more mystical: his touch casts a curious spell. There

is no other word for it. Perhaps it is the effect of his being "someone without skin" that Less can sometimes touch another and send the spark of his own nervous system into theirs. This was something Robert noticed right away; he said, "You're a witch, Arthur Less." Others, less susceptible, have paid no attention, too intent on their own elaborate needs ("Higher; no, *higher;* no, HIGHER!"). But Freddy felt it as well. A minor shock, a lack of air, a brief blackout, perhaps, and back again to see Less's innocent face above him, wreathed in sweat. Is it perhaps a radiation, an emanation of this innocence, this guilelessness, grown white-hot? Bastian is not immune. One night, after fumbling adolescently in the hall, they try to undress each other but, outwitted by foreign systems of buttons and closures, end up undressing themselves. Arthur returns to the bed, where Bastian is waiting, naked and tan, and climbs aboard. As Less does this, he rests one hand on Bastian's chest. Bastian gasps. He writhes; his breathing quickens; and after a moment he whispers: "Was machst Du mit mir?" (*What are you doing to me?*) Less has no idea what he is doing.

Less assumes, during the fourth week, that his assistant is heartbroken. Already serious in demeanor, Hans is positively morose, sitting through the lesson with two hands holding up a head that seems as heavy as bronze. Surely a girl problem, one of those beautiful, witty, chain-smoking bisexual German girls in vintage American clothes and ironed blond hair; or a foreigner, a beautiful Italian in copper bracelets who flies back to Rome to live with her parents and curate a modern-art gallery. Poor, bruised-looking Hans. Less realizes the truth only while diagramming the structure of Ford Madox Ford on the board, when he turns around to find Hans has fainted onto his desk. From his breathing and his pale complexion, Less recognizes the fever.

He calls the students to take the poor boy to the *Gesundheitszentrum* and then goes to visit Dr. Balk in his sleek modern office. It takes three repetitions before Dr. Balk, wading through the stuttered German and then sighing "Aha," understands Less needs a new teaching assistant.

The next day, Less hears Dr. Balk is down with a mysterious illness. In class, two young women quietly faint at their desks; as they collapse, their twin ponytails fly up like the tails of frightened deer. Less is beginning to see a pattern.

"I think I am a little spreading," he tells Bastian over dinner at his local *Kiez*. Less initially found the menu so baffling—divided into Minor Friends, Friends Eaten with Bread, and Major Friends—that nightly he has ordered the schnitzel over vinegary potato salad, along with a tall shimmering beer.

"Arthur, you're not making sense," Bastian says, cutting himself a piece of Less's schnitzel. "Spreading?"

"I think I am a little *illness* spreading."

Bastian, mouth full, shakes his head. "I don't think so. You didn't get sick."

"But *everyone else* is sick!" The waitress comes over with more bread and *Schmalz*.

"You know, it's a weird sickness," Bastian says. "I was feeling fine. And then you were talking to me, I felt light-headed and started burning up. It was terrible. But just for one day. I think the Brussels-sprout juice helped."

Less butters a piece of dark bread. "I did not give Brussels-sprout juice."

"No, but I dreamed that you did. The dream helped."

A perplexed look from our author. He changes the subject: "Next week I have an event."

"Yes, you told me," Bastian says, reaching to take a sip from Less's beer; he has finished his own. "You're doing a reading. I'm not sure I can make it. Readings are usually boring."

"No no no, I am not never boring. And next week a friend of mine is getting married."

The German's eyes roam to a television set, where a football match is playing. Absently, he asks, "A good friend? Is she upset that you're not going?"

"Yes, good friend. But it is a man—I do not know the German word. More than friend, but in the past." A Friend Eaten with Bread?

Bastian looks back at Less, seemingly startled. Then he leans forward, taking Less's hand, smiling with amusement. "Arthur, are you trying to make me jealous?"

"No, no. It is the ancient past." Less squeezes Bastian's hand and lets it go, then tilts his head so that the lamp lights his face. "What do you think of my beard?"

"I think it needs more time," Bastian says after some consideration. He takes another bite of Less's meal and looks at him again. He nods and says, very seriously, before turning again to the television: "You know, Arthur, you're right. You're never boring."

A phone call, translated from German into English:

"Good afternoon, Pegasus Publications. This is Petra."

"Good morning. Here is Mr. Arthur Less. I have concern about tonight."

"Oh, hello, Mr. Less! Yes, we talked earlier. I assure you everything's fine."

"But to double . . . triple-check about the time . . ."

"Yes, it's still at twenty-three hours."

"Okay. Twenty-three hours. To be correct, this is eleven at night."

"Yes, that's right. It's an evening event. It's going to be fun!"

"But it is a mental illness! Who will come to me at eleven at night?"

"Oh, trust us, Mr. Less. This isn't the United States. It's Berlin."

Arranged by Pegasus Verlag, in association with the Liberated University and the American Institute for Literature, as well as the U.S. Embassy, the scheduled reading takes place not in a library, as Less has expected, or in a theater, as Less has hoped, but in a nightclub. This also seems a "mental illness" to Less. The entrance is under U-Bahn tracks in Kreuzberg and must have been some kind of engineering shaft or East German escape route, for once Less is past the bouncer ("I am here the author," he says, sure that this is all a mistake), he finds himself inside a great vaulted tunnel covered in white tile that sparkles with reflected light. Otherwise, the room is dim and full of cigarette smoke. At one end, a mirrored bar glows with glassware and bottles; two men in ties work behind it. One seems to be wearing a gun in shoulder holster. At the other end: the DJ, in a big fur hat. The loud thrum of minimal techno beats is in the air, and people on the floor wag back and forth in the pink and white lights. In ties, in trench coats, in fedoras. One carries a briefcase handcuffed to his wrist. Berlin is Berlin, Less supposes. A woman in a Chinese dress, her red hair held up in chopsticks, approaches him with a smile. She has a pale sharp powdered face, a painted beauty mark, and matte red lips. She speaks to him in English: "Well, you must be Arthur Less! Welcome to Spy Club! I'm Frieda."

Less kisses her on each cheek, but she leans in for a third. Two in Italy. Four in Northern France. Three in Germany? He will never get this right. He says, in German: "I am surprised and perhaps delighted!"

A quizzical look, and laughter. "You speak German! How nice!"

"Friend says I speak like a child."

She laughs again. "Come on in. Do you know about Spy Club? We throw this party once a month in some secret spot or another. And people come dressed! Either CIA or KGB. And we have themed music, and themed events, like you." He looks again at the dancers, at the people gathered near the bar. In fur caps and hammer-and-sickle badges; in fedoras and trench coats; some, he thinks, seem to be carrying guns.

"I see, yes," he says. "Who are you dressing to be?"

"Oh, I'm a double agent." She stands back for him to admire her outfit (Madame Chiang Kai-shek? Burmese seductress? Nazi camp follower?) and smiles winningly. "And I brought this for you. Our American. That polka-dot bow tie is perfect." From her purse she produces a badge and pins it

to his lapel. "Come with me. I'll get you a drink and introduce you to your Soviet counterpart."

Less pulls at his lapel so that he can read what is written
there:

YOU ARE ENTERING
THE AMERICAN SECTOR

Less is told that at midnight, the music will go silent and a
spotlight will turn on over the stage where he and his "Soviet
counterpart" (really a Russian émigré, beard and *ochki,* gleefully wearing a Stalin T-shirt under his tight suit) will be
waiting, and they will then present their work to the Spy
Club crowd. They will read for four fifteen-minute seg-
ments, alternating nationalities. It seems an impossibility to
Less that club-goers will stand still for literature. It seems an
impossibility that they will listen for an hour. It seems an impossibility that he is here, in Berlin, at this moment, waiting
in the darkness as the sweat begins to darken his chest like
a bullet wound. They are setting him up for one of those
humiliations. One of those writerly humiliations planned by
the universe to suck at the bones of minor artists like him.
Another Evening with Arthur Less.

It is tonight, after all, on the other side of the world, that his
old *Freund* is getting married. Freddy Pelu is marrying Tom
Dennis at an afternoon ceremony somewhere north of San
Francisco. Less does not know where; the invitation only said
11402 Shoreline Highway, which could mean anything from a
cliffside mansion to a roadside honky-tonk. But guests are to

gather for a 2:30 ceremony, and, considering the time difference, he imagines that would be about, well, *now.*

Here, on the coldest night yet in old Berlin, with the wind howling down from Poland and kiosks set up in plazas to sell fur hats, and fur gloves, and wool inserts for boots, and a snow mountain built on Potsdamer Platz where children can sled past midnight while parents drink *Glühwein* by the bonfire, on this dark frozen night, around now, he imagines Freddy is walking down the aisle. While snow glistens on Charlottenburg Palace, Freddy is standing beside Tom Dennis in the California sun, for surely it is one of those white-linen-suit weddings, with a bower of white roses and pelicans flying by and somebody's understanding college ex-girlfriend playing Joni Mitchell on guitar. Freddy is listening and smiling faintly as he stares into Tom's eyes. While Turkish men shiver and pace in the bus stop, moving like figures on the town hall clock, ready to strike midnight. For it is almost midnight. While the ex-girlfriend finishes her song and some famous friend reads a famous poem, the snow is thickening. While Freddy takes the young man's hand and reads from an index card the vows he has written, the icicles are lengthening. And it must be, while Freddy stands back and lets the minister speak, while the front row breaks into smiles and he leans forward to kiss his groom, while the moon glows in its icebow over Berlin—it must be now.

The music stops. The spotlight comes on; Less blinks (painful scattering of retinal moths). Someone in the audience coughs.

"*Kalipso,*" Less begins. "*I have no right to tell his tale . . .*"

And the crowd listens. He cannot see them, but for almost the entire hour the darkness is all silence. Now and then lit cigarettes appear: nightclub glowworms ready for love. They do not make a sound. He reads from the German translation of his novel, and the Russian reads from his own. It seems to be about a trip to Afghanistan, but Less finds it hard to listen. He is too confused by the alien world in which he is residing: one where writers *matter.* He is too distracted by the thought of Freddy at the altar. It is halfway through his second reading when he hears a gasp and a flurry in the crowd. He stops reading when he realizes that someone has fainted.

And then another.

Three go down before the club raises its lights. Less sees the crowd, in their Cold War *Nostalgie,* their Bond-girl and Strangelove chic, caught in bright lights as in an old Stasi raid. Men come running over with flashlights. Suddenly the air is full of restless chatter, and the room seems barren with its white tile—a municipal bathhouse or substation, which, in fact, is what it is. "What do we do?" Less hears behind him in a Cyrillic accent. The Russian novelist pulls his lush eyebrows together like the parts of a modular sofa. Less looks down to where Frieda is approaching in a clatter of mincing steps.

"It's all right," she says, resting her hand on Less's sleeve while looking at the Russian. "It must be dehydration; we get that a lot, but usually much later in the evening. But *you* started reading, and suddenly . . . " Frieda is still talking, but he is not listening. The "you" is Less. The crowd has lost its shape, clotting into politically impossible groups by the bar. The lights on the tile create the awkward feeling of a night's end, though it is not even one in the morning. Less feels a tingling realization. *Then* you *started reading . . .*

He is boring people to death.

First Bastian, then Hans, Dr. Balk, his students, the crowd at the reading. Listening to his tedious conversation, his lectures, his writing. Listening to his *terrible German.* His confusions of *dann* with *denn,* of *für* with *vor,* of *wollen* with *werden.* How kind they have all been to smile and nod through his sentences, wide eyed, as if listening to a detective announce the killer before he lands, at last, on the wrong verb. How patient and giving these people are. And yet *he* is the killer. One by one, with his mistaken *blau sein* for *traurig sein,* ("I'm drunk" for "I'm blue"), *das Gift* for *das Geschenk* ("poison" for "gift"), he is committing little murders. His words, his banalities, his backward laugh. He feels drunk and blue. Yes, his gift to them is a *Gift.* Like Claudius with Hamlet's father, he is ear poisoning the people of Berlin.

Only when he hears it echoing from the tiled ceiling, and sees the faces turning toward him, does Less realize he has sighed audibly into the microphone. He takes a step back.

And there, in the back of the club, standing alone with his rare smile: Could it be Freddy? Fled from his wedding?

No no no. Just Bastian.

Is it after the minimal techno starts again, that sound that reminds Less of old New York apartments, with the pounding of pipes and the throb of your own heartbreak—or perhaps after the organizer hands him the second "Long Island"? — that Bastian comes to him with a pill and says, "Swallow this." It is a blur of bodies. He remembers dancing with the Russian writer and Frieda (two potatoes together, and they are trouble) as the bartenders wave their plastic guns in the air, and he remembers being handed an envelope with a check in the manner of a briefcase being delivered over the Potsdam bridge, but then somehow he is in a cab and then is on a kind of shipwreck where various levels of dancers and young chatting Berliners sit in clouds of cigarette smoke. Outside, on a plank deck, others hang their feet over the filthy Spree. Berlin is all around them, the Fernsehturm rising high in the east like the Times Square New Year's ball, the lights of Charlottenburg Palace glowing faintly in the west, and all around the glorious junkyard of the city: abandoned warehouses and chic new lofts and boats all done in fairy lights, concrete Honecker residential blocks imitating the old nineteenth-century buildings, the black parks hiding Soviet war memorials, the little candles somebody lights each night before the doors where Jews were dragged from their houses. The old dance halls where elderly couples, still wearing the beige of their Communist lives, still telling secrets in the learned whisper of a lifetime of wiretapping, dance polkas to live bands in rooms decorated in silver Mylar curtains. The basements where American drag queens sell tickets for British expats to listen to French DJs, in rooms where water flows freely down the walls and old gasoline jugs hang from the ceiling, lit from within. The *Currywurst* stands where Turks sift sneezing powder onto fried hot dogs, the subterranean bakeries where the same hot dogs are baked into croissants, the raclette stands where Tyroleans scrape melting cheese onto the bread and ham, decorating it with pickles. The markets already setting up in local squares to sell cheap socks, stolen bicycles, and plastic lamps. The sex dens with stop-lights signaling which clothing to remove, the dungeons of men in superhero costumes of black vinyl with their names embroidered on them, the dark rooms and back alleys where everything possible is happening. And the clubs everywhere, only just getting started, where even middle-aged married folk are sniffing lines of ketamine off black bathroom tile, and teenagers are dosing each other's drinks. In the club, as he later recalls, a woman gets onto the dance floor and really lets go during a Madonna song, really takes over the floor, and people are clapping, hooting, she's losing her mind out there, and her friends are calling her name: "Peter Pan! Peter Pan!" Actually, it isn't a woman; it's Arthur Less. Yes, even old American writers are dancing like it is still the eighties in San Francisco, like the sexual revolution has been won, like the war is over and Berlin has been liberated, one's own self has been liberated; and what the Bavarian in his arms is whispering is true, and everyone, everyone—even Arthur Less—is loved.

Almost sixty years ago, just after midnight, a few feet from the river where they danced, a wonder of modern engineering occurred: overnight, the Berlin Wall arose. It was the night of August 15, 1961. Berliners awoke on the sixteenth to this marvel, more of a fence at first, concrete posts driven into the streets and festooned with barbed wire. They knew trouble would come but expected it in degrees. Life so often arrives all of a sudden. And who knows which side you will find yourself on?

In just such a way, Less awakens at the end of his stay

to find a wall erected between his five weeks in Berlin and reality.

"You're leaving today," the young man says, eyes still closed as he rests sleepily against the pillow. Cheeks red from a long night of farewell, someone's lipstick kiss still smudged there but otherwise unmarked by excess, in the way only the young can manage. His chest as brown as a kiwi, slowly rising and falling. "We are saying good-bye."

"Yes," Less says, steadying himself. His brain feels like it's on a ferryboat. "In two hours. I must to put clothes in the luggage."

"Your German is getting worse," Bastian says, rolling away from Less. It is early morning, and the sun is bright on the sheets. Music comes from the street outside: beats from nonstop Berlin.

"You still to sleep."

A grunt from Bastian. Less leans down to kiss his shoulder, but the young man is already asleep.

As he rises to face the task of packing again, Less endures the ferryboat's tumble within himself. It is just possible to gather all his shirts, layer them carefully as pastry dough, and fold the rest of his clothes within, as he learned how to do in Paris. It is just possible to gather everything in the bathroom and kitchen, the mess of his middle-aged bedside table. It is just possible to hunt down every lost thing, to pinpoint his passport and wallet and phone. Something will remain behind; he hopes it will just be a sewing needle and not a plane ticket. But it is just possible.

Why didn't he say yes? Freddy's voice from the past: *You want me to stay here with you forever?* Why didn't he say yes?

He turns and sees Bastian sleeping on his stomach, arms spread out like those of the Ampelmännchen who signaled East Berliners: walk or don't walk. The curve of his spine, the glow of his skin, pimpled across the shoulders. In the big black iron bed of these last hours. Less goes into the kitchen and starts the water boiling for coffee.

Because it would have been impossible.

He gathers his student papers to grade them on the plane. These he carefully slips into a special compartment of his black rucksack. He gathers the suit coats, the shirts; he makes the little bundle that an earlier traveler would have hung from a stick over his shoulder. In another special place he puts his pills (the Head was right; they do indeed work). Passport, wallet, phone. Loop the belts around the bundle. Loop the ties around the belts. Stuff the shoes with socks. The famous Lessian rubber bands. The items still unused: sun lotion, nail clippers, sewing kit. The items still unworn: the brown cotton trousers, the blue T-shirt, the brightly colored socks. Into the bloodred luggage, zipped tight. All of these will circle the globe to no purpose, like so many travelers.

Back in the kitchen, he loads the last of the coffee (too much) into the French press and fills it with the boiling water. With a chopstick, he stirs the mixture and fits it with the plunger. He waits for it to steep, and as he waits he touches his face; he is startled to feel the beard, like someone who has forgotten they are wearing a mask.

Because he was afraid.

And now it's over. Freddy Pelu is married.

Less pushes down the plunger as with cartoon TNT and explodes coffee all over Berlin.

. . .

A phone call, translated from German into English:

"Hello?"

"Good morning, Mr. Less. This is Petra from Pegasus!"

"Good morning, Petra."

"I just wanted to make sure you got off okay."

"I am on the airport."

"Wonderful! I wanted to tell you what a success it was last night and how grateful your students were for the little class."

"Each one became a sick one."

"They all recovered, as has your assistant. He said you were quite brilliant."

"Each one is a very kind one."

"And if you've found you've left anything behind you need, just let us know, and we'll send it on!"

"No, I have no regrets. No regrets."

"Regrets?"

(Sound of flight being announced) "I leave nothing behind me."

"Good-bye! Until your next wonderful novel, Mr. Less!"

"This we do not know. Good-bye. I head now to Morocco."

But he does not head now to Morocco.

LESS FRENCH

HERE it comes, the trip he dreads: the one when he turns fifty. All the other trips of his life seem to have led, in a blind man's march, toward this one. The hotel in Italy with Robert. The jaunt through France with Freddy. The wild-hare cross-country journey after college to San Francisco, to stay with someone named Lewis. And his childhood trips—the camping trips his father took him on many times, mostly to Civil War battlefields. How clearly Less remembers searching their campsite for bullets and finding—wonder of wonders!—an arrowhead (time revealed the possibility his father had salted the area). The games of mumblety-peg in which clumsy young Less was entrusted with a switchblade knife, which he fearfully tossed as if it were a poisonous snake and with which he once managed to impale an *actual snake* (garter, predeceased). A foil-wrapped potato left to cook in the fire. A ghost story with a golden arm. His father's delight flickering in the firelight. How Less cherished those memories. (He was later to discover a book in his father's library entitled *Growing Up Straight,* which counseled paternal bonding for sissy sons and whose advised activities—battlefields, mumblety-peg, campfires, ghost stories—had all been underlined with a blue Bic pen, but somehow this later discovery could not pierce the sealed happiness of his childhood.) Back then, these journeys all seemed as random as the stars in the sky; only now can he see the zodiac turning above his life. Here, rising, comes the Scorpion.

Less believes he will head now from Berlin to Morocco, with a quick layover in Paris. He has no regrets. He has left nothing behind. The last sands through his hourglass will be Saharan.

But he does not head now to Morocco.

In Paris: a problem. It has been the struggle of a lifetime for Arthur Less to break the value added tax system. As an American citizen, he is due a refund of taxes paid on some purchases abroad, and in the shops, when they hand you the special envelope, the forms all filled out, it seems so simple: find the customs kiosk at the airport for a stamp, collect your refund. But Less knows the con. Closed customs offices, kiosks under repair, stubborn officers who insist he produce goods that were packed in his already-checked baggage; it is easier getting a visa to Myanmar. How many years ago was it when the information lady at Charles de Gaulle would not tell him where the detax office was? Or when he got the stamp but posted it in a deceptively labeled recycling bin? Time and again, he has been outwitted. But not this time. Less makes it his mission to get his damned tax back. Having splurged recklessly after his prize in Turin (a light-blue chambray shirt with a wide white horizontal stripe, like the bottom edge of a Polaroid), he gave himself an extra hour at the Milan airport, found the office, shirt in hand, only to have the officer sadly inform him he must wait until leaving the EU—which will take place when he concludes his layover in Paris and heads for the African continent. Less was undaunted. In Berlin, he tried the same tactic, with the same result (lady with red spiked hair, in mean Berlinese). Less remains undaunted. But at his layover in Paris he meets his match: a surprise German, with red spiked hair and hourglass spectacles, either the twin of the Berliner, or this is her weekend shift. "We do not accept Ireland," she informs him in icy English. His VAT envelope, through some switcheroo, is from Ireland; the receipts, however, are from Italy. "It's Italian!" he tells her as she shakes her head. "Italian! Italian!" He is right, but by raising his voice he has lost; he feels the old anxiety bubbling inside him. Surely she feels it. "You must now post it from Europe," she says. He tries to calm himself and asks where the post office is in the airport. Her magnified eyes barely look up, no smile on her face as she says her delicious words: "There is no post office in the airport."

Less staggers away from the kiosk, utterly defeated, and makes his way toward his gate in a numbing panic; how enviously he looks upon the smoking lounge denizens, laughing in their glass zoo. The injustice of it all weighs on him heavily. How awful for the string of inequities to be brought out in his mind, that useless rosary, so he can finger again those memories: the toy phone his sister received while he got nothing, the B in chemistry because his exam handwriting was poor, the idiot rich kid who got into Yale instead of him, the men who chose hustlers and fools over innocent Less, all the way up to his publisher's polite refusal of his latest novel and his exclusion from any list of best writers under thirty, under forty, under fifty—they make no lists above that. The regret of Robert. The agony of Freddy. His brain sits before its cash register again, charging him for old shames as if he has not paid before. He tries but cannot let it go. It is not the money, he tells himself, but the principle. He has done everything right, and they have conned him once again. It is not the money. And then, after he passes Vuitton, Prada, and clothing brands based on various liquors and cigarettes, he admits it to himself at last: It is, indeed, the money. Of course it is the money. And his brain suddenly decides it is not ready, after all, for fifty. So when he arrives at the crowded gate, jittery, sweating, weary of life, he listens with one ear to the agent's announcement: *"Passengers to Marrakech, this flight is overbooked, and we are looking for volunteers to accept a flight late tonight, with a money voucher for . . ."*

"I'm your man!"

Fate, that glockenspiel, will turn upon the hour. Not long ago Less was lost in an airport lounge, broke, robbed, defeated—and now here he is! Walking down the rue des Rosiers with a pocket full of cash! His luggage is stowed at the airport, and he has hours in the city at his own liberty. And he has already made a call to an old friend.

"Arthur! Young Arthur Less!"

On the phone: Alexander Leighton, of the Russian River School. A poet, a playwright, a scholar, and a gay black man who left the overt racism of America for the soigné racism of France. Less remembers Alex in his headstrong days, when he wore a luxuriant Afro and exclaimed his poetry at the dinner table; last time they met, Alex was bald as a malted milk ball.

"I heard you were traveling! You should have called me earlier."

"Well, I'm not even supposed to be here," Less explains, caught up in the delight of this birthday parole, knowing his words make little sense. He has emerged from the Métro somewhere near the Marais and cannot get his bearings. "I was teaching in Germany, and I was in Italy before that; I volunteered for a later flight."

"What luck for me."

"I was thinking maybe we could get a bite to eat, or a drink."

"Has Carlos got hold of you?"

"Who? Carlos? What?" Apparently, he cannot get his bearings in this conversation either.

"Well, he will. He wanted to buy my old letters, notes, correspondence. I don't know what he's up to."

"Carlos?"

"Mine are already sold to the Sorbonne. He'll be coming for you."

Less imagines his own "papers" at the Sorbonne: *The Col-*

lected Letters of Arthur Less. It would draw the same crowd as "An Evening..."

Alexander is still talking: "... *did* tell me you're going to India!"

Less is amazed how quickly intelligence moves around the world. "Yes," he says. "Yes, it was his suggestion. Listen—"

"Happy birthday, by the way."

"No, no, my birthday isn't until—"

"Look, I've got to run, but I'm going to a dinner party tonight. It's aristocrats; they love Americans, and they love artists, and they'd love for you to come. I'd love for you to come. Will you come?"

"Dinner party? I don't know if I..." And here comes the kind of word problem Less has always failed at: *If a minor novelist has a plane at midnight but wants to go to a dinner in Paris at eight...*

"It's bobo Paris—they love a little surprise. And we can chat about the wedding. Very pretty. And that little *scandal!*"

Less, at a loss, merely sputters: "Oh, that, ha ha—"

"Then you've heard. So much to talk about. See you soon!" He gives Less a nonsensical address on the rue du Bac, with two kinds of door code, then bids him a hasty au revoir. Less is left breathless below an old house all covered in vines. A group of schoolgirls passes in two straight lines.

He is certainly going to the party now, if only because he cannot help himself. A very pretty wedding. Bright promise of something—like the card a magician shows you before he makes it vanish; sooner or later, it will turn up behind your ear. So Less will mail his VAT, go to the party, hear the worst of it, make his midnight flight to Morocco. And in between—he will wander Paris.

Around him, the city spreads its pigeon wings. He has made his way through the Place des Vosges, the rows of clipped trees providing cover both from the light patter of rain and from the Utah Youth Choir, all in yellow T-shirts, performing soft-rock hits of the eighties. On a bench, perhaps inspired by the music of their youth, a middle-aged couple kisses passionately, obliviously, their trench coats spattered with droplets; Less watches as, to the tune of "All Out of Love," the man reaches into his lover's blouse. In the colonnades surrounding, teenagers in cheap plastic ponchos clump together by Victor Hugo's house, looking out at the rain; bags of gewgaws reveal they have visited Quasimodo. At a patisserie, even Less's incomprehensible French cannot prevent success: an almond croissant is soon in his hands, covering him in buttered confetti. He goes to the Musée Carnavalet and admires the decor of crumbled palaces restored, room by room, and studies a strange *groupe en biscuit* of Benjamin Franklin signing an accord with France, marvels over the shoulder-high beds from the past, and stands in wonder before Proust's black and gold bedroom: the walls of cork seem more boudoir than madhouse, and Less is touched to see Proust Senior's portrait hanging on the wall. He stands in the archway of the Boutique Fouquet when, at one o'clock, he hears a chiming throughout the building: unlike in a certain hotel lobby in New York, the ancient clocks have all been wound by some diligent worker. But as Less stands and quietly counts the chimes, he realizes they are off by an hour. Napoleonic time.

He still has hours and hours before meeting Alexander at the address he has given. Down the rue des Archives and through the small entrance to the old Jewish sector. The young tourists are lined up for falafel, the older ones seated at outdoor cafés with enormous menus and expressions of distress. Elegant Parisian women in black and gray sip garishly colored American cocktails that even a sorority girl would not order. He remembers another trip, when Freddy met him in his Paris hotel room and they spent a long indulgent week here: museums and glittering restaurants and tipsy wandering through the Marais at night, arm in arm, and days spent in the hotel bedroom, both in recreation and in recuperation, when one of them caught a local bug. His friend Lewis had told him of an exclusive men's boutique just down the road. Freddy in a black jacket, seeing himself in the mirror, transformed from studious to glorious: "Do I really look like this?" The hopeful look on Freddy's face; Less had to buy it for him, though it cost as much as the trip. Confessing to Lewis later of his recklessness, and getting the reply: "Is that what you want on your grave? *He went to Paris and didn't do one extravagant thing*?" Later, he wondered if the extravagant thing was the jacket or Freddy.

He finds the black signless storefront, the single golden doorbell, and he touches its nipple before ringing it. And is admitted.

Two hours later: Arthur Less stands before the mirror. To the left of him, on the white leather couch: a finished espresso and a glass of champagne. To the right: Enrico, the small bearded sorcerer who welcomed him and offered a place to sit while he brought "special things." How different from the Piemontese tailor (sea otter mustache) who wordlessly took his measurements for the second part of his Italian prize—a tailored suit—and then, when Arthur discovered, to his delight, a fabric in his exact shade of blue, said, "Too young. Too bright. You wear gray." When Less insisted, the man shrugged: *We shall see.* Less gave the address of a Kyoto hotel where he would be staying four months hence and headed to Berlin feeling cheated of his prize.

But here is Paris: a dressing room filled with treasures. And in the mirror: a new Less.

From Enrico: "I have . . . no words . . ."

It is a traveler's fallacy that one should shop for clothing while abroad. Those white linen tunics, so elegant in Greece, emerge from the suitcase as mere hippie rags; the beautiful striped shirts of Rome are confined to the closet; and the delicate hand batiks of Bali are first cruise wear, then curtains, then signs of impending madness. And then there is Paris.

Less wears a pair of natural leather wingtips, a paint stroke of green on each toe, black fitted linen trousers with a spiraling seam, a gray inside-out T-shirt, and a hoodie jacket whose leather has been tenderly furred to the soft nubbin of an old eraser. He looks like a Fire Island supervillain rapper. Nearly fifty, nearly fifty. But in this country, in this city, in this quarter, in this room—filled with exquisite outrages of fur and leather, subtleties of hidden buttons and seams, exclusive grays from film noir classics, with the rain-speckled skylight above and the natural fir flooring below, the few warm bulbs like angels hanged from the rafters, and Enrico clearly a bit in love with this charming American—Less looks transformed. More handsome, more confident. The beauty of his youth somehow taken from its winter storage and given back to him in middle age. *Do I really look like this?*

• • •

The dinner party is on the rue du Bac, in former maids' chambers whose low ceilings and darting hallways seem made more for a murder mystery than a banquet, and so, as he is introduced to one smiling aristocratic face after another, Less finds himself thinking of them in terms of pulp fiction: "Ah, the bohemian artist daughter," he whispers to himself as a sloppy young blonde in a green jumpsuit and cocaine-brightened eyes takes his hand, or, as an elderly woman in a silk tunic nods his way, "Here is the mother who lost all her jewels at the casino." The ne'er-do-well cousin from Amsterdam in a pinstriped cotton suit. The gay son dressed, *à l'Américain,* in a navy blazer and khakis, still reeling from the weekend's Ecstasy binge. The dull ancient Italian man in a raspberry jacket, holding a whiskey: secret former *collaborateur.* The handsome Spaniard in the corner in a crisp white shirt: blackmailing them all. The hostess with her rococo hairdo and cubist chin: spent her last penny on the mousse. And who will be murdered? Why, he will be murdered! Arthur Less, a last-minute invitee, a nobody, and the perfect target! Less peers into his poisoned champagne (his second glass, at least) and smiles. He looks around, again, for Alexander Leighton, but he is either hidden somewhere or late. Then Less notices, by the bookcase, a slim short man in tinted glasses. An eel of panic wriggles through him as he searches the room for exits, but life has no exits. So he takes another sip and approaches, saying his name.

"Arthur," Finley Dwyer says with a smile. "Paris again!"

Why is old acquaintance ne'er forgot?

• • •

Arthur Less and Finley Dwyer have, in fact, met since the Wilde and Stein Literary Laurels. This was in France before Freddy joined him, when Less was on a junket arranged by the French government. The idea was for American authors to visit small-town libraries for a month and spread culture throughout the country; the invitation came from the Ministry of Culture. To the invited Americans, however, it seemed impossible that a country would import foreign authors; even more impossible was the idea of a Ministry of Culture. When Less arrived in Paris, thoroughly jet lagged (he had not yet been introduced to Freddy's sleeping-pill trick), he took one woozy look at the list of fellow ambassadors and sighed. There on the list, a familiar name.

"Hello, I'm Finley Dwyer," said Finley Dwyer. "We've never met, but I've read your work. Welcome to my city; I live here, you know." Less said he was looking forward to all traveling together, and Finley informed him that he had misunderstood. They would not be traveling together; they would be sent off in twos. "Like Mormons," the man said with a smile. Less held his relief in check until he learned that, no, he would not be paired with Finley Dwyer. In fact, he would be paired with no one; an elderly writer had been too ill to make her flight. This did not lessen Less's joy; on the contrary, it seemed a small miracle that now he would be in France, alone, for a month. Time to write, and take notes, and enjoy the country. The woman in gold stood at the head of the table and announced where they would all be headed: to Marseille, Corsica, Paris, Nice. Arthur Less . . . she looked at her notes . . . to Mulhouse. "I'm sorry?" Mulhouse.

It turned out to be on the border of Germany, not far from

Strasbourg. Mulhouse had a wonderful harvest festival, which was already over, and a spectacular Christmas market, which Less would miss. November was the season in between: the homely middle daughter. He arrived at night, by train, and the town seemed dark and crouched, and he was taken to his hotel, conveniently located within the station itself. His room and its furniture dated from the 1970s, and Less battled with a yellow plastic dresser before conceding defeat. Some blind plumber had reversed the hot and cold shower faucets. The view out his window was of a circular brick plaza, rather like a pepperoni pizza, which the whistling wind endlessly seasoned with dry leaves. At least, he consoled himself, Freddy would join him at the end of his journey for an extra week in Paris.

His escort, Amélie, a slim, pretty girl of Algerian parentage, spoke very little English; he wondered how on earth she had qualified for this position. Yet she met him every morning at his hotel, smiling, dressed in wonderful woolens, delivered him to the provincial librarian, sat in the backseat of the car throughout their tour, and delivered him home at night. Where she herself lived was a mystery. What purpose she served was an equal one. Was he meant to sleep with her? If so, they had mistranslated his books. The provincial librarian spoke better English but seemed burdened with unknown sadnesses; in the late autumn drizzle, his pale bald head seemed to be eroding into blandness. He was responsible for Less's daily schedule, which usually consisted of visiting a school during the day and a library at night, with sometimes a monastery in between. Less had never wondered what was served in a French high school cafeteria; should he have been surprised it was aspic and pickles? Attractive students asked wonderful questions in horrible English, dropping their "aitches" like Cockneys; Less gracefully answered, and the girls giggled. They asked for his autograph as if he were a celebrity. Dinner was usually at the library, often in the only place with tables and chairs: the children's section. Picture tall Arthur Less crammed into a tiny chair, at a tiny table, watching a librarian remove the cellophane from his slice of pâté. At one venue, they had made "American desserts" that turned out to be bran muffins. Later: he read aloud to coal miners, who listened thoughtfully. What on earth was everyone thinking? Bringing a midlist homosexual to read to French miners? He imagined Finley Dwyer entertaining in a velvet-draped Riviera theater. Here: gloomy skies and gloomy fortunes. It is no wonder that Arthur Less grew depressed. The days grew more gray, the miners more grim, his spirit more glum. Even the discovery of a gay bar in Mulhouse—Jet Sept—only deepened his sorrow; it was a sad black room, with a few characters from *The Absinthe Drinkers,* and a bad pun besides. When Less's tour of duty was done and he had enriched the life of every coal miner in France, he returned by train to Paris to find Freddy asleep, fully clothed, atop the hotel bed; he had just arrived from New York. Less embraced him and began to shed ridiculous tears. "Oh, hi," the sleepy young man said. "What's happened to you?"

Finley wears a plum-colored suit and a black tie. "How long ago was it? We were traveling together?"

"Well, you remember, we didn't get to travel together."

"Two years at least! And you had...a very handsome young man, I think."

"Oh, well, I—" A waiter comes by with a tray of champagne, and both Less and Finley grab one. Finley handles his unsteadily, then grins at the waiter; it occurs to Less that the man is drunk.

"We hardly got a look at him. I recall..." And here Finley's voice takes on an old-movie flourish: "Red glasses! Curly hair! Is he with you?"

"No. He wasn't really with me then. He'd just always wanted to go to Paris."

Finley says nothing but keeps a crooked little smile. Then he looks at Less's clothes, and he begins to frown. "Where did you—"

"Where did they send you? I don't remember," Less says. "Was it Marseille?"

"No, Corsica! It was so warm and sunny. The people were welcoming, and of course it helped I speak French. I ate nothing but seafood. Where did they put you?"

"I held the Maginot Line."

Finley sips from his glass and says, "And what brings you to Paris now?"

Why is everyone so curious about little Arthur Less? When had he ever occurred to any of them before? He has always felt insignificant to these men, as superfluous as the extra *a* in *quaalude*. "Just traveling. I'm going around the world."

"Le tour du monde en quatre-vingts jours," Finley murmurs, peering up at the ceiling. "Do you have a Passepartout?"

Less answers: "No. I'm alone. I'm traveling alone." He looks down at his glass and sees it is empty. It occurs to Less that he himself might be drunk.

But there is no question Finley Dwyer is. Steadying himself against the bookcase, he looks straight at Less and says, "I read your last book."

"Oh good."

His head lowers, and Less can now see his eyes above the glasses. "What luck to run into you here! Arthur, I want to say something. May I say something?"

Less braces himself as one does against a rogue wave.

"Did you ever wonder why you haven't won awards?" Finley asks.

"Time and chance?"

"Why the gay press doesn't review your books?"

"They don't?"

"They don't, Arthur. Don't pretend you haven't noticed. You're not in the cannon."

Less is about to say he feels very much in the cannon, picturing the human cannonball's wave to the audience before he drops out of view, the minor novelist about to turn fifty—then realizes the man has said "canon." He is not in the *canon*.

"What canon?" is all he manages to sputter.

"The gay canon. The canon taught at universities. Arthur"—Finley is clearly exasperated—"Wilde and Stein and, well, frankly, me."

"What's it like in the canon?" Less is still thinking *cannon*. He decides to head Finley off at the pass: "Maybe I'm a bad writer."

Finley waves this idea away, or perhaps it is the salmon croquettes a waiter is offering. "No. You're a very good writer. *Kalipso* was a chef d'oeuvre. So beautiful, Arthur. I admired it a lot."

Now Less is stumped. He probes his weaknesses. Too magniloquent? Too spoony? "Too old?" he ventures.

"We're all over fifty, Arthur. It's not that you're—"

"Wait, I'm still—"

"—a bad writer." Finley pauses for effect. "It's that you're a bad gay."

Less can think of nothing to say; this attack comes on an undefended flank.

"It is our duty to show something beautiful from our world. The gay world. But in your books, you make the characters suffer without reward. If I didn't know better, I'd think you were Republican. *Kalipso* was beautiful. So full of sorrow. But so incredibly self-hating. A man washes ashore on an island and has a gay affair for years. But then he leaves to go find his wife! You have to do better. For us. Inspire us, Arthur. Aim higher. I'm so sorry to talk this way, but it had to be said."

At last Less manages to speak: "A bad *gay?*"

Finley fingers a book on the bookcase. "I'm not the only one who feels this way. It's been a topic of discussion."

"But . . . but . . . but it's Odysseus," Less says. "Returning to Penelope. That's just how the story goes."

"Don't forget where you come from, Arthur."

"Camden, Delaware."

Finley touches Less's arm, and it feels like an electric shock. "You write what you are compelled to. As we all do."

"Am I being gay boycotted?"

"I saw you stand there, and I had to take this opportunity to let you know, because no one else has been kind enough." He smiles and repeats: "Kind enough to say something to you, as I have now."

And Less feels it swelling up within him, the phrase he does not want to say and yet, somehow, by the cruel checkmate logic of conversation, is compelled to say:

"Thank you."

Finley removes the book from the bookshelf and exits into the crowd as he opens it to the dedication page. Perhaps it is dedicated to him. A ceramic chandelier of blue cherubs hangs above them all and casts more shadows than light. Less stands below it, experiencing that Wonderland sensation of having been shrunk, by Finley Dwyer, into a tiny version of himself; he could pass through the smallest door now, but into what garden? The Garden of Bad Gays. Who knew there was such a thing? Here, all this time, Less thought he was merely a bad writer. A bad lover, a bad friend, a bad son. Apparently the condition is worse; he is bad at being himself. *At least,* he thinks, looking across the room to where Finley is amusing the hostess, *I'm not short.*

There were difficulties, looking back, in the time after Mulhouse. It is hard to know how someone else will travel, and Freddy and Less, at first, were at odds. Though a virtual water bug in our adventures, in ordinary travel Less was always a hermit crab in a borrowed shell: he liked to get to know a street, and a café, and a restaurant, and be called by name by the waiters, and owners, and coat-check girl, so that when he left, he could think of it fondly as another home. Freddy was the opposite. He wanted to see everything. The morning after their nighttime reunion—when Mulhouse malaise and Freddy's jet lag made for drowsy but satisfying sex—Freddy suggested they take a bus to see all the highlights of Paris! Less shivered in horror. Freddy sat on the bed, dressed in a sweatshirt; he looked hopelessly American. "No, it's great, we get to see Notre Dame, the Eiffel Tower, the Louvre, Pompidou, that arch on the Champs-Ély...Ély..." Less forbade it; some irrational fear told him he would be spotted by friends as he stood in this crowd of tourists following a giant gold flag. "Who *cares?*" Freddy asked. But Less would not consider it. He made them see everything by Métro or on foot; they had to eat from stands, not from restaurants; his mother would have told him he inherited this from his father. At the end of each day, they were irritable and exhausted, their pockets filled with used subway *billets;* they had to will themselves out of their roles as general and foot soldier to even consider sharing a bed. But Freddy got lucky: Less got the flu.

That time in Berlin, taking care of Bastian—the sick man he recalled was himself.

It is all, of course, hazy. Long Proustian days staring at the golden bar of sunlight on the floor, the sole escapee from the closed curtains. Long Hugonian nights listening to echoing laughter that rang inside the bell tower of his cranium. All of this mixed with Freddy's worried face, his worried hand on his brow, on his cheek; some doctor or other trying to communicate in French, and Freddy failing, since the only available translator was on his deathbed, moaning; Freddy bringing toast and tea; Freddy in a scarf and blazer, suddenly Parisian, waving a sad good-bye as he went out; Freddy passed out, smelling of wine beside him. Less himself staring at the ceiling fan and wondering if the room was in motion below a stationary fan, or the opposite, much like a medieval man wondering if the sky moved or the earth. And the wallpaper, with its sneaky parrots hiding in a tree. The tree—Less happily identified it as the enormous Persian silk tree of his boyhood. Sitting in that tree in Delaware and looking out on the backyard and on his mother's orange scarf. Less let himself be embraced by its branches, the scent of its pink Seussian flowers. He was very far up in the tree for a boy of three or four, and his mother was calling his name. It never occurred to her that he would be up here, so he was alone, and very proud of himself, and a little scared. The sickle-shaped leaves fell from above. They rested on his pale little arms as his mother called his name, his name, his name. Arthur Less was inching along the branch, feeling the slick bark in his fingers . . .

"Arthur! You're awake! You look so much better!" It was Freddy above him, in a bathrobe. "How do you feel?"

Contrite, mostly. For being first a general, then a wounded soldier. To his delight, only three days had passed. There was still time . . .

"I've seen most of the sights."

"You have?"

"I'm happy to go back to the Louvre, if you want."

"No, no, that's perfect. I want to see a shop Lewis told me about. I think you deserve a present . . ."

This party, on the rue du Bac, is going as badly as possible. Having been approached by Finley Dwyer and informed of his literary crimes, he still cannot manage to locate Alexander; and either the mousse is off or his stomach is. It is clearly time to leave; his stomach is far too weak to hear about the wedding. His plane is in five hours, in any case. Less begins to eye the room for the hostess—hard to pick her out in this sea of black dresses—and finds someone beside him. A Spanish face, smiling through a deep tan. The blackmailer.

"You are a friend of Alexander? I am Javier," the man says. He holds in his hand a plate of salmon and couscous. Green-golden eyes. Straight black hair, center parted, long enough to push behind his ears.

Less says nothing; he suddenly feels hot and knows he has flushed bright pink. Perhaps it is the drink.

"And you are American!" the man adds.

Nonplussed, Less turns an even brighter hue. "How . . . how did you know?"

The man's eyes dart up and down his body. "You are dressed like an American."

Less looks down at his linen pants, his furred leather jacket. He understands that he has fallen under the spell of a shopkeeper, as has many an American before him; he has spent a small fortune to dress as Parisians might rather than as they do. He should have worn the blue suit. He says, "I'm Arthur. Arthur Less. A friend of Alexander; he invited me. But he doesn't seem to be coming."

The man leans in but has to look up; he is quite a bit shorter than Less. "He always invites, Arthur. He never comes."

"Actually, I was about to leave. I don't know anybody here."

"No, don't leave!" Javier seems to realize he has said this too loudly.

"I have a plane to catch tonight."

"Arthur, stay one moment. I also know nobody here. You see those two over there?" He nods toward a woman in a backless black dress, her blond chignon lit by a nearby lamp, and a man all in grays with an oversized Humphrey Bogart head. They are standing side by side, examining a drawing. Javier gives a conspiratorial grin; a strand of hair has come loose and hangs over his forehead. "I was talking with them. We all just met, but I could...sense...very quickly that I was not needed. That is why I came over here." Javier pats the stray hair back in place. "They are going to sleep together."

Less laughs and says surely they didn't say that.

"No, but. Look at their bodies. Their arms are touching. And he leans in to talk to her. It is not loud here. He is leaning in just to be close to her. They did not want me there." At that moment, Humphrey Bogart puts his hand on the woman's shoulder and points to the drawing, talking. His lips are so close to her ear that his breath blows her loose wisps of hair. Now it is obvious; they are going to sleep together.

He turns back to Javier, who shrugs: *What can you do?* Less asks, "And that is why you came over here."

Javier's eyes remain on Less. "It is part of why I came over here."

Less allows the warmth of this flattery to wash over him. Javier's expression does not change. For a moment, they are silent; time expands slightly, taking its deep breath. Less understands it is up to him to make a move. He recalls when, as a boy, a friend would dare him to touch something hot. The silence is broken only by the sound of a glass, also broken, dropped by Finley Dwyer onto the slate floor.

"And so you are flying back to America?" Javier asks.

"No. To Morocco."

"Ah! My mother was Moroccan. You are going to Marrakech, to the Sahara, then to Fez, no? It is the normal visit." Did Javier just wink?

"I guess I'm the normal visitor. Yes. It seems unfair you have me pegged, while you're a mystery."

Another wink. "I'm not. I'm not."

"I only know your mother was Moroccan."

Sexy continuous winking. "I am sorry," Javier says, frowning.

"It's good to be a mystery." Less tries to say this as sensually as possible.

"I am sorry, I have something in my eye." Javier's right eye is now blinking rapidly: a panicked bird. From its outer edge, a rivulet of tears begins to flow.

"Are you okay?"

Javier clenches his teeth and blinks and rubs. "This is so embarrassing. The lenses are new for me, and irritating. They are French."

Less does not fill in the punch line. He watches Javier and worries. He once read in a novel about a technique for removing a speck from another's eye: you use the tip of your tongue. But it seems so intimate, more intimate than a kiss, that he cannot even bear to mention it. And, being from a novel, it is possibly an invention.

"It is out!" Javier exclaims after a final flurry of lashes. "I am free."

"Or you've gotten used to the French."

Javier's face is blotched with red, tears shine on his right cheek, and his lashes are matted and thick. He smiles bravely. He is a little breathless. He looks, to Less, like someone who has run a long distance to be here.

"And there vanishes the mystery!" Javier says, resting his hand on a table and faking a laugh.

Less wants to kiss him; he wants to hold him and protect him. Instead, without thinking at all, he rests his hand on Javier's. It is still wet with tears.

Javier looks up at him with those green-golden eyes. He is so close that Less can smell the orange scent of his pomade. They stand there for a moment perfectly still, a *groupe en biscuit*. His hand on Javier's, his eyes on his. It feels possible that memory will never be finished with this moment. Then they step apart. Arthur Less has flushed as pink as a prom carnation. Javier takes a deep breath, then breaks their gaze.

"I wonder," Less begins, in a struggle to say almost anything at all, "if you have any tips about the VAT . . ."

The room, which they are blind to, is papered in green-striped fabric and hung with preliminary drawings, or "cartoons," for a greater work of art: here a hand, here a hand with a pen, here a woman's upturned face. Above the fireplace mantel, the painting itself: a woman paused in thought while writing a letter. Bookshelves go to the ceiling, and if he looked, Less would find, besides one of H. H. H. Mandern's Peabody novels, a collection of American stories in which—surprise of surprises!—one of his is featured. The hostess has not read it; she kept it because of an affair she had long ago, with another featured writer. She has read the two books of poetry two shelves above, by Robert, but she does not know that there is any connection to one of her guests. Yet here, again, the lovers meet. By now, the sun has set, and Less has found a way past the European tax system.

Less's endearing backward laugh: *AH ah ah ah!*

"Before I came here," Less is now saying, feeling the champagne taking possession of his tongue, "I went to the Musée d'Orsay."

"It's wonderful."

"I was very moved by the Gauguin carvings. But then out of nowhere there was Van Gogh. Three self-portraits. I walked up to one; it was protected with glass. I could see my reflection. And I thought: *Oh my God.*" Less shakes his head, and his eyes widen as he relives the moment. *"I look just like Van Gogh."*

Javier laughs, his hand to his smile. "Before the ear, I think."

"I thought, *I've gone crazy,*" Less goes on. "But . . . I've already outlived him by over a decade!"

Javier tilts his head, a cocker Spaniard. "Arthur, how old are you?"

Deep breath. "I'm forty-nine."

Javier moves closer to peer at him; he smells of cigarettes and vanilla, like Less's grandmother. "How funny. I am also forty-nine."

"No," Less says, truly bewildered. There is not a line on Javier's face. "I thought you were midthirties."

"That is a lie. But it is a nice lie. And you do not look close to fifty."

Less smiles. "My birthday is in one week."

"Strange to be almost fifty, no? I feel like I just understood how to be young."

"Yes! It's like the last day in a foreign country. You finally figure out where to get coffee, and drinks, and a good steak. And then you have to leave. And you won't ever be back."

"You put it very well."

"I'm a writer. I put things very well. But I'm told I'm 'spoony.'"

"I am sorry?"

"Foolish. Tenderhearted."

Javier seems delighted. "That is a nice phrase, *tenderhearted*. Tenderhearted." He takes a deep breath as if building courage. "I am, I think, the same."

Javier has a look of sadness about him as he says this. Then he stares directly into his drink. The sky out the window is lowering the last of its gauzy veils, revealing bright naked Venus. Less looks at the gray strands in Javier's black hair, the prominent rose-tinted bridge of his nose, the bent head over the white shirt, two buttons open to reveal his date-colored skin, flecked with hairs, leading into shadow. More than a few of the hairs are white. He imagines Javier naked. The gold-green eyes as the man peers up at him from a white bed. He imagines touching that warm skin. This evening is unexpected. This man is unexpected. Less thinks of when he bought a wallet in a thrift shop and in it found a hundred dollars.

"I want a cigarette," Javier says, with a child's abashed face.

"I'll join you," Less says, and together they step out of the open window, onto a narrow stone balcony where other smoking Europeans glance back at the American as on a member of the secret police. At the corner of the house, the balcony turns, offering a view of slanted metal rooftops and chimneys. They are alone here, and Javier takes out a pack and pulls on its contents so that two white tusks emerge. Less shakes his head: "Actually, I don't smoke."

They laugh.

Javier says, "I think I am a little drunk, Arthur."

"I think I am too."

Less's smile has expanded to its full size, here alone with Javier. Is it the champagne that makes him emit an audible sigh? They are side by side at the railing. The chimneys all look like flowerpots.

Looking out at the view, Javier says, "Here is something strange about growing old."

"What's that?"

"I meet new friends, and they are bald or they are gray. And I don't know what color their hair used to be."

"I never thought about it."

Now Javier turns to look at Less; he is probably the type to turn and look at you while he is driving. "A friend, I have known him for five years, maybe he is in his late fifties. And I asked him once. I was so surprised to find he was a redhead!"

Less nods in agreement. "I was on the street the other day. In New York City. And an old man came up to me and hugged me. I had no idea who he was. He was my old lover."

"Dios mío," Javier says, swallowing a gulp of champagne. Less feels his arm against Javier's, and even through the layers of fabric his skin comes alive. He so desperately wants to touch this man. Javier says, "Me, I was at dinner, and an old man was beside me. So boring! Talking about real estate. I thought, *Please, God, do not let me be this man when I am old.* Later I find out he was a year younger than I."

Less puts down his glass and, bravely, puts his hand again on Javier's. Javier turns to face him.

"And also," Less says meaningfully, "being the only single man your age."

Javier says nothing but just gives a sad smile.

Less blinks, removes his hand, and takes one half step away from the railing. Now, in the new space between him and the Spaniard, one can make out the Erector-set miracle of the Eiffel Tower.

Less asks, "You're not single, are you?"

Smoke leaks from Javier's mouth as he shakes his head gently side to side. "We have been together eighteen years. He is in Madrid, I am here."

"Married."

Javier waits a long time before he answers. "Yes, married."

"So you see, I was right."

"That you are the only single man?"

Less closes his eyes. "That I am foolish."

There is piano music inside; the son has been put to work, and whatever hangover he has does not show in the bright garlands of notes that come out the window, onto the balcony. The other smokers all turn and walk over to see and listen. The sky is now nothing but night.

"No, no, you're not foolish." Javier puts his hand on the sleeve of Less's ridiculous jacket. "I wish I were single."

Less smiles bitterly at the subjunctive but does not move his arm. "I'm sure you don't. Otherwise you would be."

"It is not so simple, Arthur."

Less pauses. "But it is too bad."

Javier moves his hand up to Less's elbow. "It is very too bad. When do you leave?"

He checks his watch. "I leave for the airport in an hour."

"Oh." A sudden look of pain in those gold-green eyes. "I am not to meet you again, am I?"

He must have been slim in his youth, with long black hair, colored blue in certain light, as in old comic books. He must have swum in the sea in an orange Speedo and fallen in love with the man smiling onshore. He must have gone from bad affair to bad affair until he met a dependable man at an art museum, just five years older, already going bald, with a bit of a belly but an easy demeanor that promised escape from heartbreak, off in Madrid, that palace of a city shimmering in the heat. Surely it was a decade or more before they married. How many late dinners of ham and pickled anchovies? How many arguments over the sock drawer—blacks mixing with navy blues—until they decided at last to have separate drawers? Separate duvets, as in Germany? Separate brands of coffee and tea? Separate vacations—his husband to Greece (completely bald but the belly in check), and he to Mexico? Alone on a beach again in an orange Speedo, no longer slim. Trash gathering along the shoreline from cruise ships, and a view of Cuba's dancing lights. He must have been lonely a long time to stand before Arthur Less and ask such a thing. On a rooftop in Paris, in his black suit and white shirt. Any narrator would be jealous of this possible love, on this possible night.

Less stands there in the furred leather jacket against the nighttime city. With his sad expression, three-quarters turned to Javier, his gray shirt, his striped scarf, his blue eyes and copper-colored beard, he looks unlike himself. He looks like Van Gogh.

A flight of starlings goes off behind him, headed to church.

"We're too old to think we'll meet again," Less says.

Javier rests his hand on Less's waist and steps toward him. Cigarettes and vanilla.

"Passengers to Marrakech . . ."

Arthur Less sits in the Lessian manner—legs crossed at the knee, free foot fidgeting—and, as usual, his long legs find themselves in the way of one passenger after another, with their rolling suitcases so enormous, Less cannot imagine what they are bringing to Morocco. The traffic is so constant that he has to uncross his legs and sit back. He still wears his new Parisian clothes, the linen of his trousers slackened from a day of use, the coat suffocatingly hot. He is weary and drunk from the party, and his face is aglow with alcohol and doubt and arousal. He has, however, succeeded in mailing his tax-free form, and for this he wears (having passed by his nemesis, the Tax Lady) the smug smile of a criminal who has pulled off one last heist. Javier promised to mail it in the morning; it is tucked inside that slim black jacket, against that firm Iberian chest. So it was not all for nothing. Was it?

He closes his eyes. In his "distant youth," he often comforted his anxious mind with images of book covers, of author photographs, of newspaper clippings. These things he can now call easily to mind; they hold no comfort. Instead, his brain's staff photographer produces a contact sheet of identical images: Javier pulling him toward the stone wall and kissing him.

"This flight is overbooked, and we are looking for volunteers . . ."

Overbooked again. But Arthur Less does not hear her, or else he cannot consider a second stay of execution, a second day of possibilities before he turns fifty. Perhaps it is all too much. Or else just enough.

The piano piece ends, and the guests break into applause. From across the roofs comes either the echo of the applause or that of another party. A triangle of amber light catches one of Javier's eyes and makes it gleam like glass. And all that goes through Less's mind is the single thought: *Ask me.* With the married man smiling and touching Less's red beard—*Ask me*—kissing him for perhaps half an hour longer, and here we have another man fallen under the spell of Less's kiss, pushing him against the wall, unzipping his jacket, touching him passionately and whispering beautiful things but not the words that would change everything, for it is still possible to change everything, until Less tells him at last that it is time to go. Javier nods, walking him back into the green-striped room and standing beside him as he says his good-byes to the hostess, and to the other murder suspects, in his terrible French—*Ask me*—taking him to the front door and walking him downstairs as far as the street, all done in blue watercolors, blurred by the mist of rain, the carved stone porticos and wet satin streets—*Ask me*—and the poor Spaniard offers his own umbrella (refused) before smiling sadly—"I am sorry to see you go"—and waving good-bye.

Ask me and I will stay.

There is a call on Less's phone, but he is preoccupied: already inside the plane, nodding to the beaky blond steward who greets him, as they always do, in the language not of the passenger, steward, or airport but of the plane itself ("Buonasera," for it is Italian), bumping his awkward way down the aisle, assisting a tiny woman with her enormous overhead luggage, and finding his favorite seat: the rightmost, rearmost corner. No children to kick you from behind. Prison pillow, prison blanket. He removes his tight French shoes and slides them under the seat. Out the window: nighttime Charles de Gaulle, will-o'-the-wisps and men waving glowing wands. He closes the shade, then closes his eyes. He hears his neighbor sitting down roughly and speaking Italian, and he nearly understands it. Brief memory of swimming in a golf resort. Brief false memory of Dr. Ess. Brief real memory of rooftops and vanilla.

"*. . . welcome you on our flight from Paris to Marrakech . . .*"

The chimneys all looked like flowerpots.

There is a second call, this time from an unknown number, but we will never know what it contains, for no message is left, and the intended receiver is already deep in takeoff slumber, high above the continent of Europe, only seven days from fifty, headed now at last to Morocco.

LESS MOROCCAN

WHAT does a camel love? I would guess nothing in the world. Not the sand that scours her, or the sun that bakes her, or the water she drinks like a teetotaler. Not sitting down, blinking her lashes like a starlet. Not standing up, moaning in indignant fury as she manages her adolescent limbs. Not her fellow camels, to whom she shows the disdain of an heiress forced to fly coach. Not the humans who have enslaved her. Not the oceanic monotony of the dunes. Not the flavorless grass she chews, then chews again, then again, in a sullen struggle of digestion. Not the hellish day. Not the heavenly night. Not sunset. Not sunrise. Not the sun or the moon or the stars. And surely not the heavy American, a few pounds overweight but not bad for his age, taller than most and top heavy, tipping from side to side as she carries this human, this Arthur Less, pointlessly across the Sahara.

Before her: Mohammed, a man in a long white djellaba and with a blue shesh wound around his head, leading her by a rope. Behind her: the eight other camels in her caravan, because nine people signed up to travel to this encampment, though only four of the camels have passengers. They have lost five people since Marrakech. They are soon to lose another.

Atop her: Arthur Less, in his own blue shesh, admiring the dunes, the little wind devils dancing on each crest, the sunset coloration of turquoise and gold, thinking at least he will not be alone for his birthday.

Days earlier—awakening from the Paris flight to find himself on the African continent: a bleary-eyed Arthur Less. Body still atingle with champagne and Javier's caresses and a rather awkward window seat, he staggers across the tarmac beneath a dyed-indigo night sky, and into an immigration line that is beyond reason. The French, so stately at home, seem instantly to have lost their minds on the soil of their former colony; it is like the redoubled madness of seeing a lover you have wronged; they ignore the line, removing the ropes from the carefully ordered stanchions, and become a mob charging into Marrakech. The Moroccan officers, in the green and red of cocktail olives, stay calm; passports are examined, then stamped; Less imagines this happens all day, every day. He finds himself shouting "Madame! Madame!" at a Frenchwoman elbowing her way through the crowd. She pouts with a shrug (*C'est la vie!*) and keeps going. Is there an invasion he has not heard of? Is this the last plane out of France? If so: where is Ingrid Bergman?

So there is plenty of time, as he shuffles with the crowd (in which, though European, he still towers), to panic.

He could have remained in Paris, or at least have accepted yet another delay (and six hundred euros); he could have tossed this whole foolish adventure aside for one even more foolish. *Arthur Less was supposed to go to Morocco, but he met a Spaniard in Paris, and no one has heard from him since!* A rumor for Freddy to hear. But if he is anything, Arthur Less is a man who follows his plan. And so he is here. At least he will not be alone.

"Arthur! You've grown a beard!" His old friend Lewis, outside customs, joyous as ever. Tarnished-silver hair worn long over the ears and bristling white on his chin; plump faced and well clad in gray linen and cotton; capillaries spreading in a fertile delta across his nose; signs that Lewis Delacroix is, at nearly sixty, a stride ahead of Arthur Less.

Less smiles warily and touches his beard. "I . . . I thought I needed a change."

Lewis holds him at a distance to study him. "It's sexy. Let's get you into some air-conditioning. There's a heat wave on, and even these Marrakech nights have been hell. Sorry your flight was delayed; what a nightmare to wait a whole day! Did you manage to fall in love with fourteen hours in Paris?"

Less is startled and says he called up Alexander. He talks about the party and Alex not showing up. He doesn't mention Javier.

Lewis turns to him and asks, "Do you want to talk about Freddy? Or do you not want to talk about Freddy?"

"Not talk."

His friend nods. Lewis, whom he met for the first time on that long road trip after college, who offered his cheap apartment on Valencia Street, above the communist bookstore, who introduced him to acid and electronic music. Handsome Lewis Delacroix, who seemed so adult, so assured; he was thirty. A generation apart back then; now they are essentially contemporaries. And yet Lewis has always seemed so much steadier; with the same boyfriend for twenty years, he is the very model of love's success. And glamorous: this trip, for instance, is exactly the kind of luxury that afforded Lewis's fascinating stories. It is a birthday trip—not for Arthur Less. For some woman named Zohra, who is also turning fifty, and whom Less has never met.

"I'd say let's get some sleep," Lewis says as they find a taxi, "but nobody at the hotel is asleep. They've been drinking since noon. And who knows what else? I blame Zohra; well, you'll meet Zohra."

The actress is the first to go. Perhaps it is the pale Moroccan wine, poured glass after glass at dinner (on the roof of the rented house, the *riad,* with a view of that upraised pupil's hand: the minaret of the Koutoubia Mosque); or perhaps the gin and tonics she requests after dinner, when she sheds her clothes (the two riad workers, both named Mustafa, say nothing) and slips into the courtyard pool, where turtles stare at her pale flesh, wishing they were still dinosaurs, the water rippling from her backstroke as the others continue to introduce themselves (Less is in here somewhere, struggling with a wine bottle between his thighs); or perhaps the tequila she discovers later, once the gin runs out, when someone has found a guitar and someone else a shrill local flute and she begins an improvisational dance with a lantern on her head before someone leads her out of the pool; or perhaps the whiskey later passed around; or the hashish; or the cigarettes; or the three loud claps of the riad's neighbor, a princess: the sign they are up too late for Marrakech—but how will we ever know? All we know is that in the morning, she is unable to get out of bed; naked, she calls for a drink, and when someone brings her water she knocks the glass away and says, "I mean vodka!" and because she is unwilling to move, and because their ride to the Sahara leaves at noon, and because her last two movies were in dubious taste, and because nobody but the birthday girl even knows her, it is in the care of the two Mustafas that they leave her.

"Will she be okay?" Less asks Lewis.

"I'm so surprised she couldn't hold her liquor," Lewis says, turning to him with his enormous sunglasses; they make him look like a nocturnal primate. They are seated together in a small bus; a freak heat wave has made the world outside shimmer like a wok. The rest of the passengers lean wearily against the windows. "I thought actors were made from steel."

"Please to all!" says their guide into his microphone; this is Mohammed, their Moroccan guide, in a red polo shirt and jeans. "Here we pass through the Atlas Mountains. They are, we say, like snake. Tonight we arrive at [*name garbled by microphone*], where we spend the night. Tomorrow is the valley of palms."

"I thought tomorrow was the desert," comes a British accent Less recognizes, from the night before, as that of the technology genius who retired at forty and now runs a night-club in Shanghai.

"Oh yes, I promise the desert!" Mohammed is short, with long curly hair, probably in his forties. His smile is quick, but his English is slow. "I am sorry for the unpleasant surprise of the heat."

From the back, a female voice, Korean: the violinist. "Can they turn up the air?"

Some words in Arabic, and the vents begin to blast warm air into the bus. "My friend said it was at top." Mohammed smiles. "But we now know it was not at top." The air does nothing to cool them. Beside them, on the road out of Marrakech, are groups of schoolchildren making their way home for lunch; they hold shirts or books over their faces to shield themselves from the merciless sun. Miles of adobe walls and, now and then, the oasis of a coffee shop where men stare at the bus as they pass. Here is a pizza joint. And here an uncompleted gas station: AFRIQUA. Someone has tied a donkey to a telephone pole in the middle of nowhere and left it there. The driver turns on music: the somehow-enchanting drone of Gnawa. Lewis seems to have fallen asleep; in those glasses, Less cannot tell.

Tahiti.

"I've always wanted to go to Tahiti," Freddy told him once, at an afternoon rooftop gathering of his young friends. A few other, older men peppered the crowd, eyeing each other like fellow predators; Less did not know how to signal that in this crowd of gazelles, he was a vegetarian. *My last boyfriend,* he wanted to tell them, *is now in his sixties.* Did any of them, like him, prefer middle-aged men? He never found out; they avoided him as if magnetically repulsed. Eventually, at these parties, Freddy would float over with a weary expression, and they would spend the last hours just the two of them, chatting. And this time—perhaps it was the tequila and sunset—Freddy had brought up Tahiti.

"That sounds nice," Less said. "But to me it seems so resorty. Like you'd never meet the locals. I want to go to India."

Freddy gave a shrug. "Well, you'd definitely get to meet the locals in India. I hear there's nothing but locals. But do you remember when we went to Paris? The Musée d'Orsay? Oh right, you were sick. Well. There was a room of carvings by Gauguin. And one said: *Be mysterious.* And the other one said: *Be in love, you will be happy.* In French, of course. Those really moved me, more than the paintings. He made the same carving for his house in Tahiti. I know I'm strange. I should want to go because of the beaches. But I want to see his house."

Less was about to say something—but just then the sun, hidden behind Buena Vista, was glorifying a fog bank, and Freddy went straight to the railing to see it. They never talked about Tahiti again, so Less never gave it another thought. But clearly Freddy did.

Because that is where he must be now. On his honeymoon with Tom.

Be in love, you will be happy.

Tahiti.

It doesn't take long to lose the next ones. The bus makes it to Ait Ben Haddou (with one lunch stop at a hallucinogenically tiled roadhouse), where they are led out of the bus. Ahead of him is a couple, both war reporters; the night before, they were regaling Less with stories of Beirut in the eighties, such as one about the bar whose cockatoo could imitate incoming bombs. A chic Frenchwoman with bobbed white hair and bright cotton slacks, a tall mustachioed German in a photojournalist jacket, they have come from Afghanistan to laugh, chain-smoke, and learn a new dialect of Arabic. The world seems to be theirs; nothing can take them down. Zohra, the birthday girl, comes over and walks beside him: "Arthur, I am so glad you came." Not tall but definitely alluring, in a long-sleeved yellow dress that shows off her legs; she possesses a unique beauty, with the long nose and shining, oversized eyes of a Byzantine portrait of Mary. Every one of her movements—touching the back of a seat, brushing her hair from her face, smiling at one of her friends—is purposeful, and her gaze is direct and discerning. Her accent would be impossible to place—English? Mauritian? Basque? Hungarian?—except Less already knows, from Lewis, that she was born right here in Morocco but left as a child for England. This is her first trip home in a decade. He has watched her with her friends; she is always laughing, always smiling, but he sees, when she walks away, the shadow of some deep sadness. Glamorous, intelligent, resilient, bracingly direct, and prone to obscenities, Zohra seems like the kind of woman who would run an international spy ring. For all Less knows, this is exactly what she does.

Most of all: she does not look anywhere near fifty, or even forty. You would never know she drinks like a sailor, as well as swears like one, smokes one menthol after another. She certainly looks younger than lined and weary, old and broke and loveless Arthur Less.

Zohra fixes her dazzling eyes on him. "You know, I'm a big fan of your books."

"Oh!" he says.

They are walking along beside a low wall of ancient bricks, and, below, a series of whitewashed houses rises from a river. "I really loved *Kalipso*. Really, really loved it. You motherfucker, you made me cry at the end."

"I guess I'm glad to hear that."

"It was so sad, Arthur. So fucking sad. What's your next one?" She flips her hair over her shoulder, and it moves in a long fluid line.

He finds himself clenching his teeth. Below, two boys on horseback are moving slowly up the river shallows.

Zohra frowns. "I'm freaking you out. I shouldn't have asked. None of my fucking business."

"No, no," Arthur says. "It's okay. I wrote a new novel, and my publisher hates it."

"What do you mean?"

"Well, they turned it down. Declined to publish it. I remember when I sold my first book, the head of the publishing house sat me down in his office, and he gave me this long speech about how he knew they didn't pay very much, but they were a family, and I was now part of that family, they were investing in me not for this book but for my entire career. That was only fifteen years ago. And bam—I'm out. Some family."

"Sounds like my family. What was your new novel about?" Catching his expression, she quickly adds, "Arthur, I hope you know you can tell me to bugger off."

He has a rule, which is never to describe his books until after they are published. People are so careless with their responses, and even a skeptical expression can feel akin to someone saying about your new lover: *Don't tell me you're dating him?* But for some reason, he trusts her.

"It was...," he starts, stumbling on a rock in the path, then starts again: "It was about a middle-aged gay man walking around San Francisco. And, you know, his...his sorrows..." Her face has begun to fold inward in a dubious expression, and he finds himself trailing off. From the front of the group, the journalists are shouting in Arabic.

Zohra asks, "Is it a white middle-aged man?"

"Yes."

"A white middle-aged American man walking around with his white middle-aged American sorrows?"

"Jesus, I guess so."

"Arthur. Sorry to tell you this. It's a little hard to feel sorry for a guy like that."

"Even gay?"

"Even gay."

"Bugger off." He did not know he was going to say this.

She stops walking, points at his chest, and grins. "Good for you," she says.

And then he notices, before them, a crenellated castle on a hill. It seems to be made of sun-baked mud. It seems impossible. Why did he not expect this? Why did he not expect Jericho?

"This," Mohammed announces, "is the ancient walled city of the tribe of Haddou. *Ait* means a Berber tribe, *Ben* means "from," and *Haddou* is the family. And so, Ait Ben Haddou.

There are eight families still living within the walls of the city."

Why did he not expect Nineveh, Sidon, Tyre?

"I'm sorry," says the tech-whiz nightclub owner. "You say there are eight families? Or Ait families?"

"Ait families."

"The number eight?"

"Once it was a village, but now only a few families remain. Eight."

Babylon? Ur?

"Once again. The number eight? Or the name Ait?"

"Yes, Ait families. Ait Ben Haddou."

It is at this point that the female war reporter leans over the ancient wall and commences vomiting. The miracle before them is forgotten; her husband runs to her side and holds back her beautiful hair. The setting sun puts the adobe scene in blue shadows, and somehow Less is taken back to the color scheme of his childhood home, when his mother went mad for the Southwest. From across the river, a cry comes up like an air raid siren: the evening call to prayer. The castle, or *ksar,* Ait Ben Haddou rises, unfeeling, before them. The husband tries, at first, a furious exchange in German with the guide, then one in Arabic with the driver, followed by French, ending in an incomprehensible tirade meant only for the gods. His command of English curses goes untested. His wife clutches her head and tries to stand but collapses into the driver's arms, and they are all taken quickly back to the bus. "Migraine," Lewis whispers to him. "Booze, the altitude. I bet she's down for the count." Less takes one last look at the ancient castle of mud and straw, remade every year or so as the rains erode the walls, plastered and replastered so that nothing remains of the old ksar except its former pattern. Something like a living creature of which not a cell is left of the original. Something like an Arthur Less. And what is the plan? Will they just keep rebuilding forever? Or one day will someone say, *Hey, what the hell? Let it fall, bugger off.* And that will be the end of Ait Ben Haddou. Less feels on the verge of an understanding about life and death and the passage of time, an ancient and perfectly obvious understanding, when a British voice intervenes:

"Okay, sorry to be a bother, just want to make sure. Once again. It's Ait..."

"Prayer is better than sleep," comes the morning cry from the mosque, but travel is better than prayer, for as the muezzin chants, they are all already packed into the bus and waiting for the guide to return with the war reporters. Their hotel—a dark stone labyrinth at night—reveals itself, at sunrise, to be a palace in a valley of lush palms. By the front door, two little boys giggle over a chick they hold in their hands. Colored a bright orange (either artificially or supernaturally), the chick chirps at them ceaselessly, furiously, indignantly, but they only laugh and show the creature to luggage-burdened Arthur Less. On the bus, he seats himself beside the Korean violinist and her male-model boyfriend; the young man looks over at Less with a blank blue stare. What does a male model love? Lewis and Zohra sit together, laughing. The guide returns; the war reporters are still recovering, he reports, and will join them on a later camel. So the bus guffaws to life. Good to know there is always a later camel.

The rest is a Dramamine nightmare: a drunkard's route up the mountain, at every switchback the miraculous gleam of geodes set out for sale, a young boy jumping at the bus's approach, rushing quickly to the roadside, holding out a violet-dyed geode, only to be covered in a cloud of dust as they depart. Here and there a casbah with fireclay walls and a great green wooden door (the donkey door, Mohammed explains), with a small door set inside (the people door), but never a sign of either donkeys or people. Just the arid acacia mountainside. The passengers are sleeping or staring out the window and chatting quietly. The violinist and the male model are whispering intensely, and so Less makes his way back, where he finds Zohra staring out a window. She motions, and he sits beside her.

"You know what I've decided," she says sternly, as if calling a meeting to order. "About turning fifty. Two things. The first is: fuck love."

"I don't know what that means."

"It means, give it up. Fuck it. I gave up smoking, and I can give up love." He eyes the pack of menthols in her purse. "What? I've given it up several times! Romance isn't safe at our age."

"So Lewis told you I'm also turning fifty?"

"Yes! Happy birthday, darling! We're going down the shitter together." She's nothing short of delighted to have learned that her birthday is the day before his.

"Okay, no romance at our age. Actually, that's a huge relief. I might get more writing done. What's the second?"

"It's related to the first one."

"Okay."

"Get fat."

"Huh."

"Fuck love and just get fat. Like Lewis."

Lewis turns his head. "Who, me?"

"You!" Zohra says. "Look how fucking fat you've gotten!"

"Zohra!" Less says.

But Lewis just chuckles. With two hands, he pats the mound of his belly. "You know, I think it's a hoot? I look in the mirror every morning and laugh and laugh and laugh. Me! Skinny little Lewis Delacroix!"

"So that's the plan, Arthur. Are you in?" Zohra asks.

"But I don't want to get fat," Less says. "I know that sounds stupid and vain, but I don't."

Lewis leans in closer. "Arthur, you're going to have to figure something out. You see all these men over fifty, these skinny men with mustaches. Imagine all the dieting and exercise and effort of fitting into your suits from when you were thirty! And then what? You're still a dried-up old man. Screw that. Clark always says you can be thin or you can be happy, and, Arthur, I have already tried thin."

His husband, Clark. Yes, they are Lewis and Clark. They still find it hilarious. Hilarious!

Zohra leans forward and puts a hand on his arm. "Come on, Arthur. Do it. Get fat with us. The best is yet to come."

There is noise at the front of the bus; the violinist is talking in hushed tones with Mohammed. From one of the window seats, they can now hear the male model's moans.

"Oh no, not another," Zohra says.

"You know," Lewis says, "I thought he would have gone sooner."

. . .

So there are only four laden camels moving across the Sahara. The male model, sick beyond all measure, has been left with the bus in M'Hamid, the last town before the desert, and the violinist has stayed with him. "He will join us on a later camel," Mohammed assures them as they board their camels and are tipped like teapots as the creatures struggle to rise. Four with humans and five without, all in a line, making shadows in the sand, and, looking at the damned creatures, with their hand-puppet heads and their hay-bale bodies, their scrawny little legs, Less thinks, *Look at them! Who could ever believe in a god?* It is three days until his birthday; Zohra's is in two.

"This isn't a birthday," Less yells to Lewis as they bob toward the sunset. "It's an Agatha Christie novel!"

"Let's bet on who goes next. I'm betting me. Right now. On this camel."

"I'm betting on Josh." The British tech whiz.

Lewis asks: "Would you like to talk about Freddy now?"

"Not really. I heard the wedding was very pretty."

"I heard that the night before, Freddy—"

Zohra's voice comes loudly from her camel: "Shut the fuck up! Enjoy the fucking sunset on your fucking camels! Jesus!"

It is, after all, almost a miracle they are here. Not because they've survived the booze, the hashish, the migraines. Not that at all. It's that they've survived everything in life, humiliations and disappointments and heartaches and missed opportunities, bad dads and bad jobs and bad sex and bad drugs, all the trips and mistakes and face-plants of life, to have made it to fifty and to have made it here: to this frosted-cake landscape, these mountains of gold, the little table they can now see sitting on the dune, set with olives and pita and glasses and wine chilling on ice, with the sun waiting more patiently than any camel for their arrival. So, yes. As with almost every sunset, but with this one in particular: shut the fuck up.

The silence lasts as long as it takes a camel to summit a dune. Lewis notes aloud that today is his twentieth anniversary, but of course his phone won't work out here, so he'll have to call Clark when they get to Fez.

Mohammed turns back and says, "Oh, but there is Wi-Fi in the desert."

"There is?" Lewis asks.

"Oh, of course, everywhere," Mohammed says, nodding.

"Oh good."

Mohammed holds up one finger. "The problem is the password."

Up and down the line the Bedouin chuckle.

"That's the second time I've fallen for that one," Lewis says, then looks back at Less and points.

There on the dune, beside the table, one of the camel boys has his arm around the other, and they sit there like that as they watch the sun. The dunes are turning the same shades of adobe and aqua as the buildings of Marrakech. Two boys, arms around each other. To Less, it seems so foreign. It makes him sad. In his world, he never sees straight men doing this. Just as a gay couple cannot walk hand in hand down the streets of Marrakech, he thinks, two men, best friends, cannot walk hand in hand down the streets of Chicago. They cannot sit on a dune like these teenagers and watch a sunset in each other's embrace. This Tom Sawyer love for Huck Finn.

The encampment is a dream. Begin in the middle: a fire pit laden with gnarled acacia branches, surrounded by pillows, from which eight carpeted paths lead to eight plain canvas tents, each of which—outwardly no more than a smallish revival tent—opens onto a wonderland: a brass bed whose coverlet is sewn with tiny mirrors, nightstands and bedside lamps in beaten metal, a washbasin and coy little toilet behind a carved screen, and a vanity and full-length mirror. Less steps in and wonders: Who polished that mirror? Who filled the basin and cleaned the toilet? For that matter: who brought out these brass beds for spoiled creatures such as he, who brought the pillows and carpets, who said: "They will probably like the coverlet with the little mirrors"? On the nightstand: a dozen books in English, including a Peabody novel and books by three god-awful American writers who, as at an exclusive party at which one is destined to run into the most banal acquaintance, dispelling not only the notion of the party's elegance but of one's own, seem to turn to Less and say, "Oh, they let you in too?" And there among them: the latest from Finley Dwyer. Here in the Sahara, beside his big brass bed. Thanks, life!

From the north: a camel bellowing to spite the dusk.

From the south: Lewis screaming that there is a scorpion in his bed.

From the west: the tinkle of flatware as the Bedouin set their dinner table.

From the south again: Lewis shouting not to worry, it was just a paper clip.

From the east: the British technology-whiz-cum-nightclub-owner saying: "Guys? I don't feel so great."

Who remains? Just four of them at dinner: Less, Lewis, Zohra, and Mohammed. They finish the white wine by the fire and stare at one another across the flames; Mohammed quietly smokes a cigarette. Is it a cigarette? Zohra stands and says she's going to bed so she can be beautiful for her birthday, good night, all, and look at all the stars! Mohammed vanishes into the darkness, and it is just Lewis and Less who remain.

"Arthur," Lewis says in the crackling quiet, reclining on his pillows. "I'm glad you came."

Less sighs and breathes in the night. Above them, the Milky Way rises in a plume of smoke. He turns to his friend in the firelight. "Happy anniversary, Lewis."

"Thank you. Clark and I are divorcing."

Less sits straight up on his cushion. *"What?"*

Lewis shrugs. "We decided a few months ago. I have been waiting to tell you."

"Wait wait wait, *what?* What's going on?"

"Shh, you'll wake Zohra. And what's-his-name." He moves closer to Less, picking up his wineglass. "Well, you know when I met Clark. Back in New York, at the art gallery. And we did that cross-country dating for a while, and finally I asked him to move to San Francisco. We were in the back room of the Art Bar—you remember, where you used to be able to buy coke—on the couches, and Clark said, 'All right, I'll move to San Francisco. I'll live with you. But only for ten years. After ten years, I'll leave you.'"

Less looks around, but of course there is no one to share his disbelief. "You never told me that!"

"Yes, he said, 'After ten years, I'll leave you.' And I said, 'Oh, ten years, that seems like plenty!' That was all we ever talked about it. He never worried about quitting his job or leaving his rent-controlled place, he never bugged me about whose pots we got to keep or whose we got to throw away. He just moved into my place and set up his life. Just like that."

"I didn't know any of this. I just thought you guys were together forever."

"Of course you did. I mean, I did too, honestly."

"Sorry, I'm just so surprised."

"Well, after ten years he said, 'Let's take a trip to New York.' So we went to New York. I'd forgotten all about the deal, really. Things were going so well, we were, you know, very very happy together. We had a hotel in SoHo above a Chinese lamp store. And he said, 'Let's go to the Art Bar.' So we took a taxi, and we went to the back room, and we had a drink, and he said, 'Well, the ten years are up, Lewis.'"

"This is Clark? Checking your expiration date?"

"I know, he's hopeless. He'll drink any old carton of milk. But it's true. He said the ten years are up. And I said, 'Are you fucking serious? Are you leaving me, Clark?' And he said no. He wanted to stay."

"Thank God for that."

"For ten more years."

"That's crazy, Lewis. It's like a timer. Like he's checking to see if it's done. You should have smacked him across the face. Or was he just messing with you? Were you guys high?"

"No, no, maybe you've never seen this side of him? He's so sloppy, I know, he leaves his underwear in the bathroom right where he took it off. But, you know, Clark has another side that's very practical. He installed the solar panels."

"I think of Clark as so easygoing. And this is—this is neurotic."

"I think he'd say it's practical. Or forward thinking. Anyway, we're in the Art Bar, and I said, 'Well, okay. I love you too, let's get some champagne,' and I didn't think about it again."

"Then ten years later—"

"A few months ago. We were in New York, and he said, 'Let's go to the Art Bar.' You know it's changed. It's not seedy or anything anymore; they moved the old mural of the Last Supper, and you can't even get coke there. I guess thank God, right? And we sat in the back. We ordered champagne. And he said, 'Lewis.' I knew what was coming. I said, 'It's been ten years.' And he said, 'What do you think?' We sat there for a long time, drinking. And I said, 'Honey, I think it's time.'"

"Lewis. Lewis."

"And he said, 'I think so too.' And we hugged, there on the cushions in the back of the Art Bar."

"Were things not working out? You never told me."

"No, things have been really good."

"Well then, why say 'It's time'? Why give up?"

"Because a few years ago, you remember I had a job down in Texas? Texas, Arthur! But it was good money, and Clark said, 'I support you, this is important, let's drive down together, I've never seen Texas.' And we got in the car and drove down—it was a good four days of driving—and we each got to make one rule about the road trip. Mine was that we could only sleep in places with a neon sign. His was that wherever we went, we had to eat the special. If they didn't have a special, we had to find another place. Oh my God, Arthur, the things I ate! One time the special was crab casserole. In Texas."

"I know, I know, you told me about it. That trip sounded great."

"It was maybe the best road trip we've ever taken; we just laughed and laughed the whole way. Looking for neon signs. And then we got to Texas and he kissed me good-bye and got on a plane back home, and there I was for four months. And I thought, *Well, that was nice.*"

"I don't understand. That sounds like you guys being happy."

"Yes. And I was happy in my little house in Texas, going to work. And I thought, *Well, that was nice. That was a nice marriage.*"

"But you broke up with him. Something's wrong. Something failed."

"No! No, Arthur, no, it's the opposite! I'm saying it's a success. Twenty years of joy and support and friendship, that's a success. Twenty years of anything with another person is a success. If a band stays together twenty years, it's a miracle. If a comedy duo stays together twenty years, they're a triumph. Is this night a failure because it will end in an hour? Is the sun a failure because it's going to end in a billion years? No, it's the fucking *sun*. Why does a marriage not count? It isn't in us, it isn't in human beings, to be tied to one person forever. Siamese twins are a tragedy. Twenty years and one last happy road trip. And I thought, *Well, that was nice. Let's end on success.*"

"You can't do this, Lewis. You're Lewis and Clark. Lewis and fucking Clark, Lewis. It's my only hope out there that gay men can last."

"Oh, Arthur. This *is* lasting. Twenty years *is* lasting! And this has nothing to do with you."

"I just think it's a mistake. You're going to go out there on your own and find out there's nobody as good as Clark. And he's going to find the same thing."

"He's getting married in June."

"For fuck's sake."

"I'll tell you the truth, it was on that road trip we met a nice young man in Texas. A painter down in Marfa. We met him together, and they kept in touch, and now Clark's going to marry him. He's lovely. He's wonderful."

"You're going to the wedding, apparently."

"I'm reading a poem at the wedding."

"You are out of your mind. I'm sorry things didn't work out with Clark. I'm heartbroken. But I know it's not about me. I want you to be happy. But you're deluded! You can't go to his wedding! You can't think it's all fine, it's all great! You're just in a phase of denial. You're divorcing your partner of twenty years. And that's sad. It's okay to be sad, Lewis."

"It's true things can go on till you die. And people use the same old table, even though it's falling apart and it's been repaired and repaired, just because it was their grandmother's.

That's how towns become ghost towns. It's how houses become junk stores. And I think it's how people get old."

"Have you met someone?"

"Me? I think maybe I'll go it on my own. Maybe I'm better that way. Maybe I was always better that way and it was just that when I was young, I was so scared, and now I'm not scared. I'll still have Clark. I can still always call Clark and ask his advice."

"Even after everything?"

"Yes, Arthur."

They talk a bit longer, and the sky shifts above them until it is quite late. "Arthur," Lewis says at one point, "did you hear that Freddy locked himself in the bathroom the night before the wedding?" But Less is not listening; he is thinking about how he used to visit Lewis and Clark over the years, about the dinner parties and Halloweens and times he slept on their couch, too tipsy to get home. "Good night, Arthur." Lewis gives his old friend a salute and heads into the darkness, so Less is left alone by the dying fire. A brightness catches his eye: Mohammed's cigarette as he moves from tent to tent, buttoning the flaps like he is tucking in sleeping children for the night. From the furthermost tent, the tech whiz moans from his bed. From somewhere, a camel complains, followed by a young man's voice soothing it—do they sleep beside the creatures? Do they sleep under this most excellent canopy, this majestical roof, this amazing mirrored coverlet, the stars? Look, you: there are enough stars for everyone tonight, and among them shine the satellites, those counterfeit coins. He reaches for, but does not catch, a falling star. Less, at last, goes to bed. But he cannot stop thinking of what Lewis has told him. Not the story about the ten years, but the idea of being alone. He realizes that, even after Robert, he never truly let himself be alone. Even here, on this trip: first Bastian, then Javier. Why this endless need for a man as a mirror? To see the Arthur Less reflected there? He is grieving, for sure—the loss of his lover, his career, his novel, his youth—so why not cover the mirrors, rend the fabric over his heart, and just let himself mourn? Perhaps he should try alone.

He chuckles to himself in the moments before sleep. Alone: impossible to imagine. That life seems as terrifying, as un-Lessian, as that of a castaway on a desert island.

The sandstorm does not start until dawn.

As Less lies sleepless in bed, his novel appears in his mind. *Swift.* What a title. What a mess. *Swift.* Where is his editor when he needs her? His editrix, as he used to call her: Leona Flowers. Traded years ago in the card game of publishing to some other house, but Less recalls how she took his first novels, shaggy with magniloquent prose, and made them into books. So clever, so artful, so good at persuading him of what to cut. "This paragraph is so beautiful, so special," she might say, pressing her French-manicured hands to her chest, "that I'm keeping it *all to myself!*" Where is Leona now? High in some tower with some new favorite author, trying her same old lines: "I think the chapter's absence will *echo* throughout the novel." What would she tell him? More likable, make Swift more likable. That's what everyone's saying; nobody cares what this character suffers. But how do you do it? It's like making oneself more likable. And at fifty, Less muses drowsily, you're as likable as you're going to get.

. . .

The sandstorm. So many months of planning, so much travel, so much expense, and here they are: trapped inside as the wind whips their tents like a man with a mule. They are gathered, the three of them (Zohra, Lewis, Less) in the large dining tent, hot as a camel ride and just as smelly, with its heavy horsehair sand door that has not been washed and three visitors who have not been, either. Only Mohammed seems fresh and cheerful, though he tells Less he was awakened at dawn by the sandstorm and had to run for shelter (for he has, indeed, slept out of doors). "Well"—Lewis announcing over coffee and honeyed flatbreads—"we are being given an opportunity for a different experience than the one we were expecting." Zohra greets this with a raised butter knife; tomorrow is her birthday. But they must submit to the sand. They spend the rest of the day drinking beer and playing cards, and Zohra fleeces them both.

"I'll get my revenge," Lewis threatens, and they go to bed to find, in the morning, that, like a bad houseguest, the storm has no intention of leaving and, moreover, that Lewis has proved prophetic: he has been afflicted as well. He lies on his mirrored bed, sweating, moaning "Kill me, kill me," as the wind shakes his tent. Mohammed appears, swathed in indigo and violet, full of regret. "The sandstorm is only in these dunes. We drive out of the desert, it is gone." He suggests they pile Lewis and Josh into the jeeps and head back to M'Hamid, where at least there is a hotel and a bar with a television, where the others, the war reporters, the violinist, the male model, are waiting. Zohra, only her eyes showing in the folds of her bright-green shesh, blinks silently. "No," she says finally, and turns to Less, ripping off her veil. "No, it's my birthday, goddamn it! Dump the others in M'Hamid. But *we're* going somewhere, Arthur! Mohammed? Where can you drive us that we wouldn't believe?"

Would you believe Morocco has a Swiss ski town? For that is where Mohammed has taken them, driving them out of the sandstorm and through deep canyons where hotels are carved into the rock and Germans, ignoring the hotels, camp beside the river in beat-up Westfalias; past villages that, as in a folktale, seem inhabited only by sheep; past waterfalls and weirs, madrassas and mosques, casbahs and ksars, and one small town (a lunch stop) where the next-door wood-carver is visited by a woman all in teal who borrows his shavings to sprinkle them on her doorstep, where, it seems, her cat has peed, and where boys are gathered in what at first seems to be an outdoor school and later (when the cheering starts) turns out to be a televised football match; through limestone plateaus; up the spiraling ziggurat roads of the Middle Atlas until the vegetation changes from fronds to needles, where, passing through a chilly pine forest, Mohammed says, "Look out for beasts," and at first there is nothing, until Zohra screams and points to where sits, on a wooden platform and turning as if interrupted at tea (or *déjeuner sur l'herbe*), a troop of poker-faced Barbary macaques, or, as she puts it: "Monkeys!" Their own troop is now far away, in M'Hamid, and Less and Zohra are alone, seated in the dark scented bar of the alpine resort, in leather club chairs with glasses of local marc, below a crystal chandelier and before a crystal panorama. They have eaten pigeon pie. Mohammed sits at the bar, drinking an energy drink. Gone is his desert costume; he has changed back into a polo shirt and jeans. It is Zohra's birthday; it will be Less's at midnight, in about two hours' time. Satisfaction has arrived, indeed, on a later camel.

"And all this," Zohra is saying, brushing her hair out of her face, "all this travel, Arthur, just to miss your boyfriend's wedding?"

"Not a boyfriend. And more to avoid the confusion," Less answers, feeling himself blushing. They are the only guests in the bar. The bartenders—two men in striped vaudeville vests—seem to be deciding on a cigarette break with the frantic whispered patter of a comedy routine. He has been telling Zohra about his trip, and somehow the champagne has let his tongue get away from him.

Zohra wears a gold pantsuit and diamond earrings; they have checked into the hotel, showered, and changed, and she smells of perfume. Surely, when she packed for her birthday trip, she picked these things for someone other than Less. But he is who she has. He wears, of course, his blue suit.

"You know what?" Zohra says, holding out the glass and staring at it. "This hooch reminds me of my grandmother in Georgia. The republic, not the state. She used to make something just like this."

"It just seemed better," Less continues, still on Freddy, "to get away. And bring this novel back to life."

Zohra sips her marc and stares at the view, such as it is at this hour. "Mine left me too," she says.

Less sits quietly for a moment, then says suddenly: "Oh! Oh no, he didn't leave me—"

"Janet was supposed to be here." Zohra closes her eyes.

"Arthur, you're here because there was an empty space and Lewis said he had a friend; that's why you're here. It's lovely to have you. I mean, you're all that's left. Everybody else is so fucking *weak*. What happened to everybody? I'm glad you're here. But I'll be honest with you. I'd rather have her."

For some reason, it never occurred to Less that she was a lesbian. Perhaps he is a bad gay, after all.

"What happened?" he asks.

"What else?" Zohra says, sipping from the little glass. "She fell in love. She lost her mind."

Less murmurs his sympathy, but Zohra is lost in herself. At the bar, the taller man seems to have won and heads out in long strides to the balcony. The short man, bald on top except for a single oasis, stares after his friend with unconcealed longing. Outside: a view perhaps of Gstaad or St. Moritz. The dark rolling forests of sleeping macaques, the Romanesque steeple of a skating rink, the cold black sky.

"She told me she met the love of her life," Zohra says at last, still staring out the window. "You read poems about it, you hear stories about it, you hear Sicilians talk about being struck by lightning. We know there's no love of your life. Love isn't terrifying like that. It's walking the fucking dog so the other one can sleep in, it's doing taxes, it's cleaning the bathroom without hard feelings. It's having an ally in life. It's not fire, it's not lightning. It's what she always had with me. Isn't it? But what if she's right, Arthur? What if the Sicilians are right? That it's this earth-shattering thing she felt? Something I've never felt. Have you?"

Less begins to breath unevenly.

She turns to him: "What if one day you meet someone,

Arthur, and it feels like it could never be anyone else? Not because other people are less attractive, or drink too much, or have issues in bed, or have to alphabetize every fucking book or organize the dishwasher in some way you just can't live with. It's because they aren't this person. This woman Janet met. Maybe you can go through your whole life and never meet them, and think love is all these other things, but if you do meet them, God help you! Because then: ka-blam! You're screwed. The way Janet is. She ruined our life for it! But what if that's real?" She is gripping the chair now.

"Zohra, I'm so sorry."

"Is it like that with this Freddy?"

"I . . . I . . ."

"The brain is so wrong, all the time," she says, turning to the dark landscape again. "Wrong about what time it is, and who people are, and where home is: wrong wrong wrong. The lying brain."

This insanity, the insanity of her lover, has her bewildered and hurt and incandescent. And yet what she has said—the lying brain—this is familiar; this has happened to him. Not exactly like this, not utter terrifying madness, but he knows his brain has told him things he has traveled around the world to forget. That the mind cannot be trusted is a certainty.

"What is love, Arthur? What is it?" she asks him. "Is it the good dear thing I had with Janet for eight years? Is it the good dear thing? Or is it the lightning bolt? The destructive madness that hit my girl?"

"It doesn't sound happy" is all he can say.

She shakes her head. "Arthur, happiness is bullshit. That is the wisdom I give you from my twenty-two hours of being fifty. That is the wisdom from my love life. You'll understand at midnight." It is clear she is drunk. Outside, the shivering bartender smokes like he means it. She sniffs the glass of marc and says, "My Georgian grandmother used to make booze just like this."

It keeps ringing in his ears: *Is it the good dear thing? Is it the good dear thing?*

"Yes." She smiles at the memory and sniffs the glass. "It smells just like my grandmother's *cha-cha!*"

The cha-cha proves too much for the birthday girl, and by eleven thirty, he and Mohammed are leading her up to her room as she smiles and thanks them. He puts her, happily drunk, to bed. She is speaking French to Mohammed, who comforts her in the same language and then again in English. As Less tucks her in, she says, "Well, that was ridiculous, Arthur, I'm sorry." As he closes her door, he realizes that he will spend his fiftieth birthday alone.

He turns; not alone.

"Mohammed, how many languages do you speak?"

"Seven!" he says brightly, striding to the elevator. "I learn from school. They make fun of my Arabic when I come to the city, it is old-fashioned, I learned in Berber school, so I work more hard. And from tourists! Sorry, still learning English. And you, Arthur?"

"Seven! My God!" The elevator is completely mirrored, and as the doors close, Less is confronted by a vision: infinite Mohammeds in red polo shirts beside infinite versions of his father at fifty, which is to say himself. "I...I speak English and German—"

"Ich auch!" says Mohammed. The following is translated from the German: "I lived for two years in Berlin! Such boring music!"

"I have been coming from there! Is excellent your German!"

"And yours is good. Here we are, you first, Arthur. Are you ready for your birthday?"

"I am fear of the age."

"Don't be frightened. Fifty is nothing. You're a handsome man, and healthy, and rich."

He wants to say he is not rich but stops himself. "How many year have you?"

"I'm fifty-three. You see, it's nothing. Nothing at all. Let's get you a glass of champagne."

"I am fear of the old, I am fear of the lonely."

"You have nothing to fear." He turns to a woman who has taken over the station behind the bar, easily his height with her hair in a ponytail, and speaks to her in the Moroccan dialect of Arabic. Perhaps he is asking for champagne for the American, who has just turned fifty. The bartender beams at Less, raises her eyebrows, and says something. Mohammed laughs; Less just stands with his idiot's grin. "Happy birthday, sir," she says in English, pouring out a glass of French champagne. "This is my treat."

Less offers to buy Mohammed a drink, but the man will indulge only in energy drinks. Not because of Islam, he explains; he is agnostic. "Because alcohol makes me crazy. Crazy! But I smoke hashish. Would you like?"

"No, no, not tonight. It makes me crazy. Mohammed, are you really a tour guide?"

"I must to make a living," Mohammed says, suddenly shy in his English. "But in truth, I am writer. Like you."

How does Less get the world so wrong? Over and over again? Where is the exit from moments like this? Where is the donkey door out?

"Mohammed, I am honored to be with you tonight."

"I am very great fan of *Kalipso*. Of course, I read not the English but the French. I am honored to be with you. And happy birthday, Arthur Less."

Probably now Tom and Freddy are packing their bags; they are many hours ahead, after all, and in Tahiti it is midday. Surely the sun is already hammering the beach like a tinsmith. The grooms are folding their linen shirts, their linen pants and jackets, or surely Freddy is folding them. He recalls Freddy was always the packer, while Less lounged on the hotel sofa. "You're too fast and sloppy," Freddy said that last morning in Paris. "And everything comes out wrinkled—see, watch this." He spread out the jackets and shirts on the bed like they were clothes for a great paper doll, placed the pants and sweaters on top, and folded the whole thing up in a bundle. Hands on his hips, he smiled in triumph (by the way, everyone is completely naked in this scene). "And now what?" Less asked. Freddy shrugged: "Now we just put it in the luggage." But of course this bolus was too large for the luggage to swallow, no matter how Freddy coaxed it, and after many tries of sitting and pressing, he eventually remade it into two packages, which he fit neatly into two bags. Victorious, he looked smugly at Less. Framed in the window, with that lean silhouette from his early forties, the spring Paris rain dotting the window behind him, Freddy's former lover nodded and asked, "Mr. Pelu, you've packed everything; now what are we going to wear?" Freddy attacked him in a fury, and for the next half an hour, they wore nothing at all.

Yes, surely Mr. Pelu is folding.

Surely this is why he never calls to wish Less a happy birthday.

And now Less stands on the balcony of the Swiss hotel, looking out over the frozen town. The railing is carved, absurdly, with cuckoos, each with a sharp protruding beak. In his glass: the last coin of champagne. Now he is off to India. To work on his novel, on what was supposed to be a mere final glaze and now appears to be breaking the whole novel to shards and starting again. To work on the tedious, self-centered, pitiable, laughable character Swift. The one nobody feels bad for. Now he is fifty.

We all recognize grief in moments that should be celebrations; it is the salt in the pudding. Didn't Roman generals hire slaves to march beside them in a triumphant parade and remind them that they too would die? Even your narrator, one morning after what should have been a happy occasion, was found shivering at the end of the bed (spouse: "I really wish you weren't crying right now"). Don't little children, awakened one morning and told, "Now you're five!"—don't they wail at the universe's descent into chaos? The sun slowly dying, the spiral arm spreading, the molecules drifting apart second by second toward our inevitable heat death—shouldn't we all wail to the stars?

But some people do take it a little too hard. It's just a birthday, after all.

There is an old Arabic story about a man who hears Death is coming for him, so he sneaks away to Samarra. And when he gets there, he finds Death in the market, and Death says, "You know, I just felt like going on vacation to Samarra. I was going to skip you today, but how lucky you showed up to find me!" And the man is taken after all. Arthur Less has traveled halfway around the world in a cat's cradle of junkets, changing flights and fleeing from a sandstorm into the Atlas Mountains like someone erasing his trail or outfoxing a hunter—and yet Time has been waiting here all along. In a snowy alpine resort. With cuckoos. Of course Time would turn out to be Swiss. He tosses back the champagne. He thinks: *Hard to feel bad for a middle-aged white man.*

Indeed: even Less can't feel bad for Swift anymore. Like a wintertime swimmer too numb to feel cold, Arthur Less is too sad to feel pity. For Robert, yes, breathing through an oxygen tube up in Sonoma. For Marian, nursing a broken hip that might ground her forever. For Javier in his marriage, and even for Bastian's tragic sports teams. For Zohra and Janet. For his fellow writer Mohammed. Around the world his pity flies, its wingspan as wide as an albatross's. But he can no more feel sorry for Swift—now become a gorgon of Caucasian male ego, snake headed, pacing through his novel and turning each sentence to stone—than Arthur Less can feel sorry for himself.

He hears the balcony door open beside him and sees the short waiter, returned from his smoke break. The man points to a cuckoo on the railing and speaks to him in perfectly understandable French (if only he understood French).

Laughable.

Arthur Less—he suddenly stands very still, as one does when about to swat a fly. Don't let it go. Distractions are pulling at his mind—Robert, Freddy, fifty, Tahiti, flowers, the waiter gesturing at Less's coat sleeve—but he will not look at them. Don't let it escape. Laughable. His mind is converging on one point of light. What if it isn't a poignant, wistful novel at all? What if it isn't the story of a sad middle-aged man on a tour of his hometown, remembering the past and fearing the future; a peripateticism of humiliation and regret; the erosion of a single male soul? What if it isn't even sad? For a moment, his entire novel reveals itself to him like those shimmering castles that appear to men crawling through deserts...

It vanishes. The balcony door slams shut; the sleeve of the blue suit remains snagged on a cuckoo's beak (a tear lies seconds in the future). But Less does not notice; he is clinging to the one thought that remains. *AH ah ah ah!* comes the Lessian laugh.

His Swift isn't a hero. He's a fool.

"Well," he whispers to the night air, "happy birthday, Arthur Less."

Just for the record: happiness is not bullshit.

LESS INDIAN

FOR a seven-year-old boy, the boredom of sitting in an airport lounge is rivaled only by lying convalescent in bed. This particular boy, one-six-thousandth of whose life has already been squandered in this airport, has gone through every pocket of his mother's purse and found nothing of interest but a keychain made of plastic crystals. He is considering the wastepaper basket—its swinging lid holds possibilities—when he notices, through the lounge's window, the American. The boy has not seen one all day. He watches the American with the same detached, merciless fascination with which he has watched the robotic scorpions that circle the airport bathroom drain. Epically tall, brutally blond, the American stands in his beige wilted linen shirt and pants, smiling at the escalator-regulations sign. The sign, so scrupulously unabridged that it includes advice on pet safety, is longer than the escalator itself. This seems to amuse the American. The boy watches as the man pats every pocket on his person, then nods in satisfaction. He looks up at a closed-circuit television to follow the fleeting romances between flights and gates, then heads down to join a line. Though everyone has already passed through at least three check-points, a man at the head of the line has everyone take out their passport and boarding pass once more. This superfluous verification also seems to amuse the American. But it is warranted; at least three people are about to board the wrong flight. The American is one of them. Who knows what adventures awaited him in Hyderabad? We will never know, for he is shown to another gate: Thiruvananthapuram. He becomes absorbed in a notebook. Soon enough, a worker is rushing over to tap the American on the shoulder, and the foreigner pops up to rush for the flight that he is yet again about to miss. They disappear together down a foreshortened corridor. The boy, already attuned to comedy at his young age, presses his nose against the glass and awaits the inevitable. A moment later, the American springs back to grab the forgotten satchel and vanishes again, this time surely for good. The boy tilts his head as boredom begins to flood. His mother asks if he needs to wee, and he says yes, but only so he can see the scorpions again.

"Here are the black ants; they are your neighbors. Nearby there is Elizabeth, the yellow rat snake, who is the parson's special friend, although he says he is happy to kill her if you want him to. But then there will be rats. Do not be afraid of the mongoose. Do not encourage the stray dogs—they are not our pets. Do not open the windows, because small bats will want to visit you, and possibly monkeys. And if you walk at night, stomp on the ground to scare off other animals."

Less asks what other animals could there possibly be?

Rupali answers, quite solemnly: "Let us never know."

A writer's retreat on a hill above the Arabian Sea, on Carlos's suggestion half a year ago—it has been a long journey, but Less has arrived at last. The dreaded birthday, the dreaded wedding, are both behind him now; ahead is the novel, and with an idea of how to go forward, he will finally have a chance to conquer it. Gone are the cares of Europe and Morocco; present still are the cares of the Delhi airport, the Chennai airport, and those of Thiruvananthapuram. In Thiruvananthapuram, he was met by a seemingly delighted woman, the manager Rupali, who graciously led him across a steaming parking lot to a white Tata driven, he was later to learn, by a relative. This driver was proud to show Less a TV set in the dashboard of his car; Less was alarmed. And off they went. Rupali, a slim and elegant woman with a neat black braid and the refined profile of a Caesar on a coin, tried to engage him with conversation about politics, literature, and art, but Less was too enchanted by the ride itself.

It was nothing like he expected, the sun flirting with him among the trees and houses; the driver speeding along a crumbling road alongside which trash was piled as if washed there (and what first looked like a beach beside a river turned out to be an accretion of a million plastic bags, as a coral reef is an accretion of a million tiny animals); the endless series of shops, as if made from one continuous concrete barrier, painted at intervals with different signs advertising chickens and medicine, coffins and telephones, pet fish and cigarettes, hot tea and "homely" food, Communism, mattresses, handicrafts, Chinese food, haircuts and dumbbells and gold by the ounce; the low, flat temples appearing at regular intervals like the colorful, elaborately frosted, but basically inedible sheet cakes displayed at Less's childhood bakery; the women sitting roadside with baskets of shimmering silver fish, terrifying manta rays, and squid, with their cartoon eyes; the countless men standing at tea shops, variety stores, pharmacies, watching Less as he goes by; the driver dodging bicycles, motorcycles, lorries (but few cars), moving frenetically in and out of traffic, bringing Less back to the time at Disney World when his mother led him and his sister to a whimsical ride based on *The Wind in the Willows*—a ride that turned out to be a knuckle-whitening rattletrap wellspring of trauma. Nothing, nothing here, is what he expected.

Rupali leads him down a path of red dirt. The ends of her pink scarf float behind her.

"Here," she says, gesturing to a purple flower, "is the ten o'clock. It opens at ten and closes at five."

"Like the British Museum."

"There is also a four o'clock," Rupali counters. "And the drowsy tree, which opens at sunrise and closes at sunset. The plants here are more punctual than the people. You will see. And this plant is more alive." She touches her *chappal* to a small fern, which instantly shrinks from her touch, folding in its leaves. Less is horrified. They arrive at a spot where the coconut trees part. "Here is a possibly inspiring view."

It certainly is: a cliff overhanging a mangrove forest, at the edge of which the Arabian Sea flogs the coast as mercilessly as an Inquisitor, foaming up in white crests against the pale and impenitent sand. Beside him, at the cliffside, the coconut trees frame a view of birds and insects, as filled with living creatures as the waters of a coral shelf: eagles, red-and white-headed, floating in pairs high above, and covens of irritated crows massing on the treetops, and, nearby, yellow-black biplane dragonflies, buzzing around in a dogfight at the entrance of a little house.

"And here is your little house."

The cottage, like the other buildings, is made in the South Indian style: all brick, with a tile roof over an open wooden lattice that lets in the air. But the cottage is pentagonal, and, curiously, rather than leave the space whole, the architects have divided it, like a nautilus shell, into smaller and smaller "rooms," until it reaches the end of its ingenuity at a tiny desk and an inlaid portrait of the Last Supper. Less stares at this curiously for a moment.

The paper trail has been lost, so it is hard to know whether, in his haste, Less missed a crucial piece of information, or whether it was delicately withheld by Carlos Pelu, but it turns out that, rather than a typical artist residency at which to finish a novel, a place full of art, providing three vegetarian meals a day, a yoga mat, and Ayurvedic tea, Arthur Less has booked himself into a Christian retreat center. He has nothing personal against Christ; though raised Unitarian—with its glaring omission of Jesus and a hymnal so unorthodox that it was years before Less understood "Accentuate the Positive" was not in the Book of Common

Prayer—Less is technically Christian. There is really no other word for someone who celebrates Christmas and Easter, even if only as craft projects. And yet he is somehow deflated. To travel to the other side of the world—only to be offered a brand he could so easily buy at home.

"Services are Sunday morning, of course," Rupali tells him, gesturing to a small gray church that, in the midst of these lively outbuildings, sits as humorless as a recess monitor. So here he will rewrite his novel. With God's happiness.

"And a note arrived for you." An envelope on the miniature desk, below the image of Judas. Less opens it and reads: *Arthur, contact me once you arrive, I'll be at the resort, I hope you arrived in one piece.* It is on business stationery, signed: *Your friend, Carlos.*

After Rupali leaves, Less takes out his famous rubber bands.

"Have you noticed," Rupali asks him a few mornings later, at breakfast, in the low brick main building, a kind of fortress above the ocean, "how the morning sounds so much sweeter than the evening?" She is talking about the birds, awakening in harmony and bedding down in discord. But Less can think only of that racket particular to India: the spiritual battle of the bands.

It seems to begin before dawn with the Muslims, when a mosque at the edge of the mangrove forest softly announces, in a lullaby voice, the morning call to prayer. Not to be outdone, the local Christians soon crank up pop-sounding hymns that last anywhere from one to three hours. This is followed by a cheerful, though overamplified, kazoo-like refrain from the Hindu temple that reminds Less of the ice cream truck from his childhood. Then comes a later call to prayer. Then the Christians decide to ring some bronze bells. And so on. There are sermons and live singers and thunderous drum performances. In this way, the faiths alternate throughout the day, as at a music festival, growing louder and louder until, during the outright cacophony of sunset, the Muslims, who began the whole thing, declare victory by projecting not only the evening call to prayer but the prayer itself in its entirety. After that, the jungle falls to silence. Perhaps this is the Buddhists' sole contribution. Every morning, it starts again.

"You must let me know," Rupali says, "what we can do to help with your writing. You are our first writer."

"I could use a freestanding desk," Less suggests, hoping to liberate himself from writing in the heart of his nautilus. "And a tailor. I tore my suit in Morocco, and I seem to have lost my sewing needle."

"We will take care of these. The pastor will know a good tailor."

The pastor. "And peace and quiet. I need that above all."

"Of course of course of course," she insists, shaking her head, and her gold earrings sway from side to side.

A writer's retreat on a hill above the Arabian Sea. Here, he will kill his old novel, tear out the flesh that he wants, stitch it to all-new material, electrocute it with inspiration, and make it rise from the slab and stumble toward Cormorant Publishing. Here, in this little room. There is so much to inspire

him: the gray-green river flows below him among the co-
conuts and mangroves. On the other bank, Less can make
out a black bull in the sun, sleek and glorious, with two
white markings like socks on its hind legs, more like a person transformed into a bull than an actual bull. Nearby, white
smoke rises from a jungle blaze. So much. He is remembering (falsely) something Robert once told him: *Boredom is the
only real tragedy for a writer; everything else is material.* Robert
never said anything of the sort. Boredom is essential for writers; it is the only time they get to write.

Looking around for inspiration, Less's eyes fall upon his
torn blue suit hanging in the closet, and he decides *this* is the
priority. The novel is set aside.

The pastor turns out to be a tanned and miniature Groucho
Marx in a cassock that buttons at one shoulder like a fast
food uniform, friendly and eager, as Rupali mentioned, to
kill his friend the snake. He also possesses a genius for invention adults only have in children's books: a house with rain
collectors and bamboo pipes, bringing water to a common
cistern, and a way to turn food waste into cooking gas, with
a hose that leads directly into his stove. And there is his three-
year-old daughter, who runs around wearing nothing but a
rhinestone necklace (who wouldn't, if they could?). She is
able to count, in English, methodically as a cart climbing uphill, up to the number fourteen—and then the wheels come
off: "Twenty-one!" she screams in delight. "Eighteen! Forty-
three! Eleventy! Twine!"

"Mr. Arthur, you are a writer," the pastor says to him
as they stand outside his house. "I want you to ask, *Why?*

Everything that seems strange here, or foolish, ask, *Why?* For instance, motorcycle helmets."

"Motorcycle helmets," Less repeats.

"You have noticed everybody wears them; it is the law. But nobody fastens the strap. Yes?"

"I haven't been out much—"

"They won't fasten it, and what's the point? Why wear it if it will fly off? Foolish, yes? It looks typically Indian, typically absurd. But ask, *Why?*"

Less can't resist: "Why?"

"Because there *is* a reason. It's not foolishness. It's because a man can't make a phone call if it's fastened. During his two-, three-hour trip home. And you're thinking, why talk while driving? Why not just stop on the side of the road? Foolish, yes? Mr. Less. Look at the road. Look." Less sees a line of women, all in saris of bright-colored cloth edged in gold thread, some carrying purses, some metal bins on their heads, making their way through the rocks and weeds beside the crumbled asphalt. The pastor spreads his arms wide: *"There is no side of the road."*

From the pastor, he learns the way to the tailor, whom he finds asleep beside his treadle, smelling distinctly of Signature whiskey. Less deliberates whether to wake him, but then a stray dog trots by, black-and-white, and barks at them both, and the man awakens of his own accord. Automatically, the tailor picks up a stone and throws it at the dog, who vanishes. *Why?* Then he notices Less. His smile tilts up toward our protagonist. He explains his unshaven chin by pointing to Less's own: "Money comes in, we will shave." Less says yes, possibly, and shows him the suit. The man waves his hand at the ease of the repair. "Come back this time tomorrow," he says, and he and the famous suit disappear into the shop. Less feels the brief pang of separation, then takes a deep breath and aims himself downhill toward town. He means to meander for fifteen minutes or so and then get straight back to work.

When he passes the shop again, two hours later, he has sweated through his shirt, and his face is aglow. His hair is clipped quite short, and his beard is gone. The tailor grins, pointing to his own chin; he has indeed himself purchased a shave. Less nods and nods and trudges up the hill. He is stopped multiple times by neighbors trying out their English, offering him tea, or a visit to their home, or a ride to church. Once back in his room, recalling there is no shower, he wearily fills the red plastic bucket, disrobes, and drenches himself in cold water. He dries himself, dresses, and sits down to write.

"Hello!" comes a call from outside his cottage. "I am here to measure you for your desk!"

"To what?" Less yells.

"To measure you for your desk."

When he emerges, in damp linen, there is indeed a portly bald man with a teenager's faint mustache, smiling and holding out a length of cloth tape. He has Less sit in the rattan porch chair as he takes his measurements; then he bows and departs. *Why?* Next comes a teenager with a grown man's mustache, who announces, "I will take your chair. There is a new chair in half an hour." Less wonders what is at work here; surely some misunderstanding, and some difficulty for the boy. But he cannot puzzle it out, so he smiles and says of course. The boy approaches the chair with the caution of a lion tamer, then grabs it and takes it away. Less watches the sea as he leans against a coconut palm. When he looks back at the house, the black-and-white dog is at the entrance, hunched over and about to excrete. It looks at Less. It takes a shit anyway. "Hey!" Less yells, and it bounds away. Deskless, he is of course unable to compose, so he watches the entertainment provided: the sea. In exactly half an hour, the boy returns . . . with an identical chair. He sets it on the porch with pride, and Less accepts it with bewilderment. "Be careful," the boy says earnestly. "It is a new chair. A new chair." Less nods, and the boy departs. He looks at the chair. Cautiously, he sits himself down, and it creaks as it takes his weight. It feels fine. He watches three yellow birds battling it out on a nearby roof, cackling and squawking and so involved in their tussle that, in a moment of unexpected slapstick, they fall together off the roof and onto the grass. Less laughs aloud—*AH ah ah!* He has never seen a bird fall before. He stands up; the chair comes up with him. It is indeed new, and the lacquer, in this climate, has not yet managed to dry.

". . . and when I had finally settled down to write, I think maybe the church let out. Because all these people started gathering around my little house. They spread out blankets, they brought out food, they had a good old picnic all around." He is talking to Rupali. It is nighttime, after dinner; the view from the window is utterly black, one fluorescent bulb lights the room, and the scents of coconut and curry leaf still ornament the air. He does not add that the ruckus on his porch was unbearable, a party going on outside his windows. He could not concentrate for a moment on this new version of his book. Less was frustrated, so furious, he even considered checking into a local hotel. But he stood there in his little Keralan house, with its view of the ocean and the Last Supper, and pictured himself walking up to Rupali and saying the most absurd sentence of his life: *I am going to check myself into an Ayurvedic retreat unless the picnicking stops!*

Rupali listens to his story about the picnic, nodding. "Yes, this is something that happens."

He remembers the pastor's advice. "Why?"

"Oh, the people here, they like to come up and look at the view. This is a good place for the church families."

"But it's a retreat..." He stops himself, then asks again: "Why?"

"Here, this special view of the sea."

"Why?"

"It is—" She pauses, looking down shyly. "It is the only place. The only place the Christians can go."

Less has gotten to the root of it at last, but again it touches something he cannot understand. "Well, I hope they had a good time. The food smelled delicious. And tonight's dinner was delicious." Less has realized that there is no refrigerator at the retreat center, so everything has been bought today at the street market or picked from Rupali's garden; everything is fresh simply because it must be. Even the coconut has been hand shredded by a congregant named Mary, an old woman in a sari who smiles at him every morning and brings his tea. *Unless the picnicking stops!* What an ass he is, everywhere he goes.

Rupali says: "I have a funny story about the dinner! This is the meal I used to bring to work when I taught French in the city. Every day, I took the train, and, you know, it is so hot! One day, there are no seats. So what do I do? I sit in on the stairs by the open doorway. Oh, it was so refreshing! Why did I not do this before? That was when I dropped my handbag right out the door!" She laughs, covering her mouth. "It was terrible! It had my school identification, my money, my lunch, everything. Disaster. Of course, the train could not stop, so I got out at the next station, and I hired a rickshaw to take me back. We were there for so long, searching for it on the train tracks! Then a policeman came out of a hut. I told him what had happened. He asked me to describe the contents. I said, 'Sir, my identification, my wallet, my phone, my clean blouse, sir.' He looked at me for a moment. Then he asked, 'And fish curry?' He showed me the handbag." She laughs again in delight. "It was all covered inside with fish curry!"

Her laughter is so lovely; he cannot bear to tell her that this is no place to write. The noise, the creatures, the heat, the workers, the picnickers—it will be impossible to write his book here.

"And you, Arthur, you had a good day?" Rupali asks.

"Oh yes." He has left out details of the barbershop he visited, in which he was shown to a windowless room behind a red curtain, where a short man in the pastor's same shirt quickly dispensed with his beard (unasked) and the hair on the side of Less's head, leaving only the blond wisp at the top, and then asked: "Massage?" This turned out to be a series of thumpings and slaps, a general pummeling, as if to extract military secrets, ending with four resounding wallops across the face. *Why?*

Rupali smiles and asks what else she can do for him.

"What I could really use is a drink."

Her face darkens. "Oh, there is no alcohol allowed on church premises."

"I'm just kidding, Rupali," he says. "Where the heck would we get the ice?"

We will never know if she gets the joke, for at that moment, the lights go out.

The outage, like most partings, is not absolute; every few minutes, the power returns, only to be lost a moment later. What follows is one of those college theatrical productions in which the lights come up spasmodically, revealing the characters in various unexpected tableaux: Rupali clutching the arms of her chair, her lips pursed in concern like a surgeonfish; Arthur Less about to step into nirvana, mistaking a window for a door; Rupali openmouthed in a scream as she touches some paper fallen on her head that surely feels like a giant fruit bat; Arthur Less, having stepped through the correct portal this time, blindly fitting his toes into Rupali's sandals; Rupali kneeling on the floor in prayer; Arthur Less out in the night, catching sight of a brand-new horror in the moonlight: the black-and-white dog trotting toward Less's cottage, carrying in its mouth a long piece of medium blue fabric.

"My suit!" Less yells, stumbling downhill and kicking off the sandals. "My suit!"

He makes his way down toward the dog, and the lights go out again—revealing, nestled in the grass, a breathtaking constellation of glowworms ready for love—so Less can only feel his way into his own cottage, cursing, carelessly stepping barefoot across the tiles, and that is when he finds his sewing needle.

I recall Arthur Less, at a rooftop party, telling me his recurring dream:

"A parable, really," he said, holding his beer to his chest. "I'm walking through a dark wood, like Dante, and an old woman comes up to me and says, 'Lucky you, you've left it all behind you. You're finished with love. Think of how much time you'll have for more important things!' And she leaves me, and I go on—I think I'm usually riding a horse at this point; it's a very medieval dream. You aren't in it, by the way, in case you're getting bored."

I replied I had my own dreams.

"And I keep riding through this dark wood and come out onto a large white plain with a mountain in the distance. And a farmer is there, and he waves at me, and he says sort of the same thing. 'More important things ahead for you!' And I ride up the mountain. I can tell you're not listening. It gets really good. I ride up the mountain, and at the top is a cave and a priest—you know, like in a cartoon. And I say I'm ready. And he says for what? And I say to think about more important things. And he asks, 'More important than what?' 'More important than love.' And he looks at me like I'm crazy and says, 'What could be more important than love?'"

We stood quietly as a cloud went over the sun and sent a chill across the roof. Less looked over the railing at the street below.

"Well, that's my dream."

. . .

Less opens his eyes to an image from a war movie—an army-green airplane propeller chopping briskly at the air—no, not a propeller. Ceiling fan. The whispering in the corner is, however, indeed Malayalam. Shadows are moving on the ceiling in a puppet play of life. And now they are speaking English. Bits of his dream are still glistening on the edges of everything, dew lit, evaporating. Hospital room.

He remembers his scream in the night, and the pastor running in (wearing only a dhoti and carrying his daughter), the kind man arranging for a church member to drive Less to the hospital in Thiruvananthapuram, Rupali's worried goodbye, the long painful hours in the waiting room, whose only solace was a supernatural vending machine that produced, in change, more than it took in, the casting call of nurses—from seen-it-all-before battle-axes to pretty ingenues—before Less was allowed an X-ray of his right foot (beautiful archipelago of bones), which confirmed, alas, a fractured ankle and, buried deep in the pad of his foot, one half of a needle, at which point he received his first procedure—done by a female doctor with collagen lips who called his injury "bullshit" ("Why does this man have a sewing needle?") and was unable to retrieve the object—and, that having failed, his foot now in a temporary splint, Less was assigned a hospital room, a chamber he shared with an elderly laborer who had spent twenty years in Vallejo, California, and had Spanish but not English, then was prepared for the next morning's surgery, requiring a variety of gurney changes and anesthetic injections until he was finally thrust into a pristine operating theater whose motile X-ray machine allowed the surgeon (an affable man with a Hercule Poirot mustache) to produce for Less, within five minutes, and with the additional use of a pocket magnet, the trifling source of his injury (held before his eyes with tweezers), after which his foot was fitted into a bootlike splint and our protagonist was given a strong painkiller, which put him almost instantly into an exhausted sleep.

And now he is looking around the room and considering his situation. His paper gown is green as the Statue of Liberty's, and his fracture is safe in its black plastic boot. His blue suit is presumably lining the den of some feral dog family. A portly nurse is busying herself with some paperwork in the corner, her bifocals giving her the appearance of the four-eyed fish (*Anableps anableps*) that can see both above and below water. He must have made noise; her head turns, and she shouts in Malayalam. Impressively, the result is that his mustachioed surgeon appears through the door, white coat swinging, smiling and gesturing at Less's foot as a plumber might at a repaired kitchen sink.

"Mr. Less, you are awake! So now you will no longer set off the metal detectors, bing bing bing! We are all curious," the doctor asks, leaning down. "Why does a man have a sewing needle?"

"To mend things. To put on missing buttons."

"This is a great hazard in your profession?"

"Apparently a needle is a greater one." Less feels he does not even sound like himself anymore. "When can I go back to the retreat, Doctor?"

"Oh!" he says, searching his pockets and producing an envelope. "The retreat has sent this for you."

On the envelope is written: *Very sorry.* Less opens it, and out flutters a scrap of bright-blue fabric. Lost forever, then. Without the suit, there is no Arthur Less.

The doctor goes on: "The retreat has contacted your friend, who will come and pick you up momentarily."

Less asks if this is Rupali or, perhaps, the pastor.

"Search me!" the doctor says, this Americanese standing out in his otherwise British English. "But you cannot return to the retreat, a place like that. Stairs! Climbing a hill! No, no, stay off the foot for three weeks at least. Your friend has accommodations. None of that American jogging!"

Cannot return? But—his book! A knock at the door as Less puzzles over where these new accommodations might be, but the answer is instantly provided as the door opens.

It is entirely possible that Less is in one of those Russian-doll dreams in which one awakens and yawns and gets out of one's childhood bunk bed, and pets one's long-dead dog, and greets one's long-dead mother, only to realize it is yet another layer of dreaming, yet another wooden nightmare, and one must go through the heroic task of awakening all over again.

Because standing in the doorway can only be an image from a dream.

"Hello, Arthur. I'm here to take care of you."

Or no, he must be dead. He is being taken from this drab-green purgatory to the special pit they have waiting for him. A little cottage above a flaming sea: the Artist Residency in Hell. The face retains its smile. And Arthur slowly, sadly, with growing acceptance of the divine comedy of his life, says the name you can by now well guess.

. . .

The driver works the horn like an outlaw at a gunfight. Stray dogs and goats leap from the road wearing guilty expressions, and people leap aside wearing innocent ones. Children stand by the roadside by the dozens, in matching red-checkered uniforms, some of them hanging from the limbs of banyan trees; school must have just gotten out. They stare at the sight of Less passing by. And all the time, he is listening to the constant bleating of the horn, the English pop music oozing like treacle from the speakers, and the soft voice of Carlos Pelu:

"...should have called me when you got here, lucky they found my note, and I said of course I'd take you in..."

Arthur Less, entranced by destiny, finds himself staring at that face he has known so well over the years. The particular Roman rudder of that nose, which used to be seen turning and turning in parties as it sought out this scrap of conversation, that eye across the room, those people leaving for a better party, the nose of Carlos Pelu, so striking in youth, unforgettable, and here in the car still holding up as perfectly as the carved teak figurehead of a ship that has been otherwise overhauled. His body has gone from sturdy youth to ample, august middle age. Not plump or chubby, not fat in the way Zohra proposed to grow fat, the carefree body that has at last been allowed to breathe; not happily, sexily, fuck-the-world fat. But majestically, powerfully, Pantagruelianally fat. A giant, a colossus: Carlos the Great.

Arthur, you know my son was never right for you.

"God, it's good to see you!" Carlos squeezes his arm and gives him a grin full of childish mischief: "I hear you had a young man singing beneath your window in Berlin."

"Where are we going?" Less asks.

"And did you have an affair? With a prince? Did you flee Italy under the cover of darkness? Tell me you were the Casanova of the Sahara."

"Don't be silly."

"Maybe it was Turin, where a boy sang under your balcony. Hopelessly in love with you."

"No one has ever been hopelessly in love with me."

"No," Carlos says. "You always gave them hope, didn't you?" The bulky frame of their car vanishes momentarily, and they are standing with glasses of white wine on somebody's lawn, young again. Wanting to dance with somebody. "I'll tell you where we're going. We're headed to the resort. I told you it was close by."

Of all the gin joints in all the world. "That's kind of you, but maybe I should check into an Ayurvedic—"

"Don't be silly. It's an entire staffed resort, totally empty. We're not opening for a month. You'll love it—there's an elephant!" Arthur thinks he means at the resort, but he follows Carlos's gaze, and his heart stops. There, just ahead of them, so age spotted and dusty it seems at first to be a cartload of white rubber made from local trees, until they lift up, the ears, like the unfolding of feathers or membranes for flight, and it is unmistakably an elephant, sauntering down the street with a bushel of green bamboo in its trunk, tail lashing, turning now to stare, with its small unfathomable eyes, at those who are staring at it—Less recognizes the stare—as if to say: *I'm not so strange as you.*

"Oh my God!"

"Bigger temples keep one. We can get around him," Carlos says, and, honking noisily, they do. Less turns his head to see the creature disappearing through the rear window, turning its head back and forth, lifting its burden, clearly aware of the commotion it is making and taking not a little joy in it. Then a crowd of men with limp Communist flags comes out of a building, smoking, and the unearthly vision is blocked.

"Listen, Arthur, I have an idea—ah, we've arrived," Carlos says abruptly, and Less can feel more than see their sharp descent toward the ocean. "Before we say good-bye, I have two quick questions. Easy questions." They pass through a gate; Less finds it hard to believe the driver is still honking.

"We're saying good-bye?"

"Arthur, stop being so sentimental. At our age! I'll be back in a few weeks, and we'll celebrate your recovery. I have business. It's a miracle we get this time together. The first is, you still have your letters from Robert?"

"My letters?" The honking stops, and the car comes to a halt. A young man in a green uniform approaches Less's side.

"Come on, Arthur, do you or don't you? I have a plane to catch."

"I think so."

"Bravo. And the other question is, have you heard from Freddy?"

Less feels the rush of hot air as the car door opens beside him. He looks and sees a handsome porter standing there, holding his aluminum crutches. He turns back to Carlos.

"Why would I hear from Freddy?"

"No reason. Keep yourself busy with your book until I get back, Arthur."

"Is everything okay?"

Carlos gestures good-bye, and then Less is outside watching the grand white Ambassador toil its way uphill into the palms until nothing is left but the constant goosing of its horn.

He can hear the sea and the voice of the porter: "Mr. Less, some of your bags have arrived. They are already in your room." But he is still staring at the palms in the wind.

Strange. It was said so casually that Less almost missed it. Sitting in the corner of the car and asking that simple question. It did not show in his face—Carlos kept the same expression of placid impatience as always—but Less could see him playing with a ring, turning and turning a lion-headed ring on his finger as his eye focused on wounded, aging, helpless Arthur Less. Less understands that the entire conversation was illusion, maya, chimera, and that Carlos's real purpose was otherwise. But he cannot decode it. He shakes his head and smiles at the porter, taking his crutches and looking up at his new white prison. Something in the way his old friend asked it, some hidden track that only a careful listener, or one who has listened for so many years, would notice, and that no one would ever suspect of Carlos: *Fear.*

For a fifty-year-old man, the boredom of lying convalescent in bed is rivaled only by sitting in church. Less is given the Raja Suite and set up in the comfortable bed with a view of the ocean marred only by a thick beekeeper's veil of mosquito net hanging from the ceiling. It is elegant, cool, well staffed, and stiflingly dull. How Less misses the mongoose. He misses Rupali and the picnickers, the battle of the bands, the pastor and the tailor and Elizabeth the yellow snake; he even misses Jesus Christ Our Savior. His only intrigue is with the porter, Vincent, who stops by every day to check in on our invalid: a clean-shaven tapered face and topaz eyes, the kind of bashful handsome man who has no idea he is handsome, and whenever Vincent pays a visit, Less prays for Jesus Christ Our Savior to extinguish his libido; the last thing he needs is a convalescent crush.

So the weeks pass in blank tedium, which turns out—finally—to be the perfect situation for Less, at last, to try to write.

It is like pouring water from an old leaking bucket into a shining new one; it feels almost suspiciously easy. He simply takes a gloomy event in the plot—say, a market owner dying of cancer—and inverts it, having Swift, out of pity, accept seven fragrant rounds of cheese, which he will then have to carry around San Francisco, growing more rank, throughout the rest of the chapter. In the sordid scene in which Swift takes a bag of cocaine to the hotel bathroom, cutting out a line on the counter, Less merely adds a motion-activated hand dryer and—whirr! A blizzard of indignity! All it takes is a pail thrown out a window, an open manhole, a banana peel. "Are we losers?" Swift asks of his lover at the end of their ruined vacation, and Less gleefully adds the response: "Well, baby, we sure ain't winners." With a joy bordering on sadism, he degloves every humiliation to show its risible lining. What sport! If only one could do this with life!

He finds himself awakening at dawn, when the sea is brightening but the sun still struggles in its bedclothes, and sits down to lash his protagonist a few more times with his authorial whip. And somehow, a bittersweet longing starts to appear in the novel that was never there before. It changes, grows kinder. Less, as with a repentant worshipper, begins again to love his subject, and at last, one morning, after an hour sitting with his chin in his hand, watching birds cross the gray haze of the horizon, our benevolent god grants his character the brief benediction of joy.

Finally, one afternoon, Vincent arrives and asks, "Please, how is your foot?" Less says he can now walk around without crutches. "Good," Vincent says. "And now, please, Arthur, get ready for an exceptional outing." Less asks, teasingly, where are they going together? Perhaps Vincent is at last going to show him some of India. But no; the man blushes and replies: "I, alas, am not going together." He says they are offering this exceptional outing to guests when the resort opens. A buzzing outside; he looks out the window to see a speedboat, helmed by two expressionless teens, approaching the dock. Vincent helps as Less limps to the boat and shakily boards. The engine starts with a tiger's roar.

The boat ride is half an hour, during which Less sees leaping dolphins and flying fish skipping like stones over the water, as well as the floating mane of a jellyfish. He recalls an aquarium he visited as a boy, where, after enjoying a sea turtle that swam breaststroke like a dotty old aunt, he encountered a jellyfish, a pink frothing brainless negligeed monster pulsing in the water, and thought with a sob: *We are not in this together.* They arrive, at last, at an island of white sand no bigger than a city block, with two coconut palms and small purple flowers. Less steps ashore gingerly and makes his way to the shade. More dolphins leap in a darkening ocean. An airplane underlines the moon. It is unmistakably paradise— until Less turns around to see the boat departing. Castaway. Is it possible this is some final plot of Carlos's? To imprison him in a room for weeks and only now, when he is one chapter away from finishing his novel, abandon him on a desert island? It is a *New Yorker* cartoon fate. Less appeals to the setting sun: He gave up Freddy! He gave him up willingly; he even stayed away from the wedding. He has suffered enough, all on his own; he is crippled, uniplegic, forsaken, and bereft of his magic suit. He has nothing left to take away, our gay Job. He drops to his knees in the sand.

A nagging hum from behind him. When he looks around, he sees another speedboat headed his way.

"Arthur, I have an idea," Carlos tells him after dinner. Carlos's assistants have made a quick campfire and grilled them two harlequined fish they speared along the reef, and Less and Carlos are sitting down among cushions to share a bottle of cold champagne.

Carlos reclines on one of the spangled cushions; he is wearing a white caftan. "When you get home, I want you to find all your correspondence about the Russian River School. From all the men we knew. The important ones, Robert and Ross and Franklin in particular."

Less, caught awkwardly between two pillows, struggles to right himself and wonders, *Why?*

"I want to buy them from you."

Above the slow washing-machine sound of the surf comes

a series of plops that must be a fish. The moon is high overhead, wrapped in a haze, casting a gauzy glow over everything and spoiling the view of the stars.

Carlos stares intently at Less in the firelight. "Everything you've got. How many do you think there are?"

"I've . . . I don't know. I'd have to look. Dozens, you know. But they're personal."

"I want personal. I'm building a collection. They're back in style now, that whole era. There are college courses all about it. And we knew them. We were part of history, Arthur."

"I'm not sure we were part of history."

"I want to get everything together in a collection, the Carlos Pelu Collection. I have a university interested; they can maybe name a room in the library after me. Did Robert write you any poems?"

"The Carlos Pelu Collection."

"You like the sound of it? You'd make the collection complete. A love poem of Robert's for you."

"He didn't write that way."

"Or that painting by Woodhouse. I know you need money," Carlos says quietly.

And so here is the plan: for Carlos to take everything. To take his pride, to take his health and his sanity, to take Freddy, and now, at last, to take even his memories, his souvenirs, away. There will be nothing left of Arthur Less.

"I'm doing okay."

The fire, made of coconut shells, finds a particularly delicious morsel and flames up in delight, lighting both of their faces. They are not young, not at all; there is nothing left of the boys they used to be. Why not sell his letters, his keep-sakes, his paintings, his books? Why not burn them? Why not give up on the whole business of life?

"Do you remember that afternoon on the beach? You were still seeing that Italian . . . ," Carlos says.

"Marco."

He laughs. "Oh my God, Marco! He was afraid of the rocks and made us go sit with the straight people. Remember?"

"Of course I remember. That's when I met Robert."

"I think about that day a lot. Of course, we didn't know it was a big storm out in the Pacific, that we were out of our minds to be on the beach! It was incredibly dangerous. But we were young and stupid, weren't we?"

"That we can agree on."

"Sometimes I think about all the men we knew on that beach."

Little parts of the memory light up now in Less's brain, in-cluding Carlos standing on a rock and staring at the sky, his trim and muscled body doubled in the tide pool below. The fire crackles, throwing helicoids of sparks into the air. Other than the fire and the sea, there is no other sound.

"I never hated you, Arthur," Carlos says.

Less stares into the fire.

"It was always envy. I hope you understand that."

A mob of tiny translucent crabs crosses the sand, making a break for the water.

"Arthur, I've got a theory. Now, hear me out. It's that our lives are half comedy and half tragedy. And for some people, it just works out that the first *entire half* of their lives is tragedy and then the second half is comedy. Me, for example. Look at my shitty youth. A poor kid come to the big city—maybe you never knew, but, God, it was hard for me. I just wanted to get *somewhere*. Thank God I met Donald, but him getting sick, and dying—and then suddenly I had a son on my hands. The ass-kicking work it took to turn his business into what I've got. Forty years of serious, serious stuff.

"But look at me now—comedy! Fat! Rich! Ridiculous! Look at how I'm dressed—in a *caftan!* I was such an angry young man—I had so much to prove; now there's money and laughter. It's wonderful. Let's open the other bottle. But you. You had comedy in your youth. You were the ridiculous one then, the one everyone laughed at. You just walked into everything, like someone blindfolded. I've known you longer than most of your friends, and I've certainly watched you more closely. I am the world's leading expert on Arthur Less. I remember when we met. You were so skinny, all clavicle and hip bone! And innocent. The rest of us were so far from being innocent, I don't think we even thought about pretending. You were different. I think everybody wanted to touch that innocence, maybe ruin it. Your way of going through the world, unaware of danger. Clumsy and naive. Of course I envied you. Because I could never be that; I'd stopped being that when I was a kid. If you'd asked me a year ago, six months ago, I would have said, yes, Arthur, the first half of your life was comedy. But you're deep into the tragic half now."

Carlos picks up the champagne bottle to refill Less's glass. "What's that?" Less asks. "The tragic—"

"But I've changed my mind." Carlos plows on. "You know

Freddy does an imitation of you? You've never seen it? Oh, you'll like it." Carlos has to get up for this one—an elaborate movement requiring him to brace himself against the palm. It is possible he is drunk. Even as he does this, he retains the same regal hauteur as when he used to pace a swimming pool like a panther. And in one nimble movement, he becomes Arthur Less: tall, awkward, bug eyed, knock kneed, and wearing a terrified grin; even his hair seems to be brushed up in that comic-book-sidekick hairstyle Less has always worn. He speaks in a loud, slightly hysterical voice:

"I got this suit in Vietnam! It's summer-weight wool. I wanted linen, but the lady said no, it'll wrinkle, what you want is summer-weight wool, and you know what? She was right!"

Less sits there for a moment and then chuckles in astonishment. "Well," he says, "summer-weight wool. At least Freddy was listening."

Carlos laughs, loses the pose, and becomes his old self again, leaning against a palm, and it flashes across his face again, briefly, the expression Less noticed in the car. Fear. Desperation. About something other than these "letters." "So what do you say, Arthur? Sell them to me."

"No, Carlos. No."

Carlos turns from the fire, asking if this is about Freddy.

Less says, "Freddy has nothing to do with this."

Carlos looks out at the moonlight on the water. "You know, Arthur, my son's not like me. Once I asked him why he was so lazy. I asked him what the hell he wanted. He couldn't tell me. So I decided for him."

"Let's back up a minute."

Carlos turns to look down at Less. "You really haven't heard?" It must be the moonlight—that couldn't be tenderness in his face.

"What was that about the tragic half?" Less asks.

Carlos smiles as if he has decided something. "Arthur, I changed my mind. You have the luck of a comedian. Bad luck in things that don't matter. Good luck in things that do. I think—you probably won't agree with this—but I think your whole life is a comedy. Not just the first part. The whole thing. You are the most absurd person I've ever met. You've bumbled through every moment and been a fool; you've misunderstood and misspoken and tripped over absolutely everything and everyone in your path, and you've won. And you don't even realize it."

"Carlos." He doesn't feel victorious; he feels defeated. "My life, my life over the past year—"

"Arthur Less," Carlos interrupts, shaking his head. "You have the best life of anyone I know."

This is nonsense to Less.

Carlos looks into the fire, then tosses back the rest of his champagne. "I'm heading back to shore; I've got to leave early tomorrow. Make sure you give Vincent your flight details. To Japan, right? Kyoto? We want to make sure you get home safe. I'll see you in the morning." And with that, he strides off across the island to where his boat waits in moonlight.

But Less does not see Carlos in the morning. His own boat takes him back to the resort, where he stays up late looking at the stars, recalling the lawn outside his cottage and how it shimmered with glowworms, and he sees one particular constellation that looks like the stuffed squirrel named Michael he had as a boy, who was left behind in a Florida hotel room. Hello, Michael! He goes to bed very late, and when he does get up, he finds that Carlos has already left. He wonders what it is he is meant to have won.

For a seven-year-old boy, the boredom of sitting in church is rivaled only by sitting in an airport lounge. This particular boy has been sitting with his Sunday-school book in his lap—a set of Bible stories with wildly inconsistent illustration styles—and staring at a picture of Daniel's lion. How he wishes it were a dragon. How he wishes his mother had not confiscated his pen. It is a long stone room with a white wood ceiling; perhaps two hundred sandals are arrayed outside on the grass. Everyone is in their best clothes; his are exquisitely hot. Fans above nod back and forth, spectators at the tennis match of God and Satan. The boy hears the parson talking; he can think only of the parson's daughter who, while only three, has completely captured his heart. He looks over, and she is on her mother's lap; she looks back and blinks. But even more interesting is the window behind her, opening onto the road, where a white Tata is stuck in traffic, and there, clearly visible in its open window: the American!

How incredible, he wants to tell everybody, but of course he's forbidden to speak; it is driving him as mad as the parson's temptress daughter. The American, the one from the airport, in the same beige linen as before. All around him, vendors are walking from car to car with hot food wrapped in paper, water, and sodas, and everywhere horns are musically honking. It feels like a parade. The American leans his head out the window, presumably to check the traffic, and then, for one, brief moment, his eyes meet those of the boy. What is contained in that blue gaze, the boy cannot comprehend. They are the eyes of a castaway. Headed to Japan. Then the invisible obstacle is removed, traffic begins to move forward, the American pulls himself back into the shadow of the car, and he is gone.

LESS AT LAST

FROM where I sit, the story of Arthur Less is not so bad. I admit it looks bad (misfortune is about to arrive). I recall our second meeting, when Less was just over forty. I was at a cocktail party in a new city, looking out at the view, when I felt the sensation of someone opening a window and turned. No one had opened a window; a new person had simply entered the room. He was tall, with thinning blond hair and the profile of an English lord. He gave a sad grin to the crowd and raised a hand the way some people do when (after being introduced with an anecdote) they say "Guilty!" Nowhere on earth could he be mistaken for anything but an American. Did I recognize him as the same man who taught me to draw in that cold white room when I was young? The one I thought was a boy but who betrayed me by being a man? Not at first. My initial thoughts were certainly not those of a child. But then, yes, on a second glance, I did recognize him. He had aged without growing old: a harder jaw, a thicker neck, a faded color to his hair and skin. No one would mistake him for a boy. And yet it was definitely him: I recognized the distinctly identifiable innocence he carried with him. Mine had vanished in the intervening years; his, strangely, had not. Here was someone who should have known better; who should have built an amusing armor around himself, like everyone else in that room, laughing; who should, by now, have grown a skin. Standing there like someone lost in Grand Central Station.

So it is that, almost a decade later, Arthur Less wears the same expression as he emerges from the plane in Osaka and, finding no one to greet him, experiences that quicksand sensation every traveler recognizes: *Of course there is no one to greet me; why would anyone remember, and what am I supposed to do now?* Above him, a fly orbits a ceiling lamp in a trapezoidal pattern, and in life's constant imitation, Arthur Less begins a similar orbit around the Arrivals terminal. He passes a number of counters whose signs, while ostensibly in English, mean nothing to him (JASPER!, AERONET, GOLD-MAN), reminding him of that startling moment while reading a book when he finds it is all complete gibberish and realizes that he is, in fact, dreaming. At the final counter (CHROME), an elderly man calls out to him; Arthur Less, by now fluent in global sign language, understands this is a private bus company and the Kyoto city council has left him a ticket. The name on the ticket: *DR. ESS.* Less experiences a brief wonderful vertigo. Outside, the minibus is waiting; it is clearly meant only for Less. A driver exits; he is wearing the cap and white gloves of a cinema chauffeur; he nods to Arthur Less, who finds himself bowing before he enters the bus, chooses a seat, wipes his face with a handkerchief, and looks out the window at this, his final destination. Only an ocean left to cross now. He has lost so much along the way: his lover, his dignity, his beard, his suit, and his suitcase.

I have neglected to mention that his suitcase has not made it to Japan.

Less is here to review Japanese cuisine for a men's magazine, in particular kaiseki cuisine; he volunteered for the gig at that poker game. He knows nothing at all about kaiseki cuisine, but he has dinner plans at four different establishments over two days, the last an ancient inn outside Kyoto, so he is expecting a wide variety. Two days, then he will be done. All he knows of Japan is a memory from when he was a little boy, when his mother drove him into Washington DC, for a special trip, and he was made to wear a button-up shirt and wool trousers, and was taken to a large stone building with columns, and stood in line for a long time in the snow before being allowed entrance to a small dark chamber in which various treasures appeared, scrolls and headdresses and suits of armor (which Less took for real people at first). "They've let them out of Japan for the first time and probably never will again," his mother whispered, apparently referring to a mirror, a jewel, and a sword on display with two very real and disappointing guards, and when a gong sounded and they were told to leave, she leaned down to him and asked: "What did you like best?" He told her, and her face twisted in amusement: "Garden? What garden?" He had been drawn not to the sacred treasures but to a glass case containing a town in miniature, to which an eyepiece was attached so that he could peer in on one scene or the next like a god, each done in such exquisite detail that it seemed he was looking in on the past through a magic telescope. And of all the wonders in that case, the greatest was the garden, with its river that seemed to trickle, filled with orange-spotted carp, and bushy pines and maples and a little fountain made from a piece of bamboo (in reality as big as a pin!) that tipped and tipped, as if dropping its load of water into the stone pool at its base. The garden enchanted little Arthur Less for weeks; he walked among the brown leaves of his backyard, looking for its little golden key. He took it for granted he would find the door.

So all this is surprising and new. Arthur Less sits in the bus and watches the industrial landscape bloom along the highway. He expected something prettier, perhaps. But even Kawabata wrote about the changing landscape around Osaka, and that was sixty years ago. He is tired; his flights and connections have felt more dreamlike than even his drugged tour of the Frankfurt airport. He did not hear again from Carlos. A piece of nonsense buzzes in his brain: *Is this because of Freddy?* But that story had reached its end, as this one almost has.

The bus continues into Kyoto, which feels like a mere elaboration on the small townlets before it, and while Less is still trying to figure out if they are in the downtown—if perhaps this is a main street, if that is in fact the Kamo River—they have arrived. A low wooden wall off the main road. A young man in a black suit bows and stares curiously at the place where Less's suitcase should be. A middle-aged woman in kimono approaches from the cobblestone court-yard. She is lightly made up, her hair pulled into a style Less associates with the early twentieth century. A Gibson girl. "Mr. Arthur," she says with a bow. He bows in return. Behind her, at the front desk, there is a ruckus: an old woman, also in kimono, chattering on a cell phone and making marks on a wall calendar.

"That is just my mother," the proprietress says, sighing. "She thinks she is still the boss. We give her a fake calendar to make reservations. The phone also is fake. Can I make you a cup of tea?" He says that would be wonderful, and she smiles handsomely; then her face darkens in terrible sorrow. "And I am so sorry, Mr. Arthur," she says, as if imparting the death of a loved one. "You are too early to see the cherry blossoms."

After the tea (which she makes by hand, whisking it into a bitter green foam—"Please eat the sugar cookie before the tea") he is shown to his room and told it was, in fact, the novelist Kawabata Yasunari's favorite. A low lacquered table is set on the tatami floor, and the woman slides back paper walls to reveal a moonlit corner garden dripping from a recent rain; Kawabata wrote of this garden in the rain that it was the heart of Kyoto. "Not any garden," she says pointedly, "but this very garden." She informs him that the tub in the bathroom is already warm and that an attendant will keep it warm, always, for whenever he needs it. Always. There is a *yukata* in the closet for him to wear. Would he like dinner in the room? She will bring it personally for him: the first of the four kaiseki meals he will be writing about.

The kaiseki meal, he has learned, is an ancient formal meal

drawn from both monasteries and the royal court. It is typically seven courses, each course composed of a particular
type of food (grilled, simmered, raw) and seasonal ingredients. Tonight, it is butter bean, mugwort, and sea bream. Less
is humbled both by the exquisite food and by the gracious-
ness with which she presents it. "I most sincerely apologize
I cannot be here tomorrow to see you; I must go to Tokyo."
She says this as if she were missing the most extraordinary of
wonders: another day with Arthur Less. He sees, in the lines
around her mouth, the shadow of the smile all widows wear
in private. She bows and exits, returning with a sake sampler.
He tries all three, and when asked which is his favorite, he
says the Tonni, though he cannot tell the difference. He asks
which is her favorite. She blinks and says: "The Tonni." If
only he could learn to lie so compassionately.

The next day is already his last, and it looks as if it will
be a full one; he has arranged to visit three restaurants. It
is eleven in the morning, and Arthur Less, still wearing his
clothes from the day before, is already on his way to the first,
recovering his shoes from the numbered cabinet where the
hotel worker keeps them when he is waylaid by the elderly
mother. She stands behind the reception desk, dwarfed and
age speckled as a winter starling, perhaps ninety years old,
and chattering, chattering away, as if the cure for his inabil-
ity to speak Japanese were the application of *more Japanese*
(a hair-of-the-dog sensibility). And yet somehow, from his
months of travel and pantomime, his pathetic journey into
the empathic and telepathic, he feels he does understand.
She is talking about her youth. She is talking about when

she was the proprietress. She pulls out a weathered black-and-white photograph of a seated Western couple—the man silver haired, the woman quite chic in a toque—and he recognizes the room where he had tea. She is saying the girl serving tea is her and the man, a famous American. There is a long expectant pause as recognition rises like a deep-sea diver, slowly, cautiously, until it surfaces, and he exclaims:

"Charlie Chaplin!"

The old woman closes her eyes with joy.

A young woman in braids arrives and turns on the little television behind the counter, changing the channels until she lands on a scene of the emperor of Japan having tea with a few guests, one of whom he recognizes.

"Is that the proprietress?" he asks the young woman.

"Oh yes," she says, "she is so sorry she could not say good-bye to you."

"She didn't tell me it was so she could have tea with the emperor!"

"It is with her great apologies, Mr. Less." There are more apologies. "I am also so sorry your suitcase is not here for you. But early this morning we had a call: there is a message." She hands him an envelope. Inside is a piece of paper with the message in all caps, which reads like an old-fashioned telegram:

ARTHUR DO NOT WORRY BUT ROBERT HAS HAD A STROKE BACK HOME NOW PLEASE CALL ME WHEN YOU CAN

—MARIAN

• • •

"Arthur, there you are!"

Marian's voice—almost thirty years since they last spoke; he can only imagine the names she called him after the divorce. But he remembers Mexico City: *She sends her love.* In Sonoma it is seven at night the previous day.

"Marian, what's happened?"

"Arthur, don't worry, don't worry, he's okay."

"What. Happened."

That sigh from across the world, and he takes a moment from his worries to marvel: *Marian!* "He was just in his apartment, reading, and fell flat on the floor. Luckily, Joan was there." The nurse. "He bruised himself a little. He's having trouble talking, a little trouble with his right hand. It's minor." She says this sternly. "It's a *minor stroke.*"

"What is a minor stroke? Does that mean it's nothing, or does that mean thank God it wasn't a major one?"

"The thank-God kind. And thank God he wasn't on the stairs or something. Listen, Arthur, I don't want you to worry. But I wanted to call you. You know you're listed first on his emergency contacts. But they didn't know where you were, so they called me. I'm second." A little laugh. "Lucky them, I've been stuck at home for months!"

"Oh, Marian, you broke your hip!"

Again the sigh. "Not broken, it turned out. But I'm bruised black and blue. What do we do? Things fall apart. Sorry I had to skip Mexico City; that would have been a nicer reunion."

"I'm so glad you're there with him, Marian. I'll be there tomorrow, I have to check on—"

"No, no, Arthur, don't do that! You're on your honey-moon."

"What?"

"Robert's fine. I'll be here a week or so. See him when you get back. I wouldn't have bothered you at all except he insisted. He misses you, of course, at a time like this."

"Marian, I'm not on my honeymoon. I'm in Japan for an article."

But there was no contradicting Marian Brownburn. "Robert said you got married. He said you married Freddy somebody."

"No no, no no," Arthur says, and finds himself getting dizzy. "Freddy somebody married somebody else. It doesn't matter. I'll be right there."

"Listen," Marian says in her administrative voice. "Arthur. Don't you get on a plane. He'll be furious."

"I can't stay here, Marian. You wouldn't stay here. We both love him, we wouldn't stay here while he's suffering."

"Okay. Let's set up one of those video calls you boys do…"

They arrange to chat again in ten minutes, during which time Less manages to find the inn's computer, which is star-tlingly up-to-date, considering the ancient room in which it sits. As he waits for the video call, he stares at a bird of paradise arranged in a bowl by the window. A minor stroke. Fuck you, life.

Arthur Less's life with Robert ended around the time he fin-ished reading Proust. It was one of the grandest and most dismaying experiences in Less's life—Marcel Proust, that is—

and the three thousand pages of *In Search of Lost Time* took him five committed summers to finish. And on that fifth summer, when he was lying abed in a friend's Cape Cod house one afternoon, about two-thirds of the way through the last volume, suddenly, without any warning at all, he read the words *The End*. In his right hand he held perhaps two hundred pages more—but they were not Proust; they were the cruel trick of some editor's notes and afterword. He felt cheated, swindled, denied a pleasure for which he had spent five years preparing. He went back twenty pages; he tried to build up the feeling again. But it was too late; that possible joy had departed forever.

This was how he felt when Robert left him.

Or perhaps you assumed he left Robert?

As with Proust, he knew the end was coming. Fifteen years, and the joy of love had long since faded, and the cheating had begun; not simply Less's escapades with other men but secret affairs that ran the course of a month to a year and broke everything in sight. Was he testing to see how elastic love could be? Was he simply a man who had gladly given his youth to a man in midlife and now, nearing midlife himself, wanted back the fortune he squandered? Wanted sex and love and folly? The very things Robert saved him from all those years ago? As for the good things, as for safety, comfort, love—Less found himself smashing them to bits. Perhaps he did not know what he was doing; perhaps it was a kind of madness. But perhaps he did know. Perhaps he was burning down a house in which he no longer wanted to live.

The real end came when Robert was on one of his reading trips, this time through the South. Robert called dutifully the first night he arrived, but Less was not home, and over the next few days his voice mail was filled, first with stories, about, for instance, Spanish moss hanging from the oaks like rotting dresses, then with briefer and briefer messages until, at last, there were none. Less was preparing himself, in fact, for Robert's return, when he was planning on a very serious conversation. He sensed six months of couples counseling, and he sensed it would end with a tearful parting; perhaps all that would take a year. But it had to start now. His heart was in a knot, and he practiced his lines as one practices a phrase in a foreign language before heading to the ticket counter: "I think we both know something isn't working, I think we both know something isn't working, I think we both know something isn't working." When, after a silence of five days, his phone rang at last, Less suppressed a heart attack and answered it: "Robert! You got me at last. I wanted to talk. I think we both know—"

But his speech was pierced by Robert's deep voice: "Arthur, I love you, but I will not be coming home. Mark will be over to get some of my things. I'm sorry, but I don't want to talk about it now. I am not angry. I love you. I am not angry. But neither of us is the man we used to be. Goodbye."

The End. And all that he held in his hand were the notes and afterword.

"Look at you, Arthur."

It's Robert. The connection is poor, but it is Robert Brownburn, the world-famous poet, appearing on the screen, and beside him (surely an effect of transmission), his ectoplasmic echo. Here he is: alive. Beautifully bald, with a baby's halo of hair. He is dressed in a blue terry bathrobe. His smile contains some of the same brilliant devilry, but today it sags to the right. A stroke. Holy shit. A tube runs under his nose like a fake mustache, his voice grates like sand, and from beside him Less can hear (perhaps heightened by the microphone's proximity) a machine's loud respiration, bringing back memories of the "heavy breather" who would sometimes call the Less house, young Arthur Less listening with fascination as his mother yelled out, "Oh, is that my boyfriend? Tell him I'll be right there!" But here is Robert. Slumped, slurring, mortified but alive.

Less: "How are you doing?"

"I feel like I've been in a bar fight. I am speaking to you from the afterlife."

"You look awful. How dare you do this," Less says.

"You should see the other guy." His words are mumbled and odd.

"You sound Scottish," Less says.

"We become our fathers." Or forefathers: his *s*'s have become *f*'s, as in old manuscripts: *When in the courfe of human events it becomes necefsary . . .*

Then the doctor, an elderly woman in black glasses, leans into view. Thin, bony, creased with lines as if crumpled in a pocket for a long time, with a wattle under her chin. A white bob and Antarctic eyes. "Arthur, it's Marian."

Oh, what jokers! Less thinks. They're kidding! There is that scene at the end of Proust when our narrator, after many years out of society, arrives at a party furious no one told him it's a costume party; everyone is wearing white wigs! And

then he realizes. It isn't a costume party. They have simply
grown old. And here, looking at his first love, the first wife—
surely they're kidding! But the joke goes on too long. Robert
keeps breathing heavily. Marian does not smile. No one is
kidding.

"Marian, you look wonderful."

"Arthur, you're all grown up," she muses.

"He's fifty," Robert says, then winces in discomfort.
"Happy birthday, my boy. Sorry I missed it." *Forry I mifsed
it. Life, liberty and the purfuit of happinefs.* "I had a rendezvous
with Death."

Marian says, "Death didn't show. I'll leave you boys alone
for a minute. But only a minute! Don't tire him out, Arthur.
We have to take care of our Robert."

Thirty years ago, a beach in San Francisco.

She vanishes; Robert's eyes watch her leave, then they return to Less. A procession of shades, as with Odysseus, and
here before him: Tiresias. The seer. "You know, it's good to
have her here. She drives me crazy. Keeps me going. There's
nothing like doing the crossword with your ex-wife. Where
the hell are you?"

"Kyoto."

"What?"

Less leans forward and shouts: "Kyoto. Japan. But I'm
coming back to see you."

"Fuck that. I'm fine. I lost my fine motor skills, not my
goddamn mind. Look at what they have me doing." In very
slow motion, he manages to lift his hand. In it, a bright-green
ball of putty. "I have to squeeze it all day. I told you this
was the afterlife. Poets have to squeeze bits of clay for eter-

nity. They're all here, Walt and Hart and Emily and Frank. The American wing. Squeezing bits of clay. Novelists have to"—and he closes his eyes and catches his breath for a moment, then continues more weakly—"novelists have to mix our drinks. Did you write your novel in India?"

"I did. I have one chapter left. I want to see you."

"Finish your fucking novel."

"Robert—"

"Don't use my stroke as an excuse. Coward! You're afraid I'm going to die."

Less cannot answer; it is the truth. *I know I'm out of your life / But the day that I die / I know you are going to cry.* In the silence, the machine breathes on and on. Robert's face crumbles a little. *Llorar y llorar, llorar y llorar.*

"Not yet, Arthur," he says briskly. "Don't be in such a fucking hurry for it. Didn't someone say you'd grown a beard?"

"Did you tell Marian I married Freddy?"

"Who knows what I said? Do I look like I know what I'm saying? Did you?"

"No."

"And now here you are. Here we both are. You look very, very sad, my boy."

Does he? Well rested and pampered, fresh from his bath? But you can't hide anything from Tiresias.

"Did you love him, Arthur?"

Arthur says nothing. There was a time—at a bad Italian restaurant in North Beach, San Francisco, basically abandoned except for two waiters and a tourist family from Germany whose matriarch later fell in the bathroom, hit her head, and insisted on going to the hospital (not comprehending the cost of American health care)—there was a time when Robert Brownburn, only forty-six years old, took Arthur Less's hand and said, "My marriage is failing, it has been failing a long time. Marian and I hardly sleep together anymore. I get to bed very late, she gets up very early. She's angry we never had children. And now that it's too late, she's even angrier. I'm selfish and terrible with money. I'm so unhappy. So, so unhappy, Arthur. What I'm saying is that I am in love with you. I was already going to leave Marian before I met you. And I *shall dance and sing for thy delight each May-morning,* I think the poem goes. I have enough to buy some shitty place somewhere. I know how to live on just a little money. I know it's preposterous. But you are *what I want.* Who gives a fuck what anybody says? You are *what I want,* Arthur, and I—" But there was no more, because Robert Brownburn shut his eyes to hold in the longing that had overcome him in the presence of this young man, clutching his hand in this bad Italian restaurant to which they would never return. The poet wincing in pain before him, suffering, suffering, for Arthur Less. Will Less ever again be so beloved?

Robert, seventy-five, breathing heavily, says, "Oh, my poor boy. A lot?"

Still Arthur says nothing. And Robert says nothing; he knows the absurdity of asking someone to explain love or sorrow. You can't point to it. It would be as futile, as unconveyable, as pointing at the sky and saying, "That one, that star, there."

"Am I too old to meet someone, Robert?"

Robert sits up slightly, his mood shifting back to merry-making. "Are you too old? Listen to you. I was watching a television show about science the other day. That's the kind of nice-old-man thing I do now. I'm very harmless these days. It was about time travel. And they had a scientist on saying that if it were possible, you'd have to build one time machine now. And build another one years later. Then you could go back and forth. A sort of time tunnel. But here's the thing, Arthur. You could never go any further back than the invention of that first machine. Which I think is really a blow to the imagination. I took it pretty hard."

Arthur says, "We can never kill Hitler."

"But you know it's like that already. When you meet people. You meet them, say, when they're thirty, and you can never really imagine them any younger than that. You've seen pictures of me, Arthur, you've seen me at twenty."

"You were a handsome guy."

"But really, really, you can't imagine me any younger than my forties, can you?"

"Sure, I can."

"You can picture it. But you can't quite imagine it. You can't go back any further. It's against the laws of physics."

"You're getting too excited."

"Arthur, I look at you, and I still see that boy on the beach with the red toenails. Not at first, but my eyes adjust. I see that twenty-one-year-old boy in Mexico. I see that young man in a hotel room in Rome. I see the young writer holding his first book. I look at you, and you're young. You'll always be that way for me. But not for anyone else. Arthur, people who meet you now will never be able to imagine you young. They can never go any further back than fifty. It isn't all bad. It means now people will think you were always a grown-up. They'll take you seriously. They don't know that you once spent an entire dinner party babbling about Nepal when you meant Tibet."

"I can't believe you brought that up again."

"That you once referred to Toronto as the capital of Canada."

"I'm going to get Marian to pull the plug."

"To the prime minister of Canada. I love you, Arthur. My point is"—and after this harangue he has apparently worn himself out, and takes a few deep breaths—"my point is, welcome to fucking life. Fifty is nothing. I look back at fifty and think, what the fuck was I so worried about? Look at me now. I'm in the afterlife. Go *enjoy* yourself." Says Tiresias.

Marian reappears on the screen: "Okay, boys, time's up. We've got to let him rest."

Robert leans over to his ex-wife. "Marian, he didn't marry him."

"He didn't?"

"Apparently I heard wrong. The fellow married someone else."

"Well, that's shitty," she says, then turns to the camera with an expression of sympathy. White hair held back with barrettes, round black glasses reflecting a sunny day in the past. "Arthur, he's worn out. It's good to see you again. We can set up another chat later."

"I'll be home tomorrow, I'll drive up. Robert, I love you."

The old rogue smiles at Arthur and shakes his head, his eyes bright and clear. "Love you always, Arthur Less."

• • •

"In this room, we take off our clothes before the meal."
The young woman pauses before the doorway, then covers
her mouth with her hand. Her eyes are wide with horror.
"Not clothes! Shoes! We take off our shoes!" It is Less's first
restaurant of three today, and, the call to Robert having already thrown off his schedule, Less is eager to begin, but
he gamely follows her ponytail to an enormous hall set
with a table and sunken seating, where an elderly man,
dressed all in red, bows and says, "Here is the banquet hall,
and you can see it transforms into a place for *maiko* dancing." He pushes a button, and as in a Bond villain's lair,
the back wall begins to tilt down, becoming a stage, and
theater lights pivot out from above. The two seem enor-
mously pleased by this. Less does not know what a maiko
might be. He is given a seat by the window and eagerly
awaits his kaiseki meal. Seven dishes, as before, taking almost three hours. Grilled, simmered, raw. And—why did
he not expect this?—again butter bean, mugwort, and sea
bream. Again, it is lovely. But, like a second date too soon
after the first, perhaps a bit familiar?

Look at me now, comes Robert's voice, haunting him from
earlier. *I'm in the afterlife.* A stroke. Robert has never been
kind to his body; he's worn it like an old leather coat tossed
in oceans and left crumpled in corners, and Less saw its marks
and scars and aches not as failures of age but the opposite:
the evidence, as Raymond Chandler once wrote, of "a gaudy
life." It is only the carrier of that wonderful mind, after all. A
case for the crown. And Robert has cared for that mind like
a tiger with her young; he has given up drinking and drugs,
kept a strict schedule of sleep. He is good, he is careful. And

to steal that—to steal his mind—burglar Life! Like cutting a Rembrandt from its frame.

The second meal of the day takes place in a more modern restaurant decorated with the unembellished severity of a Swede, in blond wood; his waiter is blond as well, and Dutch. Less is given a view of a solitary tree decorated with green buds; it is a cherry, and he is informed he is too early for the blossoms. "Yes, yes, I know," he says as graciously as he can manage. Over the next three hours he is served grilled and simmered and raw plates of butter bean, mugwort, and sea bream. He greets each dish with a mad smile, recognizing the spiral nature of being, Nietzsche's concept of eternal return. He murmurs quietly: *You again.*

When he returns to the *ryokan* to recover, the old woman is gone, but the young woman in braids is still there, reading a novel in English. She greets him with more apologies about his luggage: no suitcase has arrived. Somehow, it is more than Less can bear, and he leans against the counter. "But, Mr. Less," the woman says hopefully, "a package did arrive for you."

It is a shallow brown box postmarked from Italy, surely a book or something from the festival. Less takes it to his room, where he sets it on a table before the garden. In the bathroom, as if in an enchanted hut, a bath already awaits him, perfectly warm, and he soaks his weary body as he prepares for the next meal. He closes his eyes. *Did you love him, Arthur?* There is the scent of cedar all around. *Oh, my poor boy. A lot?*

He dries himself and puts on a gray quilted robe, preparing himself to put on the same wilted linen clothes he has worn

since India. The package sits waiting for him on the table; he
is so tired he considers leaving it for later. But, sighing, he
opens it, and inside, wrapped in layers of Italian Christmas
paper—how has he forgotten he gave his Japanese address?—
is a white linen shirt and a suit as gray as a cloud.

As a final challenge, the last restaurant of the trip sits on
a mountainside outside Kyoto, requiring Less to rent a car.
This goes more smoothly than Less imagined; his international driving permit, which looks to him like a flimsy
phony, is taken very seriously and photocopied numerous
times, as if to be handed out as keepsakes. He is shown to
a car as small, bland, and white as a hospital dessert and enters to find the steering wheel missing—then is shown to the
driver's side, all the time merrily thinking: *Oh, I guess they
drive on the other side over here!* Somehow he never thought of
it; should they give out international driving permits to people who never think of it? But he has done his time in India;
it is all a matter of Looking-Glass driving. Like laying type
for a letterpress; you just reverse your mind.

The instructions for getting to the restaurant are as mysterious as a love note or an exchange of spies—*Meet at the
Moon Crossing Bridge*—but his faith is fast; he takes the wheel
of what basically feels like an enameled toaster and follows
the clear, perfect signs out of Kyoto, toward the hill country. Less is grateful the signs are clear because the GPS, after
giving crisp, stern directions to the highway, becomes drunk
on its own power outside the city limits, then gives out
completely and places Arthur Less in the Sea of Japan. Also
unnerving is a mysterious windshield box, which reveals its

purpose when the Toaster approaches a tollbooth: it produces a high-pitched reproving female shriek not unlike his grand-mother's when she came upon a piece of broken china. He dutifully pays the toll man, thinking he has done what the machine wants, and passes into a green countryside where a river has magically appeared. But the pastoral scene does not last long—at the next tollbooth, the lady shrieks again. Surely she is berating him for not possessing an electronic pass. But could she also have discovered his other crimes and inade-quacies? How he made up ceremonies for a fifth-grade report on the religions of Iceland? How he shoplifted acne cream in high school? How he cheated on Robert so terribly? How he is a "bad gay"? And a bad writer? How he let Freddy Pelu walk out of his life? Shriek, shriek, shriek; it is almost Greek in its fury. A harpy sent down to punish Less at last.

"Take the next exit." The GPS, that rum-drunk snoozing captain, has awakened and is back in command. Mist is rising as steam rises from damp clothing set beside a fire; here, it is from the pine-dark, folded wool of the mountains. A leaden river is coiling along a bank of reeds. The Toaster passes a sake factory, or so he assumes, because here is a cheerful white barrel sitting as advertisement on the road. Some farm or other has a sign out, in English: SUSTAINABLE HARVEST. Less rolls down the window, and there is the salt-green smell of grass and rain and dirt. He rounds a corner and sees white tourist buses parked all in a row along the river, their great side mirrors like the horns of caterpillars; before them, in a military line, stand elderly people in clear raincoats, tak-ing photographs. Scattered below the steaming mountains are perhaps fifteen thatched-roof houses furred with moss.

Across from them: a bridge over the river, a wood-stone trestlework, and Less steers the car to cross it, passing tourists huddled against the rain. He imagines a boat is meant to take him upriver to the restaurant, and as he reaches the other bank and parks the Toaster (from the dashboard comes the harpy's shrill reminder), he sees a few people waiting on the dock, and among them—he recognizes her through her clear umbrella—is his mother.

Arthur, hello, honey. I just thought I'd take a little trip, he can just imagine her saying. *Have you been eating enough?*

His mother lifts the umbrella, and, free of its distorting membrane, she is a Japanese woman wearing his mother's hair scarf. Orange with a pattern of white scallop shells. How did it get all the way here from her grave? Or no, not her grave; from the Salvation Army in suburban Delaware where he and his sister donated everything. It was all done in such a rush. The cancer moved very slowly at first, then very quickly, as things always do in nightmares, and then he was in a black suit talking to his aunt. From where he stood, he could see the scarf still hanging on its wooden knob. He was eating a quesadilla; as an areligious WASP, he had no idea what to do about death. Two thousand years of flaming Viking boats and Celtic rites and Irish wakes and Puritan worship and Unitarian hymns, and still he was left with nothing. He had somehow renounced that inheritance. So it was Freddy who took over, Freddy who had already mourned his own parents, Freddy who ordered up a Mexican feast that was all prepared when Less stumbled in from the church service, drunk on platitudes and pure horror. Freddy had even hired someone to take his raincoat. And Freddy himself, in the very jacket Less bought for him in Paris, stood directly behind Less the whole time, silently, one hand resting on his left shoulder blade as if propping up a cardboard sign against the wind. One person after another came up and said his mother was at peace. His mother's friends: each with her own peculiar spiked or curled white hairdo, like a dahlia show. *She is in a better place. So glad she went so peacefully.* And when the last had gone by, he could feel Freddy's breath on his ear as he whispered: "The way your mother died was awful." The boy he met years before would never have known to say that. Less turned to look at Freddy and saw, in the close-cut hair on his temples, the first shimmer of silver.

Less had so specifically wanted to save that orange scarf. But it was a whirlwind of duties. Somehow it got bundled into the donation pile and vanished from his life forever.

But not forever. Life has saved it after all.

Less steps out of his car and is greeted by a young man in black, who holds an enormous black umbrella over our hero; Less's new gray suit is dotted with rain. His mother's scarf vanishes into a shop. He turns to the open water, where already the low dark boat of Charon is coming to carry him off.

The restaurant sits on a rock above the river and is very old and water stained in ways that would delight a painter and trouble a contractor; some of the walls seem bent with humidity, and paper hangings have taken on the crinkle Less associates with books he has left in the rain. Intact are the old tile roof, wide roof beams, carved rosettes, and sliding paper walls of the old inn this used to be. A tall stately woman meets him at the entrance, bowing and greeting him by name. On their tour of the old inn, they pass a window onto an enormous walled garden.

"The garden was planted four hundred years ago, when the surrounding area was poplar." The woman makes a sweeping gesture, and he nods in appreciation.

"And now," Less says, "it's unpoplar."

She blinks for a polite moment, then leads him into another wing, and he follows the sway of her green and gold kimono. At the portal, she slips off her clogs, and he unlaces and removes his shoes. There is sand in them: Saharan or Keralan? The woman gestures to a sniffling teenage girl in a blue kimono, who leads him down another corridor. This one is filled with hanging calligraphy and has the Alice in Wonderland effect of beginning with an enormous wooden frame and ending in a door so small that as the woman slides it sideways into a pocket in the wall, she is forced to get onto her knees to enter. It is clear that Less is meant to do the same. He supposes he is meant to experience humility; by now, he is well acquainted with humility. It is the one piece of luggage he has not lost. There, in the room, a small table, a paper wall, and one glass window so ancient that the garden behind it undulates dreamily as Less crosses the room. The room is wallpapered in large faint gold and silver snowflakes; he is told the design is from the Edo period, when microscopes made their way to Japan. Before that, no one had seen a snowflake. He takes a seat on a cushion beside a golden folding screen. The young woman exits through the little door. He hears her struggling to close it behind her; it has clearly suffered for centuries and is ready to die.

He looks around at the golden screen, the stylized snowflakes, the single iris in a vase below a drawing of a deer, the paper wall. The only sound is the breathing of a humidifier behind him, and, despite the purity of the room, the view, no one has bothered to remove from its surface the sticker DAINICHI RELIABILITY. Before him: the warped view of the garden. He starts back in recognition. Here it is.

They must have based the miniature garden of his childhood on this four-hundred-year-old garden, because it is not merely a similar garden; it is the very garden: the mossy stone path beside shaggy bamboo, wandering, as in a fairy tale, off into the dark distant pines of a mountain where mysteries await (this is an illusion, because Less knows perfectly well that what awaits is an HVAC system). The movement in the grass that could be a river, the bits of old stone that could be the steps of a temple. The bamboo fountain filling and tipping its water into the stone pool—the same, all precisely the same. The wind moves; the pines move; the leaves of the bamboo move; and, like a flag in the same wind, the memory of this garden moves within Arthur Less. He remembers that he did indeed find a key (steel, belonging to the lawn mower shed) but never the door. It was always an absurd childish fantasy that he would. Forty-five years have passed, during which he forgot all about it. But here it is.

From behind him comes the girl's sniffle; again, she struggles with the door as if with the stone of a tomb. He doesn't dare look back. At last she conquers it and appears by his side with green tea and a brown lacquered basket. She produces a worn card and reads aloud from it: English, apparently, but it makes as much sense as someone talking in a dream. He does not need a translation, anyway; it is his old pal butter bean. Then she smiles and departs. Another wrestling match with the door.

He takes careful notes of what is on his plate. But he cannot taste it. Why have these memories been brought out again, here in Japan—the orange scarf, the garden—like a yard sale of his life? Has he lost his mind, or is everything a reflection? The butter bean, the mugwort, the scarf, the garden; is this not a window but a mirror? Two birds are quarreling in the fountain. Again, as he did as a boy, he can only look on. He closes his eyes and begins to cry.

He hears the girl struggling again with the door but does not hear it open. Here comes the mugwort.

"Mr. Less," comes a male voice from behind him—from behind the door, in fact, he realizes when he turns around. Less kneels down close to it, and the voice says: "Mr. Less, we are so sorry."

"Yes, I know!" Less says loudly. "I am too early for the cherry blossoms!"

A cleared throat. "Yes, and also, also . . . We are so sorry. This door is four hundred years old, and it is stuck. We have tried." A long silence behind the door. "It is impossible to open."

"Impossible?"

"We are so sorry."

"Let's think for a minute—"

"We have tried everything."

"I can't be trapped in here."

"Mr. Less," comes the male voice again, muffled by the door. "We have an idea."

"I'm all ears."

"It is this." A whispered exchange in Japanese, followed by another clearing of the throat. "That you break the wall."

Less opens his eyes and looks at the latticed paper wall. They might as well be asking him to leave a space capsule. "I can't."

"They are simple to repair. Please, Mr. Less. If you could break the wall."

He feels old; he feels alone; he feels unpoplar. In the garden: a cluster of small birds passes like a school of colorless fish, darting back and forth before the window of this aquarium (in which it is Less who is contained, and not the birds), disappearing at last to the east with one stately gesture, and then—because life is comedy—there appears one final bird, scrambling across the sky to catch up with his mates.

"Please, Mr. Less."

Says the bravest person I know: "I can't."

It was around seven in the morning not long ago that your narrator had a vision of Arthur Less.

I was awakened by a mosquito who had, impressively, made her way past a fortress of fuming coils, electric fans, and permethrin-coated netting to settle inside my ear. I thank that mosquito every hour. If she (for humans are only hunted by females) had not been so skilled an intruder, I think I never would have seen it. Life is so often made by chance. That mosquito: she gave her life for me; I killed her with one smack of my palm. The South Pacific made a quiet rumble from the open window, and the sleeper beside me made a similar sound.

Sunrise. We had arrived at the hotel in the dark, but gradually, light began to reveal that our room was covered on three sides by windows; I realized the house was set out in the ocean itself, like a thrust stage, and that the view from every window was of the water and the sky. I watched as they took on shades of iris and myrtle, sapphire and jade, until all around me, in sea and sky alike, I recognized a particular shade of blue. And I understood that I would never see Arthur Less again.

Not in the way I had; not in the casual sprawl of all those years. It was as if I had been informed of his death. So many times I had left his house and closed the door, and now, carelessly, I had locked it behind me. Married—it seemed instantly so stupid of me. Around me everywhere, that shade of Lessian blue. We would run into each other now, of course, on the street or at a party somewhere, and maybe even get a drink together, but it would be having a drink with a ghost. Arthur Less. It could never be anyone else. From somewhere high above the earth, I began a plummeting descent. There was no air to breathe. The world was rushing in to fill the void where Arthur Less had always been. I hadn't known that I assumed he would wait there forever in that white bed below his window. I hadn't known I needed him there. Like a landmark, a pyramid-shaped stone or a cypress, that we assume will never move. So we can find our way home. And then, inevitably, one day—it's gone. And we realize that we thought we were the only changing thing, the only variable, in the world; that the objects and people in our lives are there for our pleasure, like the playing pieces of a game, and cannot move of their own accord; that they are held in place by our need for them, by our love. How stupid. Arthur Less, who was supposed to remain in that bed forever, now on a trip around the world—and who knows where he might be? Lost to me. I started shaking. It seemed so long ago I had seen him at that party, looking like a man lost in Grand Central Station, that crown prince of innocence. Watching him only a moment before my father introduced me: "Arthur, you remember my son, Freddy."

I sat upright in bed for a long time, shivering, though it was warm in Tahiti. Shivering, shaking; I suppose it was what you would call an attack of something or other. From behind me, I heard rustling and then a stillness.

Then I heard his voice, my new husband, Tom, who loved me, and therefore saw everything:

"I really wish you weren't crying right now."

And he is standing up within his paper room, our brave protagonist. He stands very still, fists clenched. Who knows what is raging through that queer head of his? They seem to echo now, the birds, the wind, the fountain, as if coming from the end of a long tunnel. He turns from the garden, which moves fluidly behind the ancient glass, and faces the paper wall. Here, he supposes, is the door. Not into the garden at all, but out of it. Nothing more than sticks and paper. Any other man could break it with a blow. How old is it? Has it ever seen a snowflake? Of all the absurdities of this trip, perhaps this is the most absurd—to be afraid of this. With one hand, he reaches out to touch the rough paper. The sunlight glows brighter behind it, making the shadow of a tree branch more distinct upon its surface—the Persian silk tree he climbed as a boy? There is no returning there. Or to the beach on a warm San Francisco day. Or to his bedroom and a good-bye kiss. In this room, everything is reflecting, but here is just the blank white wall of the future, on which anything might be written. Some new mortification, some new ridicule, surely. Some new joke to play on old Arthur Less. Why go there? And yet, despite everything, beyond it—who knows what miracle still awaits? Picture him lifting his fists above his head and, now with unconcealed pleasure, laughing, even, with ringing madness and a kind of crazed ecstasy, bringing them down with a splintering noise . . .

. . . and picture him getting out of a taxi on Ord Street in San Francisco, at the bottom of the Vulcan Steps. His plane has dutifully departed Osaka and landed on time in San Francisco; his crossing was fair, and his neighbor, who was reading the latest by H. H. H. Mandern, was even treated to a little story ("You know, I once interviewed him in New York City; he was sick with food poisoning, and I wore a cosmonaut's helmet . . . ") before our protagonist passed out from his pills. Arthur Less has completed his trip around the world; he is finished; he is home.

The sun has long since entered the fog, so the city is washed in blue as if by a watercolorist who has changed her mind and thinks it's all rubbish, rubbish, rubbish. He has no suitcase to carry; it is apparently making its own way around the world. He screws his eyes up the dark passage to home. Picture him: the balding blond of his hair, the semi-frown on his face, the wrinkled white shirt, the bandaged left hand, the bandaged right foot, the stained leather satchel, and his beautiful gray tailored suit. Picture him: almost glowing in the dark. Tomorrow, he will see Lewis for coffee and find out whether Clark has really left him and whether it still feels like a happy ending. There will be a note from Robert, to be filed with everything that will never be in the Carlos Pelu Collection: *To the boy with red toenails—thank you for everything.* Tomorrow, love will surely deepen its mystery. All that, tomorrow. But tonight, after a long journey: rest. Then the strap of the satchel catches on the handrail, and for a moment—and because there are always a few drops left in the bottle of indignity—it seems as if he is going to keep walking, and the satchel will tear...

Less looks back and untangles the strap. Fate, thwarted. Now: the long ascent toward home. Placing his foot on the first step with relief.

Why is his porch light on? What is that shadow?

He would be interested to know that my marriage to Tom Dennis lasted one entire day: twenty-four hours. We talked it all through on the bed, surrounded by the sea and the sky in that Lessian blue. That morning, when I stopped crying at last, Tom said as my husband he had a duty to stay with me, to help me work through it. I sat there nodding and nodding. He said that I had traveled an awfully long way to figure out something I should have known sooner, something people had been telling him for months, and that he should have known when I locked myself in the bathroom the night before our wedding. I nodded. We embraced and decided he could not be my husband after all. He closed the door, and I was left in that room filled side to side, and top to bottom, with the blue that signified the vast mistake I had made. I tried to call Less from the hotel phone but left no message.

What would I say? That when he told me, long ago, as I tried on his tuxedo, not to get attached, he was years too late? That it did not do the trick, that good-bye kiss? The next day, on the main island, I inquired about Gauguin's house but was informed by a local: "It is closed." For many days, I watched and was amazed by the ocean, composing endless fascinating variations on its tedious theme. Then, one morning, my father sent me a message:

Flight 172 from Osaka, Japan, arriving Thursday, 6:30 p.m.

Arthur Less, squinting up at his house. And now a security light, triggered by his movements, has come on, blinding him briefly. Who is that standing there?

I have never been to Japan. I have never been to India, or to Morocco, or to Germany, or to most of the places Arthur Less has traveled to over the past few months. I have never climbed an ancient pyramid. I have never kissed a man on a Paris rooftop. I have never ridden a camel. I have taught a high school English class for the best part of a decade, and graded homework every night, and woken up early in the morning to plan my lessons, and read and reread Shakespeare, and sat through enough conferences and meetings for even those in Purgatory to envy me. I have never seen a glowworm. I do not, by any reckoning, have the best life of anyone I know. But what I am trying to tell you (and I only have a moment), what I have been trying to tell you this whole time, is that from where I sit, the story of Arthur Less is not so bad.

Because it is also mine. That is how it goes with love stories.

Less, still dazzled by the spotlight, starts up the stairs and becomes ensnared, as he always does, in the thorns of a neighbor's rosebush; carefully he removes each spur from his shimmering gray suit. He passes the bougainvillea, which, like some bothersome talkative lady at a party, briefly obstructs his path. He pushes it aside, showering himself with dried purple bracts. Somewhere, someone is practicing piano over and over; they cannot get the left hand right. A window undulates with a watery television radiance. And then I see the familiar blond glow of his hair appearing from the flowers, the halo of Arthur Less. Look at him tripping at the same broken step as always, pausing to look down in surprise. Look at him turning to take the last few steps toward the one who awaits him. His face tilted upward toward home. Look at him, look at him. How could I not love him?

My father asked me once why I was so lazy, why I did not want the world. He asked me what I wanted, and though I did not answer then, because I did not know, and followed old conventions even to the altar, I know it now. It is long past time to answer the question—and I see you, old Arthur, old love, looking up to that silhouette on your porch—what do I want? After choosing the path people wanted, the man who would do, the easy way out of things—your eyes wide in surprise as you see me—after holding it all in my hands and refusing it, what do I want from life?

And I say: "Less!"

ACKNOWLEDGEMENTS

The author would like to thank the following people: David Ross, Lisa Brown, Daniel Handler, Lynn Nesbit, Hannah Davey, Lee Boudreaux, Reagan Arthur, Beatrice Monti della Corte and Enrico Rotelli. Much thanks also to numerous people and places around the world, but most especially to the Santa Maddalena Foundation, Arte Studio Ginestrelle, Art Castle International, the Evens and Odds, and the Dolphin Swimming and Boating Club.

ABOUT THE AUTHOR

Andrew Sean Greer is the bestselling author of five works of fiction, including *The Confessions of Max Tivoli*, which was named a best book of 2004 by the *San Francisco Chronicle* and the *Chicago Tribune*. He is the recipient of the Northern California Book Award, the California Book Award, the New York Public Library Young Lions Award, the O. Henry award for short fiction and fellowships from the National Endowment for the Arts and the New York Public Library. Greer lives in San Francisco.

Follow Andrew Sean Greer 🐦 @agreer
Follow Arthur Less 📷 @less_a_novel